Scribbles of a Mad Woman in her dressing gown

By Glynis Scrivens

Scribbles of a Mad Woman

Copyright © Glynis Scrivens 2020

All rights reserved. No part of this book may be reproduced, stored in a retrieval system, or be transmitted by any form or by any means, electronic, mechanical, photocopying, recording or otherwise, without the prior written permission of the publisher.

Glynis Scrivens asserts her moral right to be identified as the author of this book. First published 2020

Cover image by Amy Scrivens.

Paperback ISBN: 978-0-6487394-0-1
Ebook ISBN: 978-0-6487394-1-8

 A catalogue record for this book is available from the National Library of Australia

To Mum and Dad

CONTENTS

Author's note

Part I – Recipe for Life
What You See Is Who You Are 1
The Best Cobweb in the World 2
Kindred Spirits 5
Shape up, Santa 16
The Spirit of Christmas 20
Saying Goodbye 31
A Ray of Sunshine 34
Heart to Heart 38
Through a Glass Darkly 48
Did You Forget to Say Goodbye? 55
We're on the Same Wavelength 59
Hello, Stranger 67
I Can See Clearly Now 73
The Icing on the Cake 81
Recipe for Life 88
The Gift of Motherhood 94
Pyjama Party 103
A Mother's Day Present 107
Did You Forget to Tell Me? 110
All the Right Ingredients 116
Bargains 120
For Your Ears Only 124

Part II – The Language of Love
New Beginnings 130
When You Wish upon a Star 138
Short-Sighted 146

Marilyn's Alter Ego 150
A Fresh Start 156
Coffee with Bruce 165
Afternoons with Richard Gere 171
The Language of Love 175
Pieces of a Life 181
Paper Kisses 187
Flowers for Nancy 196
Holidaying with Harry 200

Part III – Murder and Mystery
Learning to Fly 212
The Poacher 218
Connie's Project 225
One Missed Call 230
Golden Opportunity 234
Eat up, Colin 238
An Open and Shut Case 245
Death Comes Silently 249
Jumping to Conclusions 255
A Deadly Dull New Year's Eve 259
A Terrible Eavesdropper 262
Which Ones Are Real? 266
Going to the Show 272
Who Is My Visitor? 275
Her Husband's Secret 283
Family Matters 291
Messenger 297
Death Claims His Prize 300
Death by Misadventure? 304

Acknowledgements 331

Author's note

My mother bought me a ream of paper because she believed I had a book in me. Something to say. I lost her before putting pen to paper. But I've never lost her belief in me. I don't think this book would exist if she hadn't given me that first ream of paper.

Some of you might recognise a scene or a character in a story. It is, after all, my own life that I draw on for inspiration. But please remember these are stories. Pieces of fiction. I've woven together random images and thoughts and moments to create something new. Something that's meant to go beyond its raw materials. Just because you recognise one detail doesn't mean any other detail in that story is true.

Happy reading!

Glynis

Part I
Recipe for Life

What You See Is Who You Are

An elderly woman held a young stranger's arm to support herself as she crossed the street.

He smilingly obliged, seeing in her a reflection of his grandmother.

She saw the willing help she'd prayed for.

Her grandson felt slighted, seeing another given preference.

Her son saw implied criticism of his negligence.

The woman's daughter saw a possible thief.

The monk saw his student practicing loving kindness.

A younger woman watching saw a reason not to offer help, and hurried on.

And in the skies above, the All-Seeing One watched – free of human blinkers.

The Best Cobweb in the World

Ten-year-old Jessie sat on the carpet by her grandmother's side, arranging balls of wool. Reds, blues, greens, purples.

"Look at my rainbow, Grandma." Her face was glowing.

Edith looked up from the shawl she was knitting. It took a moment for her eyes to adjust. She couldn't help smiling. How wonderful it was to finally be able to share her delight in the rich hues and soft tweedy texture of her favourite Shetland wools. None of her sons had shown any interest.

"Will you knit me a rainbow shawl one day, Grandma?" She held the balls up to her soft cheeks and blue eyes.

What a picture, Edith thought. "I can do something better than that, Jessie," she said. "I can teach you how to make one for yourself."

The school holidays flew by and all too soon Jessie was back at school in Glasgow, an hour's drive away. Proudly taking with her a brightly coloured scarf, knitted in plain stitch. It sagged in the middle, and the sides were uneven, where she'd lost a few stitches and then added others. But she'd made it herself and Edith felt that was more important than it looking perfect.

Edith was sitting by her fireside, wearing her shawl the following winter when a sudden sharp pain in her chest tore her from the farm and her family. It took only moments.

She gasped. The transition she'd feared more and more in recent years had actually happened. And truth be told, it'd been far less terrible than she'd imagined.

Eighty-four years on the farm, and now this.

She looked around her. It wasn't at all what she'd expected. Not that she'd had any specific ideas. But it was such a surprise to find herself so mobile. She could be at the farm, enjoying the view from the hill, then close her eyes, and here she was in Glasgow. Quite extraordinary.

They save the best until last, she thought happily. It'd been so difficult to get about in recent years, with her rheumatism and her bad legs. She couldn't resist the impulse to spread her wings… now that she had such a fine pair. She stroked them lovingly. Soft and fluffy to the touch, but wonderfully powerful. What a blessing they were.

She was so busy visiting all the places and people she'd known and loved during her lifetime, that she missed her own funeral. Never mind. She'd been to so many funerals during her lifetime, surely she could be excused this once?

The wake, on the other hand, was lively and heartwarming, a true celebration of her life. She listened with tears and pride as her sons and friends gave thanks for all the ways she'd enriched their lives.

Yet perhaps the most magical moment came when she found Jessie upstairs alone, exploring her knitting cupboard. To see her lovingly fingering the soft balls of wool made her feel that part of her was living on, in this young girl.

Jessie gently lifted up the shawl and held it up to the

light. "It's the best cobweb in the world," she whispered. "And you were the best grandmother." She buried her face in the comforting warmth, breathing in the lavender scent of the cupboard. Then she wrapped the shawl around her shoulders and went downstairs. Edith would never forget that precious moment.

She found herself reminiscing long after everyone had gone home. In fact she lost all sense of time. What with one thing and another, several decades slipped by without her being aware of it.

Until one morning she willed herself back at the farm. She wasn't sure at first whether time had moved backwards or forwards. A woman was sitting in her favourite chair, knitting a rainbow shawl. Surely this wasn't Jessie? But there was no mistaking the twinkle in those blue eyes or the rosiness of the cheeks.

And she'd become a skilful knitter.

Edith smiled contentedly as she realised who this shawl was for.

Jessie was expecting a baby.

Kindred Spirits

Make yourself a dress in your own colours.

Ellen sat up sleepily to write down the words. They puzzled her. If only she could remember more of the handwritten list Robert had shown her in her dream. He'd written down things he wanted her to do for her birthday. There were about a dozen items. One was to go to a concert. Or was it an exhibition? She couldn't be sure. But there was no doubt about the dress. He'd read it out loud to her from his list, pointing to the words to make sure they stuck in her mind.

And then he'd shown her samples of shot taffeta in a range of gleaming evening colours. She remembered seeing delicately woven gold fabric. *Fit for a princess*, she thought. The kind of gossamer Cinderella had worn to the ball.

Was Robert playing fairy godmother to her? Rescuing her from the dreariness that'd become her everyday life?

There'd been a darkness since she'd lost him. Hard to define but always there, smothering the light. An envelope of sorrow that she wore, day and night.

She rubbed her eyes, hoping it'd help her wake up. And that's when she remembered the other puzzling thing about her dream. Robert had been wearing an evening suit. Robert, who never dressed up.

How handsome he'd looked. As though it was his wedding day.

And he'd looked much younger. About forty.

She couldn't recall him ever looking more handsome. Or more pleased to see her.

Even in her dream, she'd been surprised to see him.

He'd suddenly appeared when she was talking with her friend, Linda. One moment she was listening to Linda recounting a problem, the next, Robert was leaning on the counter smiling at her.

Linda and her problems had flown out of her head.

Light-hearted, she'd looked into his loving face and wrapped her arms around him. Nothing else existed at that moment.

He'd drawn her to him, as he always did. She'd felt the strength of his arms and melted into his chest.

If only this moment could last, she'd thought. Being back in Robert's arms, feeling the love that always radiated from him.

She'd missed him terribly these past eighteen months.

And she was aware of all this while she was dreaming.

Somehow, she was both in the dream and looking on. Enjoying his embrace, but realising he was gone. It only made it all the sweeter.

Which was why it was important to write down these words. They were evidently significant.

She fossicked about for her diary. These words would

only be lost if she wrote them on a scrap of paper. Like yesterday's to-do list that she didn't find until bedtime.

"I guess this is Robert's to-do list for me," she whispered, as she wrote the words. She added "concert?" underneath.

She looked at the photograph she kept by her bed. Robert was smiling at her, one daughter on each side.

"It was lovely to see you," she said softly. She wondered whether his spirit was still in her room. For surely this had been a visit? And she'd only just woken up, so perhaps…

A half-smile played on her lips as she decided he might still be around.

"What would you say, Robert, if you were sitting up in bed beside me?"

Ellen smiled as she realised exactly what Robert would've said.

It must be nearly coffee time.

Good idea, she thought. *It'll clear my brain.* She slipped her dressing gown on and padded out to the kitchen, still groggy with sleep.

On the shelf above her cupboards, the stovetop espresso gleamed back at her. Robert always wanted "real" coffee.

She ground the beans dreamily, inhaling the intoxicating rich aroma. It'd been a few weeks since she'd made the effort to have percolated coffee. She only made it for company these days.

Maybe she should change that? "Only the best for my Ellen," Robert had always said.

Tomorrow she'd make herself real coffee again. And every other tomorrow.

She hadn't been aware until now that this was something she'd allowed to slip.

Sitting up in bed later, sipping the heady brew, Ellen felt a small cloud lifting from her mind.

The envelope had been slit open a fraction and a beam of light had been allowed in.

When she'd showered and dressed, she sprayed herself with *Romance,* his favourite perfume.

Another tentative step.

Another small beam of light.

The phone rang, dragging her back to reality.

Linda's voice sounded troubled. As it often did. "I need your advice on another problem," she began.

Ellen listened as her friend complained about a neighbour who'd heavily pruned a flowering vine that grew on their dividing fence.

Normally she'd allow Linda to talk herself out. But today she didn't want the next hour to pass in the usual way. She felt herself diluting, the new light ebbing.

So she interrupted after five minutes.

"You should invite Henry in for a pot of tea and talk through your differences," she suggested. "Maybe he isn't aware how you feel about this."

There was a shocked silence.

Before Linda could resume, Ellen added, "Must fly now. I'm going shopping this morning and want to catch the nine o'clock bus."

She'd decided on the spur of the moment to use some of Robert's superannuation on a new sewing machine. Something he'd often suggested. Her old machine had stood her in good stead over the years, but would need a major overhaul if she wanted it to do anything complicated. Like sewing an evening dress in the kind of fabric Robert had shown her. She'd baulked at the expense of repairing her old machine, and she'd shied away from learning how to use the new ones. Yet this wasn't the real Ellen, was it? The girl Robert had married all those years ago had been a spirited creature, willing to throw her heart at the world and laughing in the face of misfortune.

For a brief moment, as she walked into the sewing centre, Ellen felt a rekindling of that spirit. It was like glimpsing an old friend.

Then a sales girl approached and she felt defensive again. These machines scared her.

"You'll want one of the computerised models." Michelle, according to her name tag, seemed alarmingly unaware of Ellen's love-hate relationship with technology.

"Nothing complicated," Ellen began.

Michelle sat her down at a large table, in front of a small white plastic machine. It didn't seem nearly as sturdy as her machine at home.

"This is the one we sell to the local high school for home science classes," Michelle explained. "It's easy to learn how to use it, believe me. I used it at school last year myself." And she started pointing out the special buttonhole feature.

Ellen felt the blood rushing to her cheeks. These same schoolgirls also knew how to set up blogs and websites. It was unrealistic to compare her with this new generation.

"Is there a beginner's model?" Ellen asked. She flinched as she accidentally bit her bottom lip. How had she become so self-effacing and hesitant? She'd been a dressmaker for years. Until she'd married Robert.

Michelle patted her hand. It felt reassuring.

"I'll give you free lessons on whichever machine you choose," she said.

Ellen released a long gentle sigh. "Really? What if I need a dozen lessons? I'm not good at anything computerised."

"It's just a matter of learning what to do," Michelle said. "I've taught my own grandmother how to use this model. You couldn't be worse to teach than she was." As she smiled, Ellen noticed she was wearing braces on her teeth.

It made her feel comfortable. Michelle wasn't perfect either. But she'd taken this step to improve herself. Ellen could make an effort too.

Linda was quite put out when Ellen knocked on her front door later. Her greying blonde hair could do with a cut, Ellen noticed. And there were dark mushrooms under her eyes. If she didn't worry so much, she might get a decent night's sleep.

Then she felt immediately hypocritical. She hadn't really taken good care of herself either, had she? They'd been acting like a pair of misery bags. That's what Robert would've said.

Over a cup of tea, Linda poured cold water on Ellen's plans. "You should ask for your money back," she said.

Ellen shrugged. She hadn't mentioned her dream, of course. "It'll be fun to sew again," she said. "I popped in to see if you wanted to come to the sewing classes with me. Michelle said she didn't mind."

A strange sound came from Linda. Ellen couldn't tell if it was a snort or a grunt. "She just wants my money too."

Ellen finished her tea and stood up. "The classes are at ten o'clock every morning. Ring me if you want to come tomorrow."

As she walked down the street, she noticed Linda's next-door neighbour. Henry was spraying his rose bushes. He looked up and waved to her. He seemed friendly. Why was Linda always complaining about him?

I'll bet she didn't ask you in for a cuppa, Ellen thought.

One of Robert's sayings flashed through her mind. *You can lead a horse to water...*

Ellen felt a bit stronger. There was no need for her to take on her friend's despondency.

I'm even starting to dream about her telling me problems, she realised.

To her surprise Linda decided to join her next morning – purely as a spectator, she insisted. By the end of the hour, Ellen was able to sew straight seams and to do buttonholes. The automatic needle-threader was proving difficult but as Michelle pointed out, she'd come a long way in a short time.

After the lesson she and Linda decided to look at dress patterns and fabrics.

"Something mid-calf, I think," Ellen said, flicking the pattern book open at the tab *Cocktail and evening dresses.*

"You won't get much wear out of that, will you?" Linda said. "An everyday dress in a bright cotton would make more sense."

Ellen didn't answer. This wasn't about being sensible, was it? This was about finding herself. Wear "your own colours", Robert had said. She remembered how handsome he'd looked in the dark suit. She wanted to look her best too. That's what he wanted. She cast a careful eye over the styles. Nothing too short. Nothing too fussy.

And then she saw it. A gypsy style of dress, with a flowing mid-calf skirt, fitted bodice and waist, and matching jacket. She felt like hugging herself. She'd look pretty in this dress. It was both elegant and fun.

She bought the pattern.

"It's not my place to tell you how to spend your money." If Linda wasn't sixty years old, Ellen would swear she sounded sulky.

"This would look lovely in rich coloured silk," Michelle said next morning. "You could look for cobalt or emerald, maybe shot with maroon."

"You don't think the style's too young for me?" A few doubts had crept into Ellen's mind after Linda's lukewarm comments. "Mutton dressed as lamb?"

Michelle shook her head. "You've kept your figure. I think it'll really suit you."

Ellen told her she was planning to go to a concert next month, on her birthday. She hadn't mentioned this to Linda. Her friend had stopped going out at night since she lost her husband five years earlier and would no doubt pour cold water over that idea too.

Ellen was planning to bide her time and wait for the right moment to ask Linda to join her.

Michelle had an idea. "Why don't I help you find the right material?" she said. "It's time for my morning break. And I'll look for some for my gran at the same time."

In the third shop, Lady Luck smiled on them. There was a roll of exquisite shot silk for sale, heavily reduced. They both reached for it at the same time. Michelle held it up against Ellen and beamed. "It's perfect for both of you. You and my gran will look like twins. Would that matter?" Michelle's braces were dotted with lavender plastic, and her grin was contagious. Ellen felt years younger, beside such a light-hearted and generous creature. She'd be more than happy to look like Michelle's gran.

It was only as she lay in bed that night that Ellen remembered Robert calling her his "gypsy princess" on their first date.

Where had these lovely memories been hiding? Why had she slipped inside this dark unhappy envelope of despair since his death?

If she wasn't careful, she'd turn into someone like Linda.

She put a small swathe of the fabric under her pillow, hoping she might have another dream about Robert.

But dreams aren't always made to order.

Besides, Robert would've said she was being fanciful, she thought, as she ground beans for her coffee the following morning.

Make yourself a dress in your own colours.

So much good advice was in those few words. Robert must've seen her despondency and decided to entice back her fun-loving nature. Take his gypsy girl out of her comfort zone. Open her eyes again to the good things in life. Had he somehow known she'd been dreading another birthday without him?

The day of the concert drew near. She'd bought tickets for a symphony orchestra performing Beethoven's Pastoral Symphony.

The day before, she took her dress to show Michelle, and get her help with finishing touches.

Michelle was bursting with excitement. Her eyes shone as she carefully worked the delicate fastening on the back of the bodice. Then she noticed a slight shadow on Ellen's happiness.

"Is something the matter?" she asked.

"Linda's changed her mind about coming with me,"

Ellen said. "She doesn't think it's safe for two women our age to be out at night time."

Michelle shook her head. "Why is she leaving you on your own, if she doesn't think you'll be safe?"

"I'm beginning to realise how negative she is," Ellen said. "I'll have a good time anyway. Maybe she'll come with me next time, when she realises the bogey man didn't get me."

"That's the spirit," Michelle said. "You can lead a horse to water…"

Robert's words. And now Michelle's. Surely not a coincidence? It was as though he'd brought this young girl into her life as a breath of fresh air.

Ellen would make sure she was one of the horses smart enough to drink.

The orchestra was everything she'd hoped. Closing her eyes, she felt transported to another realm. Lifted out of herself into a fantasy of sublime sound. Her heart soared with the music.

When she opened her eyes, during a lull in the piece, she had to blink. Surely she was mistaken? Someone had sat in the empty seat beside her. Someone in a dark evening suit. A handsome man in his forties, who turned to her with eyes radiating love and pride.

As the violins led her into another flight of passion, she thought she heard a soft voice beside her and the words "my gypsy princess".

When the lights came on again at the end, the seat beside her was empty. But she thought she noticed a faint hint of the musky aftershave Robert had always worn.

She felt peaceful as she made her way to the foyer for refreshments.

Sipping a glass of chardonnay, she noticed a woman wearing a similar dress to her own. The woman waved brightly and walked up to her. She had her granddaughter's lovely smile and sparkling eyes.

"You must be Ellen," she said. "Michelle's told me all about you. I just know we're going to be friends." She clinked her glass against Ellen's. "Here's to happy days."

Ellen took another sip of the wine. "To happy days," she said softly.

Shape up, Santa

Mrs Claus watched as Santa struggled with the buttons on his red jacket. "If you don't get into shape soon, I'll put your name down for The Biggest Loser," she said. "How do you think you're going to get up and down chimneys?"

"It's not my fault," he said. "The material seems to have shrunk."

"Don't give me that excuse," she said. "You've been sitting in front of the TV for weeks, munching on chocolate cookies."

Santa stretched the black leather belt and held his breath. But it was no good. The metal eye was just out of reach of the buckle.

Outside, icicles hung from the trees and the garden was waist deep in snow. A strong wind was blowing.

Mrs Claus poured tea and set it down on the table beside the rye wafers and lettuce salad.

Santa groaned. "You can't call this lunch," he said. "Not in this weather."

"You've only got yourself to blame," she said. "Just be

grateful I'm not having fish pie and baked potatoes." She nibbled half-heartedly at a rye wafer, regretting her decision to join him in this. But what else could she do? He was unfit and out of breath all the time. How could he manage the zillion things he needed to do on Christmas Eve unless he got himself into better shape? And she was too busy answering all the children's letters and cards to sit at her sewing machine and make him a new outfit.

Santa sipped his tea and pulled a face. "You forgot the sugar."

"You're the one who needs to forget sugar." She'd sugared her own tea and added cream when her husband wasn't looking.

Santa started to protest. The effort caused one of the large red buttons to pop off his jacket and fly across the room.

He quietly helped himself to lettuce and watercress.

After lunch Mrs Claus played Bing Crosby's *White Christmas* vinyl on the old record player, and got out the photo album.

"Remember the good old days," she said.

Together they browsed through the photos. The earliest ones were in black and white, and rather eerie, showing a plump dark silhouette perched precariously on rooftops, and disappearing into chimneys.

"Children were different then," he reminisced. He pointed to a photo of his huge toy sack, with the top opened. It was the first of the colour photos. Soccer balls, cricket bats and kites protruded from the sack, and there were dozens of bubble pipes and bird whistles. "These days they ask for electronic stuff. Computer games, smart phones, games consoles. And I'm supposed to test them all."

Mrs Claus patted his hand. "Haven't you forgotten something?" she said. "You were different then too."

A puzzled look came into Santa's eyes. "What do you mean?"

She pointed to the computer, open at Santa's Facebook page. He had more friends than anyone else on Facebook and was tempted to go on Twitter as well.

"Before we had the internet, you spent all your time making toys and being jolly," she said. "Now you're either glued to the computer or testing electronic games."

"I'm just keeping up with the times," he said.

"Keeping up with the times or keeping up with the Joneses? I don't see you out on the lake, trying out ice skates. And when was the last time you kicked a soccer ball? You're not setting a very good example, are you?"

Santa's rosy cheeks went a deeper shade of red.

"But it's fun," he said in a small voice.

Mrs Claus turned off the computer and took the TV remote control. "These are banned from now on," she said sternly. "And if I catch you cheating, I'll cut off the power."

Santa whimpered.

Mrs Santa felt mean, but as she washed up the lunch things, she noticed a large red figure in the garden, throwing a soccer ball at icicles. As she watched, he was joined by some curious elves. They started kicking the ball about. More elves arrived.

Santa was out of breath and very red in the face when she called him in for dinner, but his eyes held a sparkle she hadn't seen in weeks. And he didn't complain when she served a large steaming bowl of vegetable and barley soup.

The days and weeks passed. Christmas was rapidly

approaching. Santa had cheated only once, and when she'd realised he'd gone online to buy French perfume and an Italian handbag, Mrs Claus pretended she hadn't noticed.

Christmas Eve arrived. Excitement was at fever pitch, with elves busily grooming the reindeer and giving the sleigh bells a final polish. Even Santa was gleaming, as he stood proudly in front of the mirror, admiring himself.

Mrs Claus took a photo for the album as he climbed into the sleigh. The toy sacks seemed to contain more soccer balls than last year and she'd glimpsed a last-minute delivery of cricket bats.

She smiled as Santa disappeared up into the sky, until all she could hear was a faint tinkling of bells and a cheery voice saying "Ho, ho, ho."

She went inside, made herself a large hot chocolate and sat down in front of the TV with a bag of marshmallows to watch Michael Caine in *A Christmas Carol*.

Her year's work was done. It was time to put her feet up.

The Spirit of Christmas

Freya looked at the large cardboard box sitting in the far corner of the lounge. Beside it, the spruce tree sat in a bucket of sand. Perhaps she and Karen could decorate it today?

Her granddaughter stood in the doorway, her arms full of brightly wrapped presents to place under the tree.

"It doesn't feel like a real Christmas this year, does it, Gran?" She started to cough. "Not with Grandpa in hospital." Her blonde plaits fell limply onto her shoulders as she bent down to arrange the presents.

Freya couldn't help the immediate sinking sensation in her chest, as though she'd swallowed a lump of lead. But she must be strong. She must hold onto the hope that Raymond would pull through this bout of pneumonia. The doctor in the intensive care ward had said the next twenty-four hours were critical.

Her hands shook slightly as she sipped her tea, gazing out the window at the ocean. The sun glittered off the surface of the water, reminding her of the tropical beach where Raymond had taught her to surf a lifetime ago.

But that was on the other side of the world where Christmas was a bright sunny affair and the icy shadow of fear hadn't stepped in to spoil her dreams. Her hair had been a rich auburn then.

How would Raymond answer young Karen? Freya and Raymond had enjoyed more than fifty Christmases together, none more so than their first. He considered himself an expert on the subject.

Freya held out the plate of rumballs and waited while Karen chose one. She nearly hadn't made them this year but yesterday evening there'd been Christmas carols on the TV and she'd quietly got out the ingredients with Karen bustling about happily beside her. Now she was glad she'd made the effort.

It'd been a good idea to have ten-year-old Karen here convalescing for a week after her flu. The holiday was doing them both good. It made such a change, having a youngster in the house.

Freya helped herself to a rumball and bit into the chocolaty fruit concoction. As she did, her heart lifted at the wave of memories that flooded through her.

"You know, Karen," she said at last, "sometimes the Christmases that begin by feeling the least real end up being your best ones."

Karen sat beside her on the settee. Her face was beginning to get more colour. The sea air was working its magic.

But Karen looked far from convinced. Two watery blue eyes regarded her through long lashes. "What makes a *real* Christmas, Gran?"

Raymond's face flashed across her mind, not as he'd looked earlier that day, lined and grey, but the suntanned features and boyish grin that had greeted her that Christmas in 1955, when they'd first met in Brisbane.

She'd felt lost and confused, and had asked him that same question. She'd never forget his reply, or the deep blue eyes that had regarded her so gently.

She looked at Karen now and tapped her chest, as he'd done then. "This is where the spirit of Christmas lives. Right in here. None of the other stuff matters."

Karen looked puzzled. "What about Santa Claus? And presents? And roast turkey? Can you have a real Christmas without them?"

It was her own question, but framed in childlike terms. And she knew the answer.

"All you need for a real Christmas is what lies inside your heart."

How often had Raymond said that, over the years? They'd had their own share of heartache and misfortune, but through it all there'd always been a ray of hope and joy at Christmas time. Somehow, with effort and determination, they'd always been able to rise above their circumstances and find a glimpse of something magical.

But could she really do that this year, if he was still in hospital for Christmas?

What lay inside her heart was gnawing anxiety. She knew she must make a special effort.

Karen was fidgeting. "I'm going to decorate the tree with you," she said. "Can you please help me open the box?" She slipped off the settee and started to struggle with the lid.

Ignoring the familiar twinge of pain in her wrists, Freya wrested off the lid.

Karen's face fell as her eyes cast on an assortment of shoeboxes. This wasn't what she was expecting.

"You've got the wrong one, Gran," she said. "Where are the decorations?"

Freya gave a small smile. "I like to keep them in these boxes, Karen. Otherwise they might get lost or broken." She picked up the top shoebox and opened it. Inside, carefully wrapped, was the large gold star.

"How will we put that on top of the tree?" Karen asked. "Do you have a ladder?"

"We'll wait until your Dad comes on Thursday," Freya said. She rewrapped the star. "Now it's your turn to choose."

Karen eagerly lifted the lid off the next box. Inside, she found small toy drums. She squealed in delight and attached them to the branches of the spruce tree.

"What's that, Gran?" she asked, as Freya unwrapped a wooden ornament. "It looks like a big lizard. What's it doing with the Christmas decorations?"

Freya held it in her hands. "This is a gecko. Your Grandpa carved it for me."

"I've never seen a real live gecko," she said. "And a gecko hasn't got anything to do with Christmas."

"That's what I thought too," Freya said, "before I spent a Christmas in the tropics." She remembered the rich turquoise ocean sparkling under a fierce sun, and the fine white sand that had burned her feet. It seemed a distant cousin to the chilly blue-grey expanse of water outside her window.

"Tell me about it, Gran. I want to know what a gecko has to do with the spirit of Christmas. And why did Grandpa carve it for you?" She reached over and carefully selected another rumball.

Freya traced the rough features of the gecko, remembering.

"It was 1955," she began. "I was twenty-five-years-old and desperate for an adventure. So when Aunty Elle asked me to fly out to Australia and look after her house for three months, I jumped at the chance."

"Even though it meant not being home for Christmas?" Karen asked. "And why wasn't Aunty Elle going to be home too?"

"She moved to Brisbane when she married Uncle Glen and said she was feeling homesick. She hadn't got used to Christmas being in the middle of summer. And she wanted to see all her family again."

"Didn't you think you'd get homesick too?"

Freya shook her head. "No, I don't think I really thought much about that before I set off. I just wanted to spread my wings and explore the world."

Karen giggled. Gran didn't have wings! "Then what?"

"When my plane landed and I was walking down the steps, it was like going into an oven." She remembered the thick heavy air and the tightness in her chest as she'd caught her breath.

"An oven?" Karen's voice had dropped to a whisper. "Like in *Hansel and Gretel*?"

"Yes, only muggy. More like a sauna, I suppose. I felt as though I was melting."

"How did you get into Aunty Elle's house if she wasn't there to open the door for you?" Karen looked curious. "Did she leave a key hidden somewhere? Or were you supposed to climb in a window?"

Freya smiled. "Aunty Elle asked her gardener to give me the key and show me where everything was."

She thought back to that December morning when her

taxi had pulled up to the old weatherboard home with its wide verandas and rambling garden. And the young lanky figure sitting in the big wooden chair, reading the newspaper, waiting for her. His bicycle had been propped against the battens under the house. He was wearing a white cotton singlet and denim shorts, with a broad-brimmed straw hat.

"Was it a big house?" Karen asked. "Did your Aunty Elle have any pets?"

"It was a big wooden house on stilts, and there was a veranda wrapped around two sides like a capital letter L. And the roof was made of corrugated iron. Every time there was a hail storm, the noise was deafening."

Freya sipped her tea, remembering.

"As for pets, there were chooks, two big ginger tom cats, and a pond with native fish and tadpoles for me to look after."

Karen's eyes widened. "I could look after the pets for her if she needs another holiday." She paused for breath. "What are chooks?"

"That's what everyone called hens. It's like a nickname. The hens hated storms because their run would get muddy."

"Did you have a Christmas tree?"

"Aunty Elle's gardener chopped a branch off the silky oak tree. He set it up for me on the veranda."

The watery blue eyes grew thoughtful. "But Christmas trees are spruce and they're kept inside the house."

"Not this one. You should've seen all the insects that crawled out of it over the next few days. And there was a huge spider. I was glad the tree wasn't inside the house when I saw his long hairy legs."

Karen clapped her hand across her mouth. "Did you scream?"

"Yes, and the gardener ran to see what was the matter. And do you know what he said? *What's all the fuss? It's only a huntsman.*" Freya held out her hand. "It was as big as the palm of my hand, Karen, and hairy. I was scared."

Karen shuddered. "I hate spiders, Gran. I'd have screamed too!" She picked up the wooden carving. "Were there geckos in the tree?"

Freya shook her head. "No, they walked about on the walls and ceilings inside the house. They came out every evening when all the mites and moths and little insects were flying inside, attracted by the lights. The geckos ate them for their supper."

"Were they scary?"

"Not really."

Karen blew her nose. "Did you have roast turkey with potatoes and pumpkin and brussels sprouts?"

"No, this was a long time ago, remember. Aunty Elle had an ice chest to keep her food cool. It wasn't big enough for a turkey. It was like a small fridge, and it had blocks of ice inside instead of electricity."

"No turkey?" Karen frowned. "That doesn't sound very Christmassy."

"And it didn't feel like it either. Not at first. Everything was different, and I didn't know anyone."

She helped herself to another rumball. "I made my first batch of these that Christmas. Aunty Elle used to give them as presents to all the people who helped her during the year …the rubbish man, the iceman, the fruiterer, the baker, the milkman. She must've had half a dozen tradesmen come to the house every week."

She bit into the rumball and licked the sticky chocolate off her fingers carefully. "I think they were worried they were going to miss out that year. They all dropped a hint or two the week before Christmas."

And so had someone else. Raymond had come upstairs one afternoon and found her slumped in a chair by the kitchen table, crying her eyes out. "I hate this place," she'd said. "I hate the heat, the insects, everything about it. I just want to go home." Expecting him to be sympathetic.

"If you'd stop feeling sorry for yourself, you might realise it's Christmas. And some folks around here need cheering up more than you do."

And he'd told her about the baker's wife, having a difficult pregnancy. He'd told her how the milkman had to have a second job to support his large family. By the time she'd had a cup of tea and thought about what he'd said, Raymond had produced Aunty Elle's recipe book and told her about her aunt's Christmas tradition.

And here I am, feeling sorry for myself again, she thought. Maybe there was something she could do this year that would cheer someone else up? There was always someone who was worse off.

A little hand tugged at her sleeve. "What about the gardener? Did you make him rumballs?"

Freya smiled. "Oh yes, Raymond loved rumballs."

"Raymond? Isn't that Grandpa's name? Was Grandpa the gardener?"

"Yes, I was wondering how long it'd take you to guess. I wasn't sure if I'd told you this story before." She ruffled the soft blonde hair, and kissed the top of Karen's head. "Grandpa and I met that Christmas and fell in love. It was his last Christmas in Australia. The following year he came over here to marry me."

"Did he like cold Christmases, Gran, or did he wish it was hot?"

"I was worried about that so his first year here, I surprised him by organising a Christmas in July. I bought tinned ham, made lots of salads. Just like we'd had in Brisbane. Even made him rumballs using Aunty Elle's recipe."

She remembered the blank look that'd come over Raymond's face when he'd seen the festive spread. And all of a sudden, she'd understood. What she'd done was recreate the outward show of Christmas, but she'd completely neglected the real meaning of the season. Offered him the trappings, as though they meant something by themselves. It'd been a humbling realisation.

On impulse, she'd given a plate of the rumballs to the elderly lady next door. And in the surprised pleasure and gratitude in her neighbour's eyes, she'd glimpsed something of what it was that made Christmas special. Even in July.

Perhaps there were still lessons for her to learn about Christmas? Raymond always said Christmas wasn't the weather, or the food, or the decorations. Maybe, like marriage, it could be enjoyed "in sickness and in health"? She'd never had to put it to the test before.

Freya walked over to the tree and placed the gecko on the presents, as she did every year. Raymond had handed it to her at the airport all those years ago. He'd carved it after Christmas, from the bough of silky oak.

"That Christmas started out as my worst ever. No frosts, no spruce tree, no turkey, no family. And it ended up being one of my very best."

Karen still looked doubtful. "Does that mean we can have a real Christmas this year if Grandpa's still in hospital?"

Freya looked at the pale young girl waiting so earnestly for her answer. She could almost hear Raymond's voice saying the words for her. And in her granddaughter's eyes she could see the love and hope that had bound her to Raymond that first Christmas. She mustn't let either of them down.

"Where does the spirit of Christmas live?" she gently asked.

Karen rested a hand on her chest. "In my heart," she said. "And so does Grandpa."

Freya nodded, unable to trust her voice. Quietly she took another rumball. She and Karen would make another batch when they'd finished decorating the tree. And she'd give them to her elderly neighbour.

They were rolling the rumballs in coconut that evening when the phone rang. When Raymond's doctor introduced himself, Freya felt her knees sag. Then, as he spoke, her eyes filled with tears – tears of relief and gratitude, till she thought her heart would spill over.

A sticky hand reached up to hold Freya's free hand, and two worried eyes fastened onto hers.

"Grandpa's much better," she whispered. "The doctor thinks he'll be able to come home for Christmas after all."

As Karen yelped in delight, Freya heard another voice on the phone.

"What's all the fuss?" Raymond said weakly. "It's only a dose of flu."

As Freya lay in bed later, looking through the curtains at the clear night sky, she whispered a heartfelt prayer of thanks.

A star shone brightly outside her window, a light in the darkness. A light of hope and promise.

It was suddenly quite simple. The spirit of Christmas was the spirit of love. Not just the love between her and Raymond or between her and Karen, deep though those loves were. Like the star in the night sky, which was part of a galaxy, these loves were part of a much bigger Love, more immense than she could understand. A Love big enough to embrace every human heart, just as the sky was big enough for every star.

Saying Goodbye

You hold up your Santa sack. "I guess I won't be needing this anymore."

I have to blink back the tears when I hear the slight tremble in your voice for the first time today. Neither of us has really realised until this moment that we're saying goodbye to each other. To this stage of our lives. We've been too busy packing your things together and making arrangements.

I finger the soft cotton pillowslip I sewed twenty-four years ago. Only a few months ago I filled it, knowing it'd be for the last time. All of a sudden your needs were for adult things. A recipe book. A blender. Tea towels. Cutlery. It felt strange putting it under our Christmas tree. It felt like a contradiction to put such practical everyday items into the very same pillowslip that had held your Lego kits and skateboard and cricket bat. We were play-acting this time, holding onto a past that we knew had already slipped through our fingers.

Love of course never slips through fingers. Somehow this pillowslip epitomises that. It isn't perfect, far from it.

But it's durable. There's a sameness about it that has made it irreplaceable, even when we could've afforded something better.

And apparently it has its own special smell, something it took me twenty-four years to learn.

Before handing it to me, you give it one last sniff, holding it to your face and inhaling deeply. "I love this smell," you say. "It's always been very special." And you confide that each Christmas as you sat up quietly in bed as a young boy, exploring the contents of your Santa sack in the dark, you'd first paused to breathe in its magic.

I close my eyes and breathe in. But it's not magic that I find. It's love. The bag smells of you.

Yet to an outsider, it's simply a faded homemade pillowslip, sewn from cheap fabric and looking the worse for wear.

I found the remnant of green cotton at a sale. The pattern of cheeky Santas won me over. I was pregnant at the time, and wondered whether it'd make a cool pair of rompers, or maybe a dress if my baby was a girl. Everything lay ahead of me that day as I held the fabric.

Where have these years gone?

Have I really hidden gifts in this pillowslip twenty-four times? It just doesn't seem possible. Yet here you are in front of me, a young adult leaving home to start a new phase of your life. A life where childhood things like a Santa sack and a teddy bear would take up space needed for the new life you're embarking on. It's not that you don't hold them dear. It's that you fear they'll hold you back. I understand that. And we both know that I won't throw it away.

When I was very young, my mother made reins for us,

to make sure we stayed by her side on trips into the city. She didn't have enough hands to hold onto each one of us, so this seemed the only way she could show the city sights to her curious young brood. I have no memory of wearing these reins, just the occasional reminder of them in photos.

But I clearly remember the excitement of those trips, of the department stores, of eating new foods such as frosted caramels and tropical fruit sundaes. Bustling crowds, noise, trams. The magic is still there, but the means of achieving it are long since forgotten.

I think in a way the Santa sack is also a set of reins. Something to hold you to me. Keep you within that safe loving circle of family. A rein of tradition, family rites. Yet something that as you grow older is replaced by invisible ties. Bonds of love that mature into respect, consideration, sometimes even awe. It's these invisible ones that last. We can let go of the others.

Blinking back the tears, I carefully lay the bag in the bottom drawer of my dressing table. Beside an ancient pair of reins.

A Ray of Sunshine

There's an orange on the floor in the cloakroom. And when I went into the bathroom to wash my hands, a large toy eye stared up at me from the tiled terracotta floor. It belongs to an octopus we made from an old T-shirt. The octopus though much admired didn't survive its first bathtime adventure.

The sight of these random objects in incongruous places has become the norm. What is unusual is to find anything where it actually belongs.

Take the egg-slice, for example. Until this week, it's led a mundane existence, alternating between the container on the bench top and the dishwasher. When I needed it Tuesday, to turn over two eggs, it was conspicuously absent.

Not lost, of course. Everything is found, eventually. And the egg-slice mysteriously reappeared in a toy box on Thursday, none the worse for its adventure.

I wish I could say I'm also none the worse, but I'd be lying. Being sleep-deprived has never brought out my better nature. Neither has the need to read the same book aloud twenty times. Yes, twenty. I'm not sure why but yesterday I counted.

Outside, the rain teams down into the garden, which is already a bog from last week's rain. And the week before.

I look out the bathroom window at the bedraggled remains of my lilies and roses. They thrived initially but then the soggy soil couldn't hold the lilies upright, and the roses quietly pined for sunshine.

Just like me.

Outside the kettle comes to the boil. I walk quietly down the hall to the kitchen. Careful not to walk on a toy car. My elbow is still recovering from yesterday's impromptu skating display. As is my rear end.

I was the only one who didn't see the funny side. It's hard to feel amused when your tailbone sends out shooting pain and you have trouble getting up from the floor. Well perhaps it was a bit funny. But as I lift the kettle and pour water into the mug, my elbow reminds me yet again of its presence.

Elbows aren't something I'm usually conscious of. Like tail bones, they're largely forgotten until something goes wrong.

I stir and prod the teabag, conscious that it's already seven o'clock. These precious minutes of peace are unexpected. If only I can sit down and drink my tea uninterrupted…

The kitchen at least is as it should be. I stayed up last night to make sure of that. The egg-slice is in a new position on top of the kitchen dresser just until the weekend, when it can safely descend.

There's a sticky patch on the oak table. I must've missed it when I wiped up the spilt custard.

It'll have to wait.

I take my first grateful sip of tea and lean back in the chair letting the wooden slats support my spine. Minutes pass.

The windows are a blurry mass of racing raindrops. It'll be another day indoors by the look of it. I thought the weather forecaster looked a bit shifty last night when he spoke of a break in the weather. You simply can't trust a word they say, can you? No better than our politicians.

My mind starts to come into focus. Thoughts appear. I decide to write a list. It might save some of yesterday's pandemonium.

But when I open the drawer to the dresser, my notebook isn't there. Another casualty? Surely I'd have noticed if Poppy had managed to get the drawer open? She's only just turned three. Awful possibilities crowd my mind, blanketed in feelings of guilt. I use the other drawer for cutlery. I shudder at the thought. Next time she stays there'll be some of those child-safety things in the kitchen.

Another sip of tea brings back a vague memory of using the notebook. We'd been drawing around the outlines of our hands the other day. I can now remember writing down the date too. Feeling overwhelmed by memories and wanting to preserve this one. I know only too well how quickly time races by. It can't really be twenty-five years since I made pastry hands, lining up the kids and getting them to place their hands on the sheets of pastry, fingers outstretched. I'd always use the bluntest bread knife. And they'd always move their fingers at a critical moment so we'd have to reposition them. When there was finally a line of pastry hands of various sizes, we'd grate cheese on top and sprinkle paprika.

Ten minutes in the oven and I'd have something everyone would eat, and the oven would warm up the kitchen.

A tear unexpectedly trickles down my cheek.

I sip tea. It feels comforting. Something that has stayed the same. Just like this oak table.

I've changed. I know that. I realised it only too clearly yesterday, as I was slow to get off the floor.

Where have the years gone?

Where has my energy gone too?

Things I took in my stride now occupy far too much of my time. It leaves less room for the other things. The ones memories are built on.

Next door's car comes to life. I watch as it swims onto the road and causes tiny waves to appear in its wake. Like the thoughts that ripple through my mind. Thoughts and images of the future.

Swimming lessons. School. Driving lessons. All these things lie ahead for Poppy.

How much of these times will I be privileged to share?

A little voice disturbs my thoughts. Poppy's standing in the doorway, her wispy blonde curls dishevelled, her eyes blank, not yet focussed, still only semi awake.

Smiling I rush over and lift her, sore tailbone forgotten. Elbow forgotten. Even the rain doesn't touch the happiness I feel at that moment.

Holding my granddaughter in my arms, her soft warm cheek resting against mine, my world is filled with sunshine.

Poppy nestles against me.

Another day has begun.

Heart to Heart

Brenda glanced nervously at her watch. Three o'clock. Her daughter Alice would be here any moment. She hadn't seen her for nearly twelve months. Was it really that long ago that Alice had stormed off, to live with her aunt in Surrey? Originally it was to be for a week, but her aunt had needed a hip replacement and Alice had offered to stay and help. Then she'd found a job locally.

The odd postcard had arrived, with snippets of news, and they'd exchanged birthday presents, but Brenda hadn't really felt they'd communicated. Not until last night's phone call when Alice had said she was driving up to see her. There'd been a wariness and tension in Alice's voice, but something else as well.

Was it possible after all this time that Alice too was hoping to find a bridge to link their troubled hearts?

She looked at the quilted wall hanging, which she'd made in the weeks after Alice had moved out. When her own heart had ached and swelled with grief.

A car pulled up outside. Brenda wiped the palms of her hands onto her jeans.

The first thing she noticed about Alice as she walked up the driveway was her hair. It was blonde, just as it'd been when she was young. She stood by the window to watch the sunlight glinting off her daughter's hair.

Somehow she'd never got used to seeing Alice with black hair. Never understood the need to cover up who she was.

Alice had always covered things up. That'd been the problem.

And Brenda had never really felt able to deal with the sorry situations that'd resulted.

Maybe the blonde hair was a reflection of other changes? A small ray of hope entered her heart.

The doorbell rang, and Brenda hurried down the hall.

She clasped Alice in her arms. "I love your hair," she managed.

Alice shrugged. "I wanted a change." Her voice was subdued.

Brenda led her into the kitchen. She knew Alice hated any kind of fuss, so she started to make coffee. She'd let her daughter do the talking. It'd be silly to get the visit off on the wrong footing after all this time. She'd never quite known what to say to her, even now.

Alice sat down at the wooden table and looked around.

Brenda carefully measured the coffee beans into her old-fashioned grinder. It looked as though it belonged in another century. To a time when people weren't always in a hurry. When there was time for families to sit around the kitchen table and sort out their differences. When people spent more time simply talking to each other. And listening. That's why she'd bought it, when she'd seen it in the charity shop. To remind herself to walk through time, not run.

There'd been plenty of time to think once Alice had moved out. She wanted to learn from the mistakes she'd made.

Soon the air was rich with the fresh intoxicating aroma of the ground coffee.

"What's your news?" Brenda reached into the cupboard for cups and saucers. Another old-fashioned choice. Everyone else seemed to use mugs for their coffee now. But these cups were a rich buttercup with bright daisies. Too cheerful to resist. And big enough for a decent-sized coffee.

"I'll wait until you're sitting down."

Brenda's heart hovered slowly in mid-air. She felt the heat rising from her chest and suffusing her face. She'd noticed Alice's complexion was pale and there were dark circles under her eyes. She daren't think what it might mean.

"Don't look like that, Mum," Alice said. "It's nothing bad. I just don't want to shock you."

"My heart can't take much." Brenda sat down at the table, beside her daughter.

"Your heart's pretty tough," Alice said. "It's needed to be, hasn't it?"

Words didn't come. All Brenda could do was nod. Why had Alice come today? What was she trying to tell her?

She didn't have to wait. The words tumbled out.

Alice reached across and held her hand. "I'm going to have a baby."

The tears fell of their own accord, as Brenda's arms wrapped her daughter close in an awkward embrace.

"I didn't even know you were in a relationship. Who is the father?" More questions flooded her mind, before Alice could begin to answer. *How will you be able to support a baby? Are you still living in Surrey?*

"His name is Max and he's a high school teacher. I want you to meet him."

Brenda sipped her coffee. "Maybe I could drive down to Surrey for a few days?"

Alice's eyes sparkled. "We're decided to move back here. Max's got a transfer to my old high school." She paused. "I know it's a lot to grasp but I'm hoping you'll be okay with it all."

Brenda gave a deep sigh and felt her shoulders relax. "You had me worried when you said I'd need to be sitting down. I thought you'd lost your job, or decided to live the other side of the world."

"I'm moving, but it's to be closer to home, not further away. I don't know anything about babies. And neither does Max."

The word 'home' lingered in Brenda's mind. "Just learn to trust your instincts. That's what worked for me." She paused, "And I learnt to listen to my own mother."

Alice pouted, as if to protest, but her lips twitched into a smile. The smile grew, until the tongue stud appeared.

They were both conscious of it.

"I put you through a lot, didn't I?" Alice was suddenly serious again.

Brenda looked for words to explain the gulf between her expectations and the angry young life she'd produced. "It wasn't easy. I had to do a lot of soul-searching. We're such different people."

Alice held her hand tightly. "Thanks for never giving up on me."

"I think I should say the same to you. We've both had to learn a lot, haven't we?"

Alice's eyes suddenly lit up. "That's one of the reasons I came today," she said. "I want to learn how to sew."

Brenda wiped her eyes. "I've waited years to hear you say that." She bit her tongue. "That sounds all wrong, doesn't it? I don't mean I expected you to be like me. It's just that I've wanted something to share with you and with all your artistic talent, sewing seemed something we could have in common."

"I was too stubborn to see that," Alice said. "I always felt you wanted a clone and that I didn't fit the bill."

"That's my fault. I was so worried about your father's health that I couldn't see the impact it was having on you."

"Let's not talk about fault. We all made mistakes. I've gone through it all with Max and he's helped me realise that."

"Your Max sounds as though he's good for you."

Alice's eyes glistened. "He's helped me turn my life around."

"How did you two find each other?"

"I've been working part time in the admin section at the same school where Max teaches," Alice said. "Once we got talking, he suggested I study art in the evenings so I could find work that's more suited to my talents."

"How does he feel about the baby?" Brenda couldn't help asking.

"It's come as a huge surprise to us both, but he's very practical." Alice smiled. "And he's excited. He wants to be a hands-on dad."

"What about your art?"

"Max suggested we both work part-time once the baby's old enough." She held Brenda's hand. "There's something else I want to tell you, and I hope it doesn't upset you. If the baby's a boy, we'd like to name him after Dad."

Brenda wiped her eyes, but there was a smile on her face. "When's your baby due?"

"I've only just found out that I'm two months pregnant."

"That gives us lots of time for you to learn how to sew."

"I really want to be able to sew clothes for my baby, Mum. Learn to mend. All that stuff."

"We can start on the basics today, if you've got time."

Alice looked at the quilted wall hanging, behind Brenda. "Do you think I'll ever be able to make a quilt like that?"

Brenda bit the inside of her bottom lip. *I hope you never need to*, she thought. Perhaps she should've put it away this morning?

The quilt had evolved from a period of intense heartache and despair. A time when Brenda had felt there was no one she could turn to for solace. Somehow she'd simply needed to work things out in this way. It was her life depicted on this quilt, in a form she could understand. By hanging it on the wall in the living room, it reminded her that anything could be dealt with. Its presence reassured her whenever life threw something seemingly impossible in her path.

She looked at the quilt, touching the line of black embroidery that stretched across the width.

"This stitch is easy to learn," she said. "It's similar to blanket stitch."

Alice drew her arm through Brenda's.

"Is that an old-fashioned clothes line?" she asked. "Why are there hearts on it?"

Brenda shook her head and felt her eyes moistening. "It's barbed wire," she said softly. "Our hearts were all on barbed wire. And they were hurting. That's what I wanted to show."

Brenda felt Alice's arm tighten around her, before being released.

She watched as her daughter rolled up the sleeves of her cardigan.

They both looked at her forearms. Over the years the crisscross scars had faded to a soft pearl. But in Brenda's memory they were still raw and angry, as the day she'd first seen them.

"My life felt like barbed wire too," Alice said. "I think I must've been suffering from depression to do this to myself."

"That's what I worried about. And you seemed to blame yourself for your father's heart attack."

Alice nodded. "When I came home from work and saw an ambulance parked outside, I freaked out. I'd argued with him that morning."

"We should've told you earlier about his heart condition but we didn't want to worry you."

They both looked quietly at the quilt.

"Why did you make your heart different to everyone else's?" Alice asked.

Brenda looked at the four hearts sitting on a line of barbed wire. With a trail of tiny hearts raining down from one of the hearts. That heart was Brenda's.

"My heart broke when I found out that you'd cut yourself. I felt very alone. These tiny hearts are meant to symbolise what was going on inside me."

Alice brushed her eyes. "It was me I hated, never you. I blamed myself for his death."

"I felt that, but my heart kept leaking tears, I didn't seem to have any control over it." She paused. "I was so overwhelmed by my own emotions that I didn't really grasp what you must've been going through."

"I wasn't exactly approachable."

"No, but if I had my time over again, I'd try harder to find help for you."

"Don't beat yourself up about it, Mum. I don't think I'd have opened up to anyone back then."

Alice gently traced the bright cherry-coloured outline of Brenda's heart with her forefinger.

The tenderness in the gesture brought fresh tears to Brenda's eyes. She tried to will them away, as she watched her daughter.

The years peeled away. She remembered sitting here at the dining room table, a piece of soft red cloth in front of her. On the table were hearts in all shapes and sizes. Choosing which heart would represent each of them had been the hardest part. She'd wept silently for the loss of innocence. For the hurt. For the disillusion.

She'd found a sturdy-looking heart for Daniel, to reflect his strength of character. Her son's was solid too, but slighter. He'd grow into the sturdiness over time. It was already in his eyes.

She'd noticed one of the pieces had fallen onto the floor. When she picked it up, the fabric had crush marks. She'd tried to smooth them out with her hand, but they'd resisted. *This one is Alice's*, she'd thought. She knew she should iron it but couldn't bring herself to do it. Solutions couldn't be forced on Alice's heart. She'd have to find a gentler way. And there'd been one. She'd carefully rubbed it and stretched it around her hot tea cup. That'd smoothed out the worst of the crush marks.

Love always found a way, she reflected, as she watched her daughter now.

Alice was still looking intently at the row of hearts, sitting on the barbed wire.

"I've only just noticed something," she said. "Why is your heart a bit bigger than the others?"

Brenda had instinctively chosen this heart to reflect her own that sad afternoon. It'd only been later that she too had noticed that it was slightly more substantial than the others. She was glad Alice was looking at the quilt closely enough to see this subtlety. But she felt self-conscious too. Her heart was no bigger or better than anyone else's. It'd simply felt swollen at the time. Now she saw it differently. Perhaps all mothers needed to develop more heart, as they learnt to grow into the role?

"Your heart will grow too, as you help your baby through life," she said. "Just enjoy every moment with your baby. Those early years seem to pass very quickly."

"Did you enjoy your moments with me? Despite everything?"

Brenda took her into her arms, this slight girl who would soon become a mother herself. Alice's blonde head sank into her shoulder, leaving a sweet scent of fresh shampoo. She held tightly to Brenda in a way that was breath taking. Opening so many doors that'd been closed and locked in recent years. It was a warm heartfelt hug, one she'd waited years to receive.

And for the first time she realised that true healing had taken place, transforming the angry wounds into pearly scars. On Alice's arms. And also on her own heart.

"We had good times," Brenda answered. "Remember our

beach holidays? We all seemed to relax as soon as we saw the ocean."

"Maybe we should've lived by the sea?" Alice said. "It might've suited us better."

"Too late now for what ifs. We've got a whole new future opening up."

She thought back over the years.

There'd been good moments when she'd felt she didn't deserve so much happiness. And there'd been terrible times when she'd felt crushed and completely inadequate. And now a new baby was coming into their lives, another heart that'd need to be looked after and nurtured. This time by her daughter.

Brenda realised it was time she made another quilt.

She'd need to find a new way of expressing this insight. Of showing how pearls of wisdom came into being.

Perhaps she'd use oyster shells this time? They could be nestled in a bed of sand, in the warm nurturing waters of the ocean.

She could throw away the black cotton, and buy some gold silk.

Through a Glass Darkly

Robyn wasn't religious but she couldn't help feeling this was a miracle. Only yesterday her world was dark and unfocussed. Now, lying in the recovery area of the eye hospital, she had glimpses of a crystal-clear lighter world. One she'd lost sight of several years ago, so gradually that she hadn't been aware how significant the changes had become.

How blue the sky now looked. Not the dark grey-blue of yesterday but a lighter more cheerful shade. Her left eye was covered by a clear plastic protective shield, attached to her face by white taping. It was in the spaces between this taping that she could see a new world.

Patrick would be waiting outside for her, in the sitting room where patients were taken. At least, she hoped he'd be there. He hadn't been too good this morning when he'd brought her here. Down in the mouth, his eyes with that so-familiar dull darkness. He'd lost his cheerfulness over recent years just as she'd lost her normal vision.

Two of a kind, she thought.

But immediately dismissed the thought. She'd never experienced the kind of internal battles he was experiencing and didn't really understand them. How could he be depressed when he had everything he'd always wanted? A good job, a lovely home, two vibrant grown-up children, and even a small cottage by the sea where they could go fishing and have holidays. How could he not be happy when he possessed so much? But unhappy he clearly was, and he didn't show any signs of doing anything to improve his state of mind.

Never mind Patrick, she'd just enjoy these glimpses of blue sky that heralded a promise of things to come. She'd be back here in a fortnight's time to have the cataract removed from her right eye as well. After that, there'd be no stopping her.

Would she stay with Patrick if he continued to be like this? The thought of leaving him had crossed her mind more than once, especially at those times when he'd been adamant that he didn't need any help. Where was the happy loving man she'd married? How did his work colleagues cope with him? But then again, they didn't see him at his worst, did they? He seemed to unravel when it was just the two of them, shrugging off the veneer of fake cheerfulness he assumed when he was socialising. It was unconvincing, but preferable to the blackness of his mood on those days when he'd lie in bed, curtains drawn, not speaking. Then she'd feel sucked into the despair he was suffering, as though he was a vacuum of misery drawing her towards the abyss where his soul dwelt.

She had no idea how long she lay there, wondering at the glimpses of lightness and thinking about Patrick's darkness. Her mind drifted, as it emerged from the anaesthetic. Surfacing for a while then slipping back into a dream state.

Then she became aware of a nurse beside her stretcher, measuring her blood pressure. She had a vague memory that this had happened a few times already. There was something familiar about it. But this time the nurse noticed she was more alert and spoke to her.

"Are you ready for a cup of tea or coffee?" she asked.

Robyn nodded, and allowed the nurse to help her off the stretcher. They made their way slowly to the sitting area where she was assisted into a big comfortable armchair.

"Coffee would be lovely," she said. Adding that she liked milk and one teaspoon of sugar.

She rested against the comfort of the supportive chair, and looked around. The woman sitting opposite her was eating a sandwich. Like her, she had a plastic shield over one eye. Robyn was surprised how young she looked. She'd always associated cataracts with older people. The attentive young man by her side reminded her of how solicitous Patrick used to be.

The nurse returned with a mug of coffee. To Robyn's surprise it was good percolated coffee, café standard. For some reason she'd expected instant coffee. Her spirits rose. And there was a plate of cheese and lettuce sandwiches.

As she took a first grateful sip of the coffee, she heard the nurse speaking over the phone to Patrick, letting him know it was time for him to collect her. The coffee tasted wonderful, all the more so because she'd had to fast before the procedure.

She was finishing the last mouthful of sandwich when her husband arrived. She could immediately tell he was making an effort to sound cheerful. It was a good sign, but what would he be like when they were home again, just the two of them?

He sat down in an armchair beside her. The nurse came over. *How considerate*, Robyn thought, as more coffee arrived. She didn't feel quite ready to go back to the domestic situation which faced her. Better to linger here a while longer until she felt her strength returning.

Patrick was curious to hear about her experience. As they drove home and he asked question after question, she was surprised how animated he was.

Was this a good time to raise the difficult issue of his own health problem? Or should she just enjoy the change in his manner while it lasted?

She was still undecided when they arrived back home. Patrick parked in the garage, and came around to her side of the car to help her. Leaning on him, she walked back inside.

It was such a relief to have the operation behind her. To know everything had gone well.

"I think I'll lie down for a while," she told him.

This was a turnaround. Usually it was Robyn bustling around the house while Patrick lay on the bed, staring at the ceiling.

Where will he lie today if he feels unwell, she thought? Hopefully not here, beside her. She needed to recuperate, not be dragged down.

Today was all about recovering from the darkness that had been clouding her vision. There was no room for anyone else's darkness.

But there was a gentleness in his manner that she hadn't felt for a while. And a look of genuine concern in his blue eyes. They weren't inward-looking at the moment. It made a nice change.

"How do you feel?" he asked. "You're pale."

"Sleepy," she said. Adding "but also excited."

He placed a warm wrap over her and quietly withdrew. She could hear him in the kitchen, loading the dishwasher. The next sound she was aware of was the kettle coming to the boil. She opened her eyes. How long had she been asleep? She reached over to her bedside table until she found her alarm clock. It was already four o'clock. She must've been asleep for three hours. No wonder she felt hungry.

"I thought I heard you stirring." Patrick was standing in the doorway with two cups of tea.

Even Patrick looked different, though not so dramatically different as the sky had been. And the blue checked shirt he was wearing made him seem lighter than usual.

She wouldn't mention it. He wouldn't understand.

She and Patrick didn't have those kinds of conversations any more.

He put the tea down so he could arrange some pillows behind her back. *It does him good to focus on someone else's needs*, she thought. It brought out a different side to his personality.

Even more surprising was the chocolate gingerbread muffin he brought her a few moments later. "I made these myself," he said, a new tone of pride in his voice. Usually Robyn did all the cooking. This was a new recipe. Had he found it on one of those cooking websites?

She bit into the muffin, aware of him watching her. "It's absolutely delicious," she said.

The muffin was still warm. She tried to guess which spices he'd used. There was definitely a lot of cinnamon and ginger, and another flavour. Was it cardamom? She was impressed.

"We'll have to keep this recipe," she told him.

And maybe I'll keep you as well, she couldn't help thinking.

After the tea and muffin, it was time to take off the shield and apply eye drops. A loud gasp escaped her lips as she saw the room properly for the first time. The curtains such a lovely sage green, the wooden frames around the windows a lighter and gentler shade of brown than she was accustomed to seeing. The embroidery threads in her mother's framed tapestry on the wall were subtle and clear. Everything fresh and transformed.

"It's a new world," she said happily.

"I wish I could see a new world," Patrick blurted out. Reverting to his usual "I" sentences where everything was about him.

"Maybe you could?" she said softly, taking his hand in hers. "We could find someone who might be able to help you?"

He took a deep breath. She was expecting him to say something else but he didn't. But he didn't look glum either. That was a good sign.

"I'm not sure anyone could help me," he said after a pause.

"You won't know until you try." She pressed his hand. "It'd be hard to ask for help, I know that. But I'd come with you to the appointment, if that'd make it easier."

He sipped his tea, staring out the window, lost in thought.

"Anything's worth a try," she persisted. Now they'd actually begun this difficult conversation, she wanted it to lead to something positive. At least an acknowledgement on his part that his state of mind needed to change. Either through his own efforts or with assistance from an expert in the field.

Quietly he ate his muffin, ignoring the crumbs that fell onto his shirt.

Robyn had noticed the way the muffins were a bit too crumbly. She'd find a way to adjust the recipe. Maybe adding an extra egg would help? She was good at adapting things. And good at adapting to situations, she realised. She'd adapted to the way her eyesight had gradually deteriorated. And she'd adapted to the way Patrick's moods had changed.

Could she help him adapt to change? Or was this something that had to come from within the person?

"You won't know until you try," she repeated.

His eyes flickered as he turned towards her. "Do you really think so?" he said.

It wasn't the *no* she'd been half expecting.

"I'm going through these operations so I can have my sight restored," she said. "Why don't you try to have your way of seeing restored as well?"

He breathed out deeply. "And you'd be happy to come with me?"

She nodded.

He gave a small smile. "So you think I have emotional cataracts? Ones that darken how I feel?"

"We both know it's true," she said. "Let's not shut our eyes to your problems. That won't solve anything."

"Well, you've set me a good example," he said. "I know you were worried about today even though you tried to hide it."

While he finished his muffin, Robyn lay down again and inserted the eye drops. The first one stung her eye. She wasn't looking forward to doing this for the next four weeks. Change came at a price. And maybe she'd been underestimating Patrick's feelings about therapy?

But they'd both made a good start on the road to recovery.

Did You Forget to Say Goodbye?

To someone you love, it's the hardest word to say. Fingertips touching and gently letting go. Eyes locking for a lingering moment of union. A teary bear hug before boarding a plane.

Life is full of farewells. They come in all shapes and sizes. And when they're least expected.

We say countless little goodbyes every day. Moments of perfection we know can never last. The dew on a rosebud that tomorrow will unfurl, and again, until it has no more tomorrows.

For tomorrow always comes, awakening in its freshness, releasing all which yesterday was lost.

As I lost you, only yesterday.

A phone call plucked you from my life, as a strong breeze will blow a leaf from a branch. As a gale will fell a mighty tree.

Today the ground's covered with the leaves of my memories. I'm walking knee-deep through these freshly fallen twigs and leaves, looking for something to hold onto.

Did you forget to say goodbye?

There are no goodbyes here where the tree once stood. I pick up a leaf, flecks of green in many shades, marked with an intricate pattern of veins. I touch the surface with my finger, marvelling at its perfection. One of a myriad of leaf memories of the time we spent together.

The first time it happened, I was angry with you. I was only eight-years-old, too young to understand, but old enough to feel betrayed.

"Where's Grandpa?" I asked, when you didn't come down to breakfast.

You must've slept in, I thought. Or perhaps you'd caught a cold? I'd seen you blowing your nose the night before.

No one explained to me that your sister had suffered a sudden heart attack and died. You had to suffer my silent rejection.

I didn't talk to you for several days. Until you sat me on your knee one afternoon in the garden. It must've been autumn because I clearly remember the reds and yellows and browns. Our garden was a fairyland that afternoon.

You had two leaves in your hand to show me, a fresh green one from the lemon tree, and a brilliant red one from the ground.

You broke the lemon leaf in half and got me to sniff.

"This is my heart," you said. "It's broken in half because you've stopped talking to me."

I sniffed it again, trying to disguise the upset feelings overwhelming me. It'd never occurred to me I could break the heart of a grown-up. I was afraid of what I'd done, and didn't know how to make things right again.

"What's this one?" I pointed to the red one, wanting to get onto safer ground.

"That's another piece of my heart," you said. "It's no longer part of the tree but it's complete and it's beautiful."

I didn't know what to make of this and just looked at it quietly, waiting for you to explain.

"Aunty Grace is in heaven," you said. "We were lucky to have so many good times with her."

You got me to collect a basket of red leaves.

"These are our memories of Aunty Grace. There's more than we can ever hold in our arms, but in our heart there's always room."

We both looked at the broken lemon leaf. "What can we do about this?" I asked. "Leaves can't be mended, can they?"

"Try kissing it better," you said, "and close your eyes."

The leaf tasted bitter and my lips felt funny but when I opened my eyes you were holding a brand-new leaf in your hand.

I threw my arms around your neck and kissed you better too. I promised myself I'd taken better care of your heart.

I wonder now where you hid the second green leaf. Was it in your shirt pocket? I wish I'd asked you when I was older. But life tumbled along and was too exciting for me to stop and tie up loose ends. Always the future beckoned.

The next time you went away for a while without saying goodbye, I was in my twenties, too full of my own concerns to give it much attention. I was sharing a house with friends from university. This night I'd dropped by home. Fridays, roast chicken followed by apple pie. Not something you forget lightly when you're living away from home.

"Where's Grandpa?" I asked, noticing your empty place at the dining table.

Mum had a weary look in her eyes, and ran her hand through her hair. I was afraid she was going to cry.

"He didn't want to worry you," she began.

And I coaxed out the details of your open-heart surgery. After dinner we drove to the hospital. When the nurse in the intensive care ward wasn't watching, I put a green lemon leaf in your hand.

Your lips twitched into a small smile. When I saw your fingers curl over the leaf, I knew everything would be alright. You'd pull through.

What happened this time? Did you not want to worry me? Did Aunty Grace take your hand and lead you to a higher garden, where rosebuds never lose their promise?

I'm sitting on the wooden bench in the garden, under the lemon tree. I've kicked the ground, spraying leaves into the air. Nothing I do helps me understand, takes away the anger. The hurt that pushes everything else from my heart.

My toe nudges the pile of leaves under the bench. They're in all shapes and sizes, reds, browns, speckled green and yellow.

A little cluster of shiny green leaves catches my eye. I bend down for a closer look. There's something about the leaves that chokes me. I gently break off a small leaf, and break it in half, sniffing. It's a new lemon tree, grown from a seed inside one of last year's lemons.

I raise it to my lips, close my eyes, and kiss it.

You don't reappear. My heart doesn't mend.

My lips get that funny tingly sensation. It travels through my entire body. Carefully, making sure none of the delicate roots is damaged, I gather up this tiny plant. There's an old basket on the bench, big enough to hold this piece of your heart.

There's room in my garden for a lemon tree, and my heart is big enough to hold all the leaf memories of you.

We're on the Same Wavelength

When the images flashed through my mind, I immediately knew something was wrong. Irreparably wrong. Everyone knew your life flashed through your mind as you died.

But I wasn't dying. And the images weren't of my life.

They were images of your life, Robert.

So what were they doing in my mind?

I sat up in bed and checked the clock. I'd slept away half the afternoon. It was three o'clock here in Brisbane. That meant it must be five o'clock in the morning in England. I couldn't phone at that hour. On the off chance everything was okay, I'd give you a scare. And if it wasn't? How could a phone call help?

My breath caught in my throat. Inside me the baby pushed and shoved. Fred the Footballer I nicknamed him. Every time I tried to rest, he decided it was party time.

I flinched as a little foot made firm contact with my aching diaphragm.

Could my pregnancy explain the images? Nightmares were becoming a regular occurrence. Only last night I'd had an awful dream about Daniel. In my dream we'd been living in a posh house set in acreage. I was standing on a balcony, looking up at the terraced gardens behind the house. Daniel leapt from a diving board into a swimming pool on the upper level. Then I'd heard a voice, "But there's no water in the pool". Followed by a soft thud.

I'd woken with palpitating heart and hot sweaty body to hear him breathing softly beside me. It'd taken ages for my heart to stop racing and beat normally again.

Could these images of your life be another way my psyche was playing tricks with me, Robert? Daniel reckoned it was all to do with me needing security. In his case, my husband. Maybe a twin brother fitted into the security need too?

"What do you think, Fred?" I asked my heavy belly. "Can I blame these images of Robert on my hormones?" I stumbled into the kitchen for a glass of water. Maybe I was a bit dehydrated? That'd been another problem recently.

It was a typical sauna afternoon, the sort Brisbane specialised in over summer. I was having trouble getting used to it, now that I was home all day. In the university administration building where I'd worked, it'd been air-conditioned. Almost too cold. We'd all worn cardigans, then melted in the heat when we stepped outside.

The kettle gleamed a welcome at me from the bench. Maybe a cup of tea would help?

My brain kept replaying the images, like a broken record player caught on a scratch. They'd been too real, that was the problem. I'd seen Robert as a child and then as a young man, standing in the front garden of the council home where we'd grown up. The dry gravel, the straggly bushes, even the broken section of fence near the front gate – the details were just too accurate.

And there was something else that unnerved me. I'd sensed myself in the background *as a minor character*. An onlooker. How could I explain that away, except as a direct transfer from your brain to mine?

We'd always said we were on the same wavelength. But I'd never entertained the thought that it could be literally true. Not until now. The implications filled me with an unnamed dread.

The kettle came to the boil and clicked itself off. I poured the boiling water onto a teabag, and tried to hurry it along by dunking it up and down. Impatient, like Fred the Footballer.

The minutes ticked slowly by. It was still too early for me to phone.

By four o'clock I'd drunk three cups of tea, and couldn't wait any longer. It'd be six o'clock in your little cottage in Devon. Hopefully not too cold or bleak a morning, because I had to get you out of bed. Hear your voice.

I tapped in the long series of numbers, and waited.

The seconds ticked by. A tingle ran along my spine as it always did when I phoned you.

Then I heard your voice. But not what I wanted to hear. "You have dialled… Sorry but we are unable to come to the phone…"

I could've thrown the phone onto the floor in my helpless anger. The phone was my only way of contacting you, and it'd let me down.

Fortunately, I clung onto what was left of my adult self.

I'd barely replaced the receiver when the phone startled me by ringing. For a moment I just stared at it blankly. Then

I grabbed it and pressed it to my ear. Sally's anxious voice spelt out my fears.

"I'm phoning from an ambulance," she gasped. "It looks like Robert's having a heart attack."

The stammered details drilled holes in my brain, etching a picture I couldn't bear to look at.

Until avoidance became impossible.

"It started just on five o'clock this morning," she said. "He started complaining about having indigestion. We didn't realise it was his heart."

In other words, Robert had become ill at three o'clock this afternoon, Brisbane time. At three o'clock he'd had images of his childhood flash through his brain. Somehow managing to transmit them to me. Beam them across the ocean and across the time zones, defying all logic. Had it been intentional? Had he had a sudden premonition and thought of me? I clung onto that thought. There was comfort in it. And comfort was in scant supply. Not just that afternoon but for the dark hours that followed, lapsing into days. Days, nights, phone calls at all hours. Life ceased to have any semblance of normalcy. We were stranded on a sandbar of despair, clinging to whatever hope drifted by. Buoyed one day by an optimistic prognosis. A prognosis that changed like the tide from one extreme to the other. Then despair became hope, almost a sense of complacency as Robert's doctor talked of an operation. I'd even started sleeping properly. Felt okay enough to complain. What an awful time we'd been through, I told Sally. It was only considered a relatively mild heart attack, but the underlying problem was much more serious and could've proved fatal without treatment.

Everything seemed to be on track.

Until it happened a second time.

It was a Sunday night. I'd gone to bed early, trying to catch up on sleep. A hopeless ask that night, with little Fred determined to leap about and kick me under the ribs. My body felt strained and uncomfortable. I was exhausted.

My eyes were closed. Then I saw the images again, almost an exact replay. The gravel, the bushes, the broken fence. And you and me, standing in the garden talking. This time I was even slower to work out what it could mean. Or maybe it was my subconscious trying to cushion the blow? For once again I found my rational explanation. I was simply reliving the experience, I told myself. It was seven-thirty at night. Nine-thirty in the morning, in England.

Nothing bad happened then, did it?

Didn't it?

I still hadn't said anything to Daniel about the first time I saw these images. Now it felt too late to say anything. They were too precious for me to let them be pigeonholed along with my nightmares, cast as a by-product of overactive hormones. And they were too precious to share. I didn't want to dilute the intensity of the experience, which I knew must happen.

They'd have to be my secret, something to ponder over and revisit for the rest of my life. But now, I must go to hospital. I knew that, without any doubt. The reason was quite simple. These were my own images, not Robert's – they'd been different this time. I'd been the one at the centre. That made me realise it was me who needed help.

The discomfort I'd dismissed as indigestion wouldn't go away. I remembered you'd mentioned this feeling, Robert, and it dawned on me that perhaps we shared a similar medical condition. All those nights when my heart had raced, I'd put it down to my pregnancy or to the nightmares I'd been having. The warnings had been there and I hadn't understood them.

I called out to Daniel and asked him to phone an ambulance for me.

Soon I was lying in the coronary unit at the Mater Hospital, while a heart specialist explained to Daniel that I was suffering a mild heart attack. It all sounded so terribly familiar. So we mentioned your underlying condition, Robert, and that ended up saving my life.

Semi-conscious, I seemed to be floating.

Daniel was stroking my forehead, making soothing noises. He seemed glued to the present, to reality, whereas you and I were travelling through time and space, independent of the normal realities.

For we were in this together, weren't we, Robert? And somehow in life's irony, our operations were scheduled within hours of each other. Your heart operation and my caesarean.

Just a few more days of waiting. More hours to fill. More long hot nights with just an invisible struggling shape to keep me company in the dark.

Thursday was the big day. *I'll be alright once it's over*, I kept telling myself.

And was overjoyed when my bedside phone rang on Wednesday evening and it was you.

"We'll be as good as new again, Sis," you said. "That's what my specialist says."

"I wouldn't even have recognised my symptoms as a

heart problem," I said. "You've saved my life, Robert. My heart would never have coped with a natural birth."

"Are the doctors sure you'll manage a caesarean?" you asked.

"They keep saying how lucky I am to have an identical twin," I said. "I'll be fine. And they're expecting to cure my heart condition with a minor operation in a few months' time."

There was a pause. I knew there were tears in your eyes. Mirrors of my own. "We'll have to say in better touch," you said. "Once life's back to normal again."

Your words were music to my ears. I'd been worried we might drift apart, living on opposite sides of the world. And now I was about to become a mother, I'd be busier than ever.

"My baby will need a godfather," I suggested. "When we've both recovered, we'll have a special Christening service. Bring the whole family together again."

"I'd be honoured to be your baby's godfather," you said. "Nothing would mean more to me."

A warm feeling of inexplicable fullness grew in my heart. For the first time in days, I felt a deep glow of contentment that reached to the very core of my being.

The truth slowly dawned on me. All these years, we'd intuitively known each other's thoughts and feelings without the need for words. It was something we simply took for granted. Somehow we really had been on the same wavelength.

And we still were.

Living on opposite sides of the world hadn't been able to alter the bond between us. It was something that transcended normal boundaries. Why hadn't I fully realised this before?

As I lay down to rest again a few moments later, I rested my hand on my swollen belly.

I hadn't said anything to Robert on the phone just now, but we'd noticed during the ultrasound that the baby I was carrying was a boy.

"We'll call him Daniel," I'd said.

But my husband had gently taken hold of my hand. "That might be a bit confusing, to have two of us with the same name," he'd said. "Perhaps he should be called Robert Daniel? I'll never be able to properly thank your brother for saving your life."

"Goodnight, little Robert," I said, patting my belly. "I can't wait to meet you tomorrow."

Hello, Stranger

It's all the things that no longer happen that hurt - and there are constant reminders of them. The empty space beside me on the bed where you used to lie, sleepily telling me your dreams every morning, still in your pyjamas.

The hand you no longer hold to cross the road. The kite that gathers dust. Shaped like a fire-breathing dragon, it sits undisturbed against the wall in your bedroom. It hasn't scared a butterfly for years.

Then there are the dolls going mildewy in the bathroom cupboard since your last clean out. Next stop for them is the charity bin at our local supermarket.

It's sneaked up on me this time, Melissa, which it shouldn't have done. You're my youngest. I've already been through this twice. I haven't learnt much about coping, though, if this emptiness inside is anything to go by.

You're in front of your mirror, applying make-up. Totally absorbed in choosing a lip-gloss, you haven't noticed me enter the room. How could you hear anything above that music? I have to knock these days. There's an invisible sign on your door that says *Keep Out. Do Not Enter Unless Invited.*

Am I invited? Sometimes. You seem to vacillate between being my girl and being a stranger. I never know who I'll find.

I can relate to my girl. She talks to me, confides in me, *needs* me. The stranger's a newcomer. She's a bit intimidating, to tell the truth. More sophisticated. Very independent. Even speaks differently, especially when she's on the phone. And she wears lots of perfume and make-up. Her lovely face doesn't need foundation, blush, mascara, and eye shadow.

It's hard to recognise you under the layers of make-up. And your light blonde hair is a dark shade of brown now, and you spend hours straightening it. I've burnt myself on that appliance more times than I'd care to say. Do you ever remember to turn it off?

But I won't be saying anything. I had my head snapped off last time.

Sometimes the stranger will be here, and something happens that brings my girl back. Maybe our dog Spirit will come to the door to say hello. He seems to have the knack of finding you under the make-up, under the fashionable clothes, under all the props you use to signpost this new phase of your life.

But tonight he's out of luck. He's whining. You've forgotten to take him for a walk. Or to give him dinner.

I slip out of your room. I've forgotten what I was going to say to you.

He and I look at each other. He misses you too.

I get him his dinner, and while he wolfs it down, I find his lead. It's still light enough to take him on a walk around the neighbourhood. Freshen up both our moods. I've noticed he's been looking down in the dumps. His life's got empty spaces in it too, where you used to be.

By the time we get back, you've finished applying your make-up. You're on the phone. It seems to have become magnetised to your ear.

I fix dinner. It's Saturday so I make your favourite - chicken curry with basmati rice. The kitchen fills with the exotic aroma. It can simmer while I watch the TV news.

I'm ready to dish up when you finally hang up the phone.

"Dinner's ready," I say cheerfully.

"I've already eaten."

Except you haven't, have you? You've been at work from eleven o'clock until three. And since you got home, you've been in your room.

Without looking at me, you tell me you're going Latin dancing with Anna tonight.

"I haven't got time to eat," you say, without realising the contradiction. "Anna's father's picking me up at half past six."

"Why didn't you say something earlier?" I begin. My cheerful voice has deserted me. I'm trying not to sound upset but my heart's sinking. We used to be so close, now I find things out as they're happening. If then.

"Keep me some. I might be hungry when I get back."

You're looking at me as you speak. I recognise the I-need-a-favour look in your eyes. No amount of blue eye shadow and mascara can conceal it.

"Can you give me and Anna a lift home at ten o'clock?"

"Why didn't you ask earlier?" I say. "I didn't even know you were going out."

"I'm asking you now," you say with a too-bright smile as you take my hand. "Please, Mum."

Knowing the smile and contact will get you a *yes*. Knowing instinctively it's what I need.

Outside a car horn toots.

"Ten o'clock?" you say, walking down the hall.

And as you close the car door and drive off, I realise with a pang that you haven't kissed me goodbye.

I touch my cheek - another empty space.

I eat my curry and watch Inspector Morse on TV. Then I make coffee. I'm not the night owl I once was. If I don't have coffee, I might doze off.

Ten o'clock sees me at the Latin dancing studio. You've got me well trained - and I'm looking forward to hearing about your evening. Hundreds of people pour out of the studio onto the pavement. It takes you a while to spot the car.

"Anna wants to sleep over," you say, as you both sit in the back of the car. Now I feel like a chauffeur, not a mother. And the seat beside me is empty, too.

I pretend I haven't heard you above the car radio. Surreptitiously, I turn it up.

But it doesn't work.

Anna comes back to our place. She eats the curry I've kept for you. "Not bad," she says.

"Yes, my mum makes a great curry," you say, making a toasted cheese sandwich.

I have to bite my lip and leave the room. Otherwise, I'll say something I'll regret later. My words have developed the nasty habit of sitting wedged between us.

So I pour a bath and add Relax bubble bath. There's a full moon tonight, shining through the window onto the rippling water. I turn off the light and enjoy the simple pleasure of watching the reflections bounce as the water continues to pour. A nice steamy aroma is rising from the bath and I begin to relax. My jaw muscles slacken and I slowly undress.

In another moment, I'm lying in the bath, wondering what I was like as a teenager. Did I just dump Mum for a while the way my kids seem to do? Of course things were different back then, but some things never change.

When I think back, I can remember sitting with friends in the kitchen at home, making impromptu suppers, while Mum had a long bath. I can remember being proud of her cooking. And I can remember asking for lifts at the last moment. I wonder now what she must have been feeling. Left out? Or just tired? Waiting for me to go to bed so she could make sure I'd turned everything off. Did she feel alone, I wonder?

Of course, she had my father, but he'd always be in bed asleep when I got home. Not a worrier, like Mum.

It's too late now to phone. She's no more a night owl than I am. But first thing in the morning I'll give Mum a ring and see if she's busy. When I drop Anna home in the morning, I'll drive on to Mum's and see how she is. Make sure there are no empty spaces in her life. And let her know there are spaces in mine I'd like to share with her.

Maybe next Saturday, Melissa, when you're off Latin dancing with Anna – yes! I overheard you talking in the back of the car just now - maybe I could visit Mum and watch the Saturday night movie with her? I noticed there are some classic films starting up next week. We haven't seen a Cary Grant movie together for years.

We'll set her alarm clock for half past nine in case we both doze off. And we can have coffee. I'll make extra chicken curry and basmati rice so I can take her some to reheat for her Sunday lunch. And there'll be enough for you too, Melissa, as well as Anna next Saturday.

Problem solved. For the time being, anyway.

I lie back in the bath, relaxing fully for the first time all evening. Lazily I gather up handfuls of the bubbles and hold them up to the light - and see a myriad of sparkling rainbows. Hundreds of tiny empty spaces that are now made beautiful.

I Can See Clearly Now

Wendy walked about the optometrist's waiting room, praying that her six-month-old son Oliver would doze off on her shoulder. *Where's Mum?* she thought. Her appointment was in ten minutes' time. What could she do? Her baby wouldn't stop crying. She jigged him up and down with her tired arms. Her head was pounding.

Unexpectedly, silence. She relaxed, her shoulders sagging. She peeped at her cherub. He was gleefully waving about a fashionable pair of oblong red frames with thick purple side arms. He must've quietly grabbed them from the display as she was walking past.

She had no choice but to untangle them from his chubby fingers while ignoring his cries of protest. She hoped the sales assistant wouldn't notice they'd become a little sticky. *At least he hasn't broken them,* she thought.

As he'd broken hers, just yesterday, when he'd woken from his afternoon nap in a grisly mood. Sucking his fist and howling. She'd walked up and down the hallway, singing Twinkle Twinkle Little Star. Her glasses had ended up in three pieces before she'd realised what he was up to. His little fingers were so quick, she couldn't keep up with him.

Now she felt at her wits' end. Yesterday's headache was still brewing in her head, a combination of Oliver's crying and her eyestrain. And she'd had yet another nearly sleepless night.

He'd been crying, as he was now. She'd put teething gel on his sore gums, and noticed the edge of a tooth finally cutting through.

The familiar high-pitched protest was at deafeningly close range. Maybe she should walk outside for a moment? That might distract him. It was so embarrassing.

Everyone thinks I don't know how to look after my baby.

She glanced at her watch. Five minutes to ten. *Where are you, Mum?* she thought. Her tired eyes were rewarded by the sight of a silver-haired figure hurrying along the pavement towards her. Her mother was short and fairly slight inside her layered cardigans, but at this moment she seemed like a tower of strength. Wendy felt her facial muscles relax, and realised how tense she'd been. She hugged her mother with her free arm, and rested her head for a moment on her mother's shoulder.

Oliver wriggled with excitement. Two chubby arms stretched towards his grandmother.

"Sorry I'm late. The bus was caught in traffic," Joyce said. Then her attention turned to Oliver. She held two sticky hands in hers, and kissed him on both cheeks. His big blue eyes were fastened onto hers, as she took him into her arms.

"Thanks for coming at such short notice," said Wendy. "This was the only free appointment today. I'm lucky there was a cancellation."

Her mother's eyes lingered on Wendy's face. "You look worn out," she said.

Wendy smiled wryly. "I didn't think it'd be so hard with Elliot away. At least his conference finishes on Friday."

"Four more days to go. Maybe I can help out?"

"Just seeing you makes me feel stronger. I haven't adjusted to not getting enough sleep."

"We'll make sure you have time to rest today. Put your feet up. Paint your fingernails."

"I won't have much time. Claire phoned last night. She's booked a restaurant for eight o'clock tonight. Invited the usual gang."

"It's alright for Claire," Joyce said. "She's still single. Now you've got Oliver, you need to start putting yourself first."

"I felt about a hundred listening to Claire. At the moment my idea of a good night is settling down with a cup of tea and a magazine."

"Maybe you'd enjoy yourself if you had a sleep this afternoon? What does your heart tell you?"

Wendy shook her head. "It's my brain doing the talking. The place she's booked was written up in the weekend paper. It's very upmarket. I can't afford it this month and I didn't know how to tell Claire. I'm sick of sounding like a wet blanket."

Joyce looked thoughtful. "First things first. Let's see if your glasses can be mended. Otherwise you'd need to factor in a taxi fare as well."

"I'm just praying they don't need replacing. My budget wouldn't cope with the ridiculous price of new frames."

She could hear the flatness in her voice and hoped her mother hadn't noticed.

"What you need is a holiday."

Her mother had suggested a few days at the beach in her

holiday cabin. Just the three of them. That was out of the question now. With her glasses broken, she couldn't drive. If only her mother had a driving licence.

Life could be so unfair. And it was darned expensive.

She checked the time. It was 10 o'clock.

"Thank goodness you're here, Mum. Will you be okay with Oliver?"

Then Wendy smiled. Her question was superfluous. Grandmother and baby were totally rapt in each other. Oliver lifted a piece of red floral fabric out of Joyce's blouse pocket. She always kept tempting pieces of brightly coloured material within reach of her favourite pickpocket.

"We'll meet you in the café over the road," Joyce said. "You look as though you could do with coffee."

Thankful, Wendy went back inside. How peaceful it seemed. She walked casually over to the display of frames and unobtrusively wiped a tissue over the red frames.

Soon she was sitting in the optometrist's raised chair, watching as he put horizontal and vertical lines across her vision. Answering the usual array of questions. Which is darker, the horizontal or the vertical? And the lenses would be shuffled about until both sets of lines were equal.

It always felt like an invasion of her personal space, sitting here, inches away from him. She could feel his warm breath on her face.

He wrote her prescription on the card and compared it with her existing one.

"No need to make any changes this time, Wendy." He was sitting at his desk now, their personal space re-established, the intrusive moment gone.

She handed him the three pieces of frame that until

yesterday had been her glasses. "Can you do anything with these, Andrew? I really can't afford to replace them, but I'm not sure they can be mended."

He inspected the broken plastic, twisting it one way and another. "It's not as bad as it looks," he said at last. "A screw has fallen out, and if we're lucky, we'll be able to glue this other piece back where it belongs. Shouldn't take long."

Wendy sat in the waiting room again feeling relieved. What if she'd had to wait days for new glasses to be made? It was a huge weight off her mind.

Relaxed, she found herself enjoying the fuzziness created by her myopia. Without her glasses, the rows of frames on the wall opposite looked like an array of colourful butterflies.

It brought back memories of her childhood. Nights when she'd sat in the back seat of her father's car, looking up at the sky through the rear windscreen. How wonderful the stars had seemed, so large and luminous. They'd been gleaming streams of light stretching across the sky. Even better on nights when it was raining and the raindrops on the windscreen added to the effect.

One night at bedtime, she'd mentioned to her mother that she had another headache. A few days later she'd found herself on the raised chair in the optometrist's office with Andrew putting a large metal contraption in front of her eyes to test different lenses. It'd been a revelation. No more peering at bus numbers. No longer having to sit in the front row at school.

But Wendy also remembered the disappointment when she'd first seen stars through her new glasses. Little cold orbs - nothing like their glorious counterparts. She'd taken off her glasses when her parents weren't looking so she could still enjoy them in their fuzzy splendour.

Yes, sometimes it was nicer when the world was fuzzy. When things weren't as clearly defined as they were in the world of adults.

She couldn't help wondering what adulthood would be like if she could take off the invisible glasses of responsibility now and again. It'd be lovely to enjoy the fuzziness of sensations again, the way she had as a child. Of walking along her favourite beach, dragging her toes in the sand. Of sitting on the rocks at the headland, eating fish and chips. Life had been so hard with Elliot away. Especially with Oliver teething. It felt like all work and no fun.

Motherhood. It'd certainly meant a lot of growing up on her part.

"Having a good day?" the young receptionist asked brightly, as Andrew emerged from his office. The girl flashed her a bright smile. Her hair had streaks of copper and brown through the ash blonde. Her makeup was perfect, straight from the cover of the magazine Wendy hadn't found time to read yet.

She bit the inside of her lip and nodded. The girl would be horrified if she knew the half of it.

"You're in luck," Andrew said, very pleased with himself. "You'll need to be careful till the glue dries. And in future, keep them out of reach of that beautiful baby of yours."

He turned to his receptionist. "There's no charge for the mending."

Wendy's spirits rose as she crossed the road to the café. Her mother had ordered her a cappuccino and raisin toast. A dribbling Oliver was slumped on her shoulder, one sticky hand clutching a piece of bright material.

"Is there anything you want to do while he's asleep?" Joyce asked.

Wendy contentedly skimmed a spoonful of the aromatic froth and licked it from the spoon. A delicious blend of chocolate and cinnamon. She stirred a sachet of sugar into her coffee, and buttered the hot toast.

"I don't have anything to wear to Claire's dinner tonight."

Wendy felt her mother's gaze taking in her saggy eyes and limp hair. She tried to sit up straight.

"Do you really want to go?" Joyce said.

"I can't afford it. But you know Claire, she expects everyone to jump when she clicks her fingers. She's invited a dozen people tonight."

"That doesn't sound like a *yes*, Wendy."

She looked at her mended glasses, which were drying on the table. Oliver dozed contentedly. Did she really have to go out tonight?

When she put on her glasses, would that make it clearer? Or should she make a decision now, when everything was still delightfully fuzzy? How tempting that was. To allow herself to stay in the in-between zone where she could pretend she was a child again.

The urge was irresistible.

She took out her phone and texted Claire. *I'm afraid Oliver's got a temperature. I won't be able to make it tonight.*

She smiled and looked at her mother. "That wasn't really a lie. Everyone has a temperature, don't they?"

Joyce sipped her tea thoughtfully. "We could be at the beach by lunchtime. Stay at my cabin for a few days. What do you think?"

"That sounds too good to be true."

"I'll take *that* as a yes. I'll help you pack."

Underneath the table Wendy slipped off her shoes and curled her toes. This afternoon she'd write her name in the hard wet sand of the shoreline. She couldn't wait, even though she knew the waves would wash the letters away by morning, as they always did. But at least it'd be an assertion. A promise to herself. To the child in herself.

And tonight, when her mother wasn't looking, she'd take off her glasses and gaze at the stars.

The Icing on the Cake

My sister Fran peeps in the kitchen door. "You've made Mum's boiled fruit cake," she says.

The knife slips from my hand and clatters onto the wooden floorboards. She's taken me by surprise. I've been half-expecting her not to come.

This is the first time she's spoken to me in weeks. It breaks the ice. I've been wondering how I'd get through the afternoon without talking to her.

I turn on the kettle for the first pot of tea of the afternoon, and hunt for some clean mugs. When I look up, she's rinsing the old teapot, the green pottery one Mum bought me as an engagement present. The big new metal one I bought for today sits in gleaming splendour on the bench.

Perhaps it's a good thing that Fran's here?

It's not easy to avoid someone at a family reunion. Especially with a family as small as ours. And everyone will be here at my place because it's turned into a rainy weekend. Eleven people in one cottage doesn't allow for such luxuries as not speaking to someone.

I wonder why Fran has come early? I wasn't expecting

anyone for at least another hour or so. That's why I'm in old jeans and bare feet, unloading last night's dinner dishes from the dishwasher. She certainly knows how to make me feel lousy, I think, taking in her carefully groomed appearance. What I'd give to be able to afford those Italian jeans and cashmere sweater she's wearing. Not to mention that hairstyle and the pearl earrings. I've never been able to wear my hair in a braid. Stray bits always spoil the effect.

I don't answer her, just keep unloading the china and cutlery.

It's hard to know what to say when someone who should know better sits back in judgment on you. Doesn't try to see things from your point of view.

"It's all your own fault," she'd said when I told her Emily had left home. I'd simply hung up the phone. Speechless.

Five weeks ago now. The pain already overshadowed by the subsequent discovery that my daughter's pregnant. *Is that my fault too, Fran?*

I haven't found the words to tell her.

Or anyone else, for that matter. I'm still trying to get my head around the idea myself. Not just that my unmarried daughter is going to have a baby when she's not much more than a child herself. But that I'm going to become a grandmother, when I'm still looking for Mr Right myself. The version I found at her age didn't turn out to be the real thing.

What a pair we are! Everything in our lives seems to be happening in the wrong order.

No wonder Fran sits back smugly, safe in her marriage and her perfect children. Maybe I'd be smug too, if I'd married an intellectual property lawyer and my daughter got As for maths. *Emily hasn't even worked out that one plus one equals three*, I think grimly.

Everything's always fallen into place in Fran's life. She's living out the ideal script. Me? I'm living in one of the afternoon soaps. And without Mum to turn to for advice any more, things have been rough.

But that doesn't excuse Fran. Not in my eyes. Things might be going well for her, but she's forgetting she was a tearaway.

When she blames me for my daughter's behaviour, is she forgetting all the heartbreak we put Mum through when we were seventeen? We had some pretty narrow escapes without realising it. When we hitched a ride to the coast one summer weekend, forgetting to leave a note behind to let her know where we were. Wondering why she'd looked so terrible when she opened the door to us the following evening. "I thought you were the police," she'd said, hugging us so hard we squirmed. The guilt too late, the understanding aeons away.

Just relief not to find ourselves grounded. She'd been too relieved to punish us.

Where have these experiences been filed in Fran's brain?

When I opened my heart to her, unburdened myself the way I'd been able to with Mum, why did she turn away? I thought there was something there I could rely on. Some trace of the old Fran. The pre-respectable Fran. The one who'd treated me as an equal.

What did I find? *It's all your own fault.*

Those words have ended any real relationship we might've had. Shut the door to any further communication. Made me realise loud and clear that my sister is no substitute for Mum. That was just wishful thinking on my part.

Am I being too hard on her?

All she's done is say exactly what I've been telling myself every night as I lie staring at the ceiling. But surely she could see that I needed something else? Some reassurance that trying and caring matter. That I'm not a terrible mother. I know I can never measure up to Mum when it comes to parenting, but I need to know I'm okay. Why couldn't Fran say that at least?

I didn't even bother to phone her when Emily turned up home the next night. Just as we'd done.

And how could I? Poor Emily had clung to me, exhausted and nauseous. I'd recognised her symptoms at once. I wasn't much older than her myself, but at least I was married. Or I was, by the time she was born.

Fran hadn't known. Just me and Mum. One of many secrets we were able to share.

I cut a slice of the fruitcake and quietly offer it to my sister. We're still in the kitchen. I've found a clean plate for her in the dishwasher.

Fran closes her eyes as she bites into the crumbly cake. "I thought about making one of these for today but I couldn't face it. But I'm glad you did." She takes another bite, and a question appears in her brown eyes. "Why didn't you ice it, Jess? You know, the lemon icing she always made."

"I couldn't face icing it," I mutter. "Smelling it cooking last night was bad enough."

No, that wasn't quite true. If anything, I'd found it comforting to smell the currants and sultanas simmering away on the stove with the butter and spices. I'd sat in the lounge watching TV and nursing a cup of tea. It'd brought back so many happy childhood memories.

I'd bought the lemon and the icing sugar yesterday but when I looked at them this morning, I couldn't face the prospect of icing the cake. Maybe it was too soon? Or did my subconscious feel it'd be presumptuous to try to replicate something that over the years had become almost a symbol of Mum? I can't remember a family gathering when one of her famous boiled fruitcakes wasn't the centre piece of the spread.

Fran spoons some tea leaves into the pot and pours on the boiling water. For a blink, it's like having Mum here. But I'm not going to fall into that trap again.

She hands me a mug of milky tea. "I needed to see you before everyone gets here," she says. And before I can wonder how to react, tears are pouring down her cheeks. Washing me away.

Awkwardly I put my arm around her shoulders. Something I haven't done in ages. Not since that last reunion. The one where we had to say goodbye to Mum.

When she looks up, the mascara has run down her cheeks in a purple river, which threatens to dribble into the corner of her mouth. I quickly fetch a tissue and wipe it away.

"Is it the cake that's upset you?" I ask. "Maybe I shouldn't have made it today. I wasn't sure."

She blows her nose on the tissue. There's a little smudge of mascara left on her nose. It makes her look vulnerable.

"Remember that game we used to play?" she asks, looking up at me with her pink mottled face. "Judge and jury."

Her words stir a distant memory. Of sitting at the table with straw on my head as a wig, and a plastic hammer in my hand, ready to pronounce a verdict. I used to drape a black cloth over my shoulders and wear black-rimmed glasses we'd found in a charity shop. Fran would pretend to be all sorts of different criminals, whatever we'd heard on the news the night before. We used words like arson, rape and murder, with no real idea what we were talking about. The game used to worry Mum to bits. "Can't you girls play something different?" she'd say, after we'd spent an entire weekend committing offences and getting sent to gaol.

It's been years since I've remembered that game.

"I forgot my role," Fran says softly. She reaches out and takes my hand. "Thought I was the judge this time."

Now there's a lump in my throat and it's choking me. I'm having trouble breathing.

"You're entitled to your opinion," I manage at last.

She shakes her head, and a few dark strands of hair skip out of her braid. "I've been trying to work out how to fix things up," she says. "Can you forgive me, Jess?"

This is all getting too much for me. But I need to be honest with her now, or we'll just keep on having problems. "How could you understand?" I ask her. "Your life's so perfect. We live in different worlds."

"We didn't used to," she says. "And I don't want to now." There's a pause. "I don't know why you think my life's perfect. Alan's never home any more. And the kids don't need me. Joseph told me to get lost yesterday when I said he had to do his homework. And Sophie spends the whole night on the phone to her friends."

My heart soars. So Fran is human after all. And she's ready to admit it.

"Things get worse before they get better," I say, quoting Mum.

"The darkest hour comes before dawn," says Fran, completing it for me.

We both smile, remembering.

Then Fran opens my cupboard door and pokes around.

"What are you looking for?" But I don't need to ask. I fossick among my drawer of pots and pans, emerging triumphant with a china mixing bowl.

She turns, a bag of icing sugar in one hand, and a wooden spoon in the other.

Without another word, I get the lemon from my fruit bowl. As she melts butter in a saucepan, I juice the lemon.

Together we ice the cake. Some of the icing drizzles down where the slice is missing.

The cake isn't perfect. And neither are we.

But that doesn't really matter.

Recipe for Life

Is this really something you've created? I can't recognise you here, Beatrice.

I'm sitting down on an old wicker chair that used to belong to my grandmother. She'd sit on our front steps watching life go by every afternoon. Now the chair is hidden by bushes and palings, in the back corner of the garden under the old apple tree. It's not here for watching life, but for hiding from it.

What's gone wrong in your young life that could produce this den in the garden?

A den. Somewhere for a wounded animal to shelter.

And to drink, it seems. There's an empty vodka bottle and a port bottle with a few dead flies drowned in the last dregs. Cigarette butts. Empty beer bottles.

Not all yours, of course. Your friends also hide here, running away from the reality of their own lives and the wishes of their families.

A generation in hiding.

It's not uncomfortable here. The old rug from the living room sits incongruously under the tree, colourful woollen grass, soft underfoot. There's an old floral cushion. And you've been using my blue sleeping bag, bought for the only attempt I ever made at camping. Made colourful with a thick layer of fallen jacaranda flowers.

I'm not meant to know this place exists. And it's taken me a few weeks to cotton onto it. The back garden is protected from prying parental eyes by tall evergreen bushes we planted twenty years ago when we toyed with the idea of a hedge.

Last night's conversation washes through my tired brain. It'll be the only words from you that I hear today, I expect. But I've chewed them over most of the night and regurgitated them without finding any answers. I need to know more, but where will I find it? I sip my coffee, and look around me. Reminding myself not to leave my mug here, betraying my presence.

A presence no longer what it was. No longer one of comfort. This worm has finally, belatedly, turned. Its eyes opened. Its thoughts expressed.

I'd gone into your bedroom to say goodnight. At first I thought you were asleep but then I heard the tinny echo of the music coming from your phone and noticed the white ear plugs. So I gently tapped your shoulder. You flinched, looked up, and turned over to face the wall.

I should've given up then.

"Good night," I said.

"Good-bye," you said. "Get out of my room."

Banished.

My sin?

Letting you know after dinner that I disapproved of the way you've behaved lately. Friends arriving with alcohol when I was in pyjamas, ready for bed. Too much drinking. And more. Things I'm not game to say, even to myself. Things I dare not grace with acknowledgement.

I'd like to run away from reality myself.

But I'm your mother. I'm where the buck stops.

And now that I've confronted you, voicing concerns that have gathered momentum in recent weeks, I'm struggling to deal with the fallout.

My words leap back at me, dealing karate chops.

"This is no way to find happiness." What did I hope to achieve by saying that? Have I become some pseudo new age enlightened mother, preaching ancient wisdom? Or have I simply lost the plot?

I skirted around the real issues. Kept it in the safety of philosophy.

You were having none of it.

I foolishly stood my ground. Tears far too close for my brain to hold its own in this unequal contest. Why couldn't I have waited? Just kept my thoughts to myself until I'd worked out a reasonable way of approaching you.

No, I launched forth.

"This isn't right. And I can't let it continue." Words that finally led me into the topic of drinking and boys and late nights.

I kick the vodka bottle. Who sold this to a seventeen-year-old? What were they thinking?

How much alcohol was still poisoning your brain when you said you wouldn't be spending Christmas with the family?

My stomach tightens.

"This is the last place I want to be on Christmas Day.

And you're the last person I want to spend it with." And you reached down to turn up the volume.

Loud tinny Chili Peppers music filled the air. Wrecking your eardrums. Wrecking the fragile relationship we've built up over the years.

I take another sip of my coffee, but it's lukewarm now. I tip it behind one of the bushes.

Noises inside the house. You're in the kitchen. I can hear the clank of china. Cutlery.

Are you cleaning up after breakfast? Dare I hope you too want to restore peace between us?

Or are you packing a few essentials? Planning to leave today and move in with Karen's family, as you threatened to last night?

Maybe I'll stay where I am. I've done enough damage already, and anyway, I'd rather not know yet. I'd rather cling onto the few illusions I have left.

My thoughts return to my grandmother. You wear her name. Beatrice.

For some reason I spent my early childhood believing her name was Beetroot.

I've got no idea where that came from. And since I didn't mention it to anyone, it persisted until I was nearly ten.

My false label didn't get in the way of her love. Not a mother's love, but something that combined practicality and perspective and timelessness. She was the perfect supplement to my own mother. A warm comforting presence that made home feel like a place of safety, somewhere where the world could be kept at bay.

How odd that her chair serves that purpose for you now. I wonder what she'd make of that?

And suddenly I realise she'd see the positive in this sorry situation. "At least she's home, so you have some peace of mind," she'd have said. "You know where she is and you know she's safe. Some mothers don't have that comfort."

What else would you say, Gran?

"Go to her," comes the answer. "You two need to talk things through. She'll be an adult one day and it might be too late then."

I look up at the house. I can see my daughter through the kitchen window.

What if I get it wrong again? I ask my memory of my grandmother. *What if I just make things worse?*

"You're entitled to let your daughter know when you disapprove of what she's doing," comes the imagined reply. "You're her guide, not her friend, so don't confuse the two." It rings true. I can remember overhearing her say these very words to my own mother one night, when I'd arrived home well after midnight from a party.

I remember my heart dropping at the sound of my mother's sobs. I'd thought things would never be right between us again.

If only my mother and grandmother were here now to guide me. A female bloodline of wisdom to tap into.

Yet I can feel them gently prodding me. "Go to her," they say. "You need to talk this through."

So I do. I gather my mug and leave behind this secret haven that I've stumbled on.

My footsteps sound too loud on the fallen leaves but I don't want to be quiet either. Perhaps that extra minute will make a difference to your response.

I open the back door.

There's an open bottle of brandy on the bench.
At the sight, the words dry out in my throat.
You're bending over, reaching into the cupboard.

As you straighten, my eyes are awash with relief. It isn't a glass in your hand, as I feared. It's my grandmother's bowl, the one we always use for making our Christmas puddings.

"It's November and we haven't made the plum pudding yet." Your voice is soft and questioning, your eyes young and vulnerable. "I can't find the recipe."

I find my voice. "That's because we never wrote it down. We just seemed to make it up as we went along every year. That's how my grandmother cooked."

A bit like mothering, I thought. Something to sweeten it, something to hold it together, something to give nourishment.

"All I could remember was the brandy." You look sheepish.

Suddenly we both laugh.

A tinkle.

Like a Christmas bell.

I rummage around producing currants and sultanas and eggs and sugar. All the essentials. With a wooden spoon to bind them together.

"We could do with a recipe ourselves, couldn't we?" I look at Beatrice.

"The puddings turn out pretty well every year without one," you say. "I don't see why we can't."

"Maybe if we put our heads together, we'll get this right?" And I help my daughter measure ingredients into the bowl. A touch of spice, a touch of love, and a touch of Christmases past.

We find our recipe for love. It was in our hearts all along.

The Gift of Motherhood

My sister Jamie was waiting for me at Brisbane International airport when I finally emerged from Customs.

Even from seven yards away I could feel the sadness and uncertainty in her eyes, before they revealed it themselves.

It puzzled me.

Till I noticed that three-year-old Tom wasn't beside her. Perhaps he'd caught a virus? Or maybe he was still asleep?

Nobody told planes to respect normal working hours. They always seemed to arrive in the dead of night or the crack of dawn. Long-haul flights, that was. My flight from Edinburgh was four hours late.

"You're here at last, Kerry," she said. And I was enveloped in her welcoming arms. My head rested on her shoulder. Her hair smelt of fresh shampoo. She still had shoulder length hair, I noticed, and felt a bit envious of its rich chestnut colours. And she seemed to have put on a bit of weight. Last time I was here, her shoulders had felt a bit bony when we'd said goodbye. Mind you, I was quite well padded myself then, so perhaps I was the one who'd changed. I was two whole dress sizes smaller this time.

We waited by the luggage carousel. Neither of us had much to say. I was exhausted from the flight. Even standing here waiting felt like an effort. And Jamie had dark shadows under her eyes as though she hadn't been sleeping very well. She seemed a little tense too, as though she'd been under a bit of strain lately. I decided to talk to her about it later. Once things had settled down a bit. We had a lot of catching up to do.

"What a pair we are," I said, when we were finally seated in her blue Ford, driving along the river to the southern suburbs where she lived. Jamie was married to a civil engineer and they'd recently bought a wooden home on stilts. I couldn't wait to see it. Previously, they'd rented a trendy riverside apartment in New Farm. The night time views had been fabulous - the lights of the Story Bridge reflecting on the inky surface of the Brisbane River, with a steady stream of City Cat ferries. But somehow the apartment had lacked that homely feeling. They lived on the other side of the river now.

Jamie talked about their plans for the new house and the garden, and I found myself becoming a bit impatient. It felt as though we were skirting around all the important stuff. Emails and phone calls were never enough when we were separated but now that I was here, it felt as though neither of us was ready to talk about those things that lay close to our hearts.

When she finally paused, I asked, "How's Tom?" There was a slight flicker in her eyes. "A bundle of mischief," she said. "He's a real live wire. Just like his dad."

Jamie had never been a live wire. Or a bundle of mischief. And neither had I. Looking back, we seemed to travel through childhood unscathed. No emergency trips to the hospital, no major problems at school, nothing to give a parent grey hair.

Jamie's husband, from all accounts, had been the exact opposite. Once he'd gone on a church camp – to keep him out of mischief, his mother had said. He'd nearly chopped off his big toe with an axe, trying to help make firewood when the supervisor wasn't around. The supervisor, handing him back to his parents again, had sighed, "Tom's guardian angel had to work overtime!" It seemed ironic that his son was turning out the same.

"Does he still try to sail paper boats on the river?" I had a photo of my nephew launching one of these boats, on my dressing table in Edinburgh.

Jamie nodded. "The boats are made of balsa these days. He's enlisted help from his dad."

I tried to picture the scene. I imagined my brother-in-law was able to construct some pretty impressive miniature boats. Maybe we could all go to New Farm Park one day and sail his toy boats on the river? Or perhaps it'd be safer to go to the lakes on the university campus? And Tom could feed the ducks and water hens.

My three weeks of holiday stretched before me like a path full of sunshine and fresh air and adventure. It was my first real opportunity to get to know young Tom. He'd only been eight weeks old when I'd moved to Edinburgh and it'd taken me this long to save up enough for a flight home. There'd been other considerations too, of course. And I'd spent my first few vacations exploring the museums and neighbouring towns. My teaching position had proved demanding too. But now that I was here, I couldn't wait. The strength of my anticipation took me by surprise.

"I can't tell you how good it is to be here," I said. "I should've come sooner."

Jamie smiled. We were pulling into the driveway. The house reminded me of something out of a fairy tale. Lots of hidden nooks and crannies, a couple of chimneys, a tiny attic, and a big rambling garden full of flowers and butterflies and palm trees full of noisy colourful parrots.

There was a loud whoop, as I got out of the car. A dog started barking, and a red-haired little boy threw himself into my arms. I held him tight. But he wasn't still for long. Soon he was squirming and looking over his shoulder. A plump sticky hand dragged me into the garden where a young blue heeler pup struggled against his chain.

My brother-in-law was woken by the racket and came out to greet me. He was 6'4" and had the same red hair, tousled now by sleep. For the umpteenth time I felt grateful that Jamie had met such a wonderful husband. Men like Tom were rare, as I'd discovered. He should've been cloned.

Tom senior held me in a bear hug that almost took my breath away.

Jamie went to release the pup. "We tie him up at night time," she explained. "He started chewing up the bulbs and generally wrecking the garden while we were asleep."

Soon my hands and arms were being licked, and a fluffy tail thrashed the air around me. At the same time, two chubby hands stretched out, as a little red-haired boy tried to regain the pup's affection.

"Benny's my dog." He sounded a bit put out.

Jamie told me that this scene was re-enacted every time they had a visitor.

"It doesn't hurt him to learn to share," she said. "I don't want him growing up expecting the world to revolve around him."

"There's nothing worse than a spoilt child," I said.

Tom senior theatrically covered his ears. "You girls are talking about me, I can tell." And he carried my big suitcase into the house. Behind him came a small set of legs almost hidden by my overcoat. The sleeves trailed along the steps behind him.

Jamie moved to rescue it from him. "It'll get dirty," she said. "And it's such lovely wool."

But I held back her hand. "I can get it dry-cleaned before I go home." I looked around at the morning. It was 7 o'clock, and the skies were endlessly blue. Sun shone onto my upturned face. I breathed in the warm moist scented air and listened to the choir of insects and birds. This was home.

Jamie saw the expression on my face and squeezed my hand. "I'll bet you've missed the warm winters and the sunshine."

"I've missed everything," I told her. "And everyone. More than I was expecting." There'd been a lot of emotional upheaval in the family around the time I'd left for Edinburgh and I hadn't really thought about the move as much as I otherwise might have done. And the impact of the Scottish weather on my lifestyle hadn't occurred to me.

All this was forgotten now as I absorbed the scents and sounds of home. Children, dogs, gum trees, magpies - each awoke fresh memories. Jamie and I spent the whole morning reminiscing, till my body suddenly reminded me that in Edinburgh it was the wee hours of the morning.

When I woke, it was dark and the house was quiet. I had

absolutely no idea what time it was. A mosquito buzzed annoyingly around my head. I swiped at it. Another dive-bombed me. Now I was fully awake and realised that I was ravenous.

As quietly as possible, I made my way into the kitchen to find the kettle. Soon I was sitting out on the veranda with a mug of tea and a plate of toast, thickly spread with Vegemite. Something else I'd missed.

It was a dark night and the stars winked brightly at me. High in the sky was a configuration I hadn't seen for three years. No one had told me that you couldn't see the Southern Cross in the northern hemisphere. With my mouthful of toast, I smiled at the familiar friendly kite shape.

I was still sitting on the veranda when the magpies started their song. They were joined by crows, and before long a whole chorus of birds was telling the world the sun was about to rise. The air smelt clean and sweet. Untouched. Dark shapes gradually acquired details, and as the sun became stronger, my eyes started to grow heavy. As I pulled the sheet over me again, I heard Jamie turning on the kettle.

We crisscrossed each other's paths for a few days while my body complained about the changes in time zone.

But there were magical moments to compensate for the hours lost.

Every afternoon I took Tom and his pup for a walk. He told me about his friends at kindergarten, and let slip a few embarrassing family tales. I took him to my heart. Life back home would feel empty without him, I realised.

"He's pretty full-on, isn't he?" Jamie and I were watching Tom playing boisterously with the pup. The two wrestled on the grass. "I don't think I'm ready for one of my own yet."

At my words, her bottom lip faltered. Her eyes brimmed over with relief. "I've been wanting to talk to you about that," she said.

"What do you mean?"

Jamie started to speak but the words didn't come. Her shoulders shook and the tears flowed, as I took her in my arms. When she finally quietened down and looked at me, her eyes were shining. "I don't know how it's happened but … we've proved the doctors wrong."

The words slowly sank in. "You don't mean you're …" I couldn't say the word in case I was mistaken.

But there was no mistaking the happiness in her eyes. "Yes, I'm actually pregnant. We only found out last week." She paused. "I haven't told anyone in case something goes wrong. It feels too good to be true."

"But that's wonderful news. You always wanted to have a big family. Maybe you will after all?"

"I'm not game to think that far ahead. We're just taking one day at a time." She paused, suddenly very serious. "But it changes things, doesn't it?"

"It certainly will. You won't have two seconds to yourselves once the baby's born. Especially if this little person is anything like Tom." No doubt she felt daunted by the prospect of another ball of energy in her life. And I could understand that. I'd realised this week just how incredibly demanding motherhood was. It was my first real up-close experience with a young child. "Won't Tom be excited to have a little brother or sister?"

Jamie's shoulders relaxed. "I expect it'll put his nose out of joint to start with. We've tried not to spoil him, but after all the trouble we had, he's been such a blessing." She reached over to hold my hand. "But that's not what I meant. We've been wondering how you'd feel when you heard our news."

"I couldn't be happier. Truly."

Jamie persisted. "But doesn't it change things?" There was an anxious tone in her voice.

I suddenly realised why Jamie's eyes had held that sad look. And recognised it properly for the first time. It was the look of anticipated loss.

"It only changes things for the better." I held my sister in my arms and gently stroked her hair as she started to sob again. "I'd never dream of taking Tom back, if that's what you've been worried about. It wouldn't matter if you had ten babies of your own."

She wiped her eyes, and reached for a tissue. "I haven't been able to sleep properly. I've been feeling as if we asked you under false pretences."

"You weren't to know," I said. "Goodness knows you'd been trying to have a baby for years. And of course you believed the doctors when they said that you wouldn't be able to have one of your own."

My mind was whirling. Poor Jamie must've been nursing this fear all week. No wonder she'd had black circles under her eyes. If only I'd been a bit more intuitive. It'd never occurred to me that she was living with such a deep-rooted anxiety. And seeing me enjoying getting to know young Tom would've just made her feelings of guilt intensify.

"Carrying your baby for you and Tom is the only unselfish thing I've ever done in my life." I carefully lifted her hair out of her eyes. "And even then, it wasn't entirely unselfish. I was giving myself a wonderful nephew."

Jamie's bottom lip was still wobbling. "When you moved

to Edinburgh almost straightaway, I was a bit confused. I wondered if you had regrets." Her tears fell freely once more. "I wondered if you wanted your baby back."

"He's yours, and he'll always be yours. I went to Edinburgh to give you all a chance to gel as a family. I thought it'd be easier for all of us."

She took another tissue. "And you didn't have any regrets?" Her eyelashes were wet and stuck together. But there was a glimmer of joy in her eyes for the first time.

I remembered the ache of separation. The pain of saying goodbye to the little person who'd lived inside me for those nine months.

But I remembered also the depth of love in my sister's eyes when I'd placed him in her arms. The look on my brother-in-law's face when he'd held his son for the first time. For he was their son. The glorious result of their gene pool. I'd merely been the go-between. A safe place for their seed to grow and develop.

"I'd do it again tomorrow," I said.

And then I remembered the morning sickness. The tiredness. The bad dreams. The kicking that seemed to start as soon as I lay down at night.

"Luckily I don't have to," I said. "This time I can cheer from the sidelines."

Pyjama Party

Lisa tried not to stare when Gene walked into the kitchen. It was hard enough getting used to the fact that her daughter's boyfriend had started sleeping over. But this morning he'd taken things one step further – he was wearing her Snoopy pyjama pants.

She quickly poured two mugs of tea. "Good morning," she managed, before hurrying to the safety of her own bedroom.

"What do you mean he's wearing Harriet's pyjamas?" Tom sat bolt upright in bed, suddenly fully awake. "What's wrong with the boy? Does he bat for the other side as well?"

She shook her head. "He's one of these sensitive poetic types. Has a well-developed feminine side." Lisa took a sip of the strong black tea. She was right, wasn't she? Truth was Gene made her feel ancient and out of touch. This new generation was just a bit too different to hers. Every time she thought she'd become unshockable, something else happened to prove her wrong.

"Which ones is he wearing?" Tom asked. "Nothing see through or frilly? If he is, I'll turf him straight out into the street."

"Nothing like that, thank goodness." Lisa paused. "Luckily she doesn't wear that sort of stuff."

"Is that all he wears of Harriet's?" Tom looked worried. "He doesn't borrow he r bras or knickers, does he?"

Lisa shook her head. "Course not." But Tom had sown the seed of doubt in her mind. Pyjamas weren't all that different to undies, were they? Where would Gene draw the line?

Then Tom thought of something that made them both feel better. "Maybe this is like what happens in the footy," he suggested. "Like the way the players swap jerseys at the end of a game these days."

Or take them off, she thought, her mind drifting back to the closing moments of the soccer last night on TV. David Beckham looked a bit of all right under that jersey. All those tattoos … in all the right places. She wouldn't mind if Harriet lent her Snoopy pyjamas to David Beckham.

Hypocrite, she whispered to herself. But let the image linger in her mind.

Metrosexual. That's the word she kept reading in magazines to describe blokes like Becks. Could Gene be one of these too? Or was it one set of rules for the rich and famous and another for mere mortals?

She decided to ask Harriet about it after Gene had ridden off on his motorcycle.

Her daughter was wearing her old pyjamas and had a dreamy smile on her face.

"Is Gene metrosexual?" Lisa asked, handing her a cup of tea.

"What on earth are you talking about?" Harriet eyed her warily.

"Boys didn't wear their girlfriend's pyjamas in my day."

"Don't be so ridiculous. He didn't have any so I lent him mine." She headed back to her room. "Stop looking for things to criticise."

Her door was shut before Lisa could say anything else.

Next day it was Tom's turn to make their morning cuppa.

He was so agitated he burnt his fingers on the hot tea sloshing out of the mugs.

"That boy is unbelievable," he spluttered. "He's gone too far this time."

"What's he wearing? Harriet's baby doll pyjamas?"

Tom could barely speak. "*Your* dressing gown."

"*Mine?*"

"He said it was a bit chilly. As though that was an explanation."

Lisa offered to make them a second cuppa, just so she could see for herself. But she was too late. The dressing gown and Snoopy pants were on the floor outside the bathroom. She could hear the shower running.

"Remember the water restrictions," she called out. "Keep it under four minutes."

Harriet's head popped around the door. "What are you doing here, Mum? Stop embarrassing me in front of Gene."

The door closed gently in Lisa's face.

She picked up her purple dressing gown. David Beckham would look stunning in this … but Gene wasn't going to wear it again.

She picked up the Snoopy pants. She'd make sure they disappeared into the deep recesses of the washing basket this morning. Harriet would never look in there for them.

"Two can play this game," she told Tom, when she eventually returned with their cups of tea. She hid the dressing gown in the bottom drawer of the old-fashioned wardrobe she'd inherited from her grandmother. She'd turn in her grave if she knew the half of it, Lisa thought.

"I don't see how." Tom innocently drank his tea, blissfully unaware of the role he was about to play.

Next morning couldn't come fast enough for Lisa.

"But I made tea yesterday," Tom grumbled when she poked him in the ribs at 7 o'clock.

"Have you forgotten?" she said.

"Take a look at yourself." And she swept the sheet off him.

He lay there, exposed. Draped in the black negligee she'd bought when she was pregnant.

"I can't believe I agreed to this."

Lisa pushed him out of bed. "Off you go. Just wish I could see Gene's face."

Tom disappeared.

There were gasps and laughter from the kitchen. And a loud wolf whistle.

He returned very quickly, empty-handed.

"Well? What happened?"

A pale-faced Tom sank back onto the bed.

"Gene didn't sleep over last night," he said. "It was one of Harriet's girlfriends."

A Mother's Day Present

Cheryl was carefully arranging the lavender and white chrysanthemums in a glass vase, when there was a knock on the kitchen door.

"Can I come in please, Mrs Knightly?"

It was her eleven-year-old neighbour, Billy, hair untidy, slightly out of breath. She'd seen him playing cricket in his back yard while she'd been cutting the flowers.

"Your bowling's improved," she said. "I saw you take three wickets."

He looked pleased. Then the worried crease returned on his forehead. "I've got a big problem," he said. "I'm hoping you can help me."

"It's Saturday afternoon, a beautiful autumn day, and you've had your friends over to play," she said. "How could anything be wrong?"

"Thing is I haven't got any money and it's Mother's Day tomorrow." He bit his lip. "I was wondering if I could maybe do some jobs for you and earn enough to get a present for Mum."

"You've left it a bit late, haven't you?"

He looked down. "I'd saved up enough for a bunch of flowers but I bought a cricket ball instead yesterday cos my mates were coming over."

"I don't have much money either," she said. "I have to live off my pension."

He turned to go, shoulders slumped. "Sorry to bother you," he mumbled.

"Sit down, Billy, let's see if we can solve your problem." She turned on the kettle. "Two heads are better than one."

"Not when one of them's mine," he said. "How could I have been so dumb?"

"We all make mistakes," she said.

And made a pot of tea.

Billy looked around her tidy kitchen. "You don't look as though you need any help," he said.

Cheryl smiled. "I could do with some help in the garden," she began. "But I couldn't give you any money."

Billy looked crestfallen.

She sipped her tea. "We'll pick off the dead roses and collect the basil seeds. Then you can help me plant my bulbs," she said. "And I think between us we might find an answer to your problem."

He hesitated. "All right," he said. "I'll still have time to do some jobs after that. Maybe one of the other neighbours will be home by then."

She collected together a few pots, spades and secateurs, and two straw hats for them to wear.

Billy dug up the flowerbeds, added the seaweed fertilizer, and made little signs to show where the different bulbs were planted. Daffodils, freesias and tulips.

"We've done a good job," he said proudly. His face was flushed.

"There's one more job before we're finished," said Cheryl.

He looked puzzled. "I thought that was everything."

Cheryl walked to the back of the garden where chrysanthemums rioted over a rockery near the hen house. Dozens of smiling petals of all colours.

"Are we going to pick some for my Mum?" Billy asked hopefully.

"We're going to give her something better than that." Cheryl carefully separated one of the plants and pushed the spade deep under the roots. "Hand me that pot," she said.

Billy watched as she settled the plant into the pot and gently pushed down the soil. They watered it in.

"Now your mother will have chrysanthemums every Mother's Day," she said. "Just as I do."

He looked at the plants wonderingly. "Did you get these one Mother's Day too?" he asked.

Cheryl remembered that Sunday all those years ago when she'd given her own mother a pot plant for Mother's Day. She'd helped her divide out the clump the following year, and her mother had given her one to bring home.

"That white one is from my own mother's garden," she said softly. And picked a spray for Billy to give his mother.

Mother's Day wasn't about expensive presents. It was about love and memories and appreciation. It wasn't too early for Billy to learn that.

Did You Forget to Tell Me?

You're my daughter and I can see you struggling. I'm here for you, Katie. Just a word or a smile away. Waiting with a lifeline I'm not allowed to throw.

All I've been allowed to do is drive you to the medical centre today. A long quiet journey through drizzling rain. Neither of us knowing how to break the silence.

Sitting here in the waiting room I can't help feeling envious when I see young girls holding their mother's hands. In our lives this open trust has floundered since you hit adolescence five years ago.

You're in the doctor's surgery. A problem you can't talk to me about. You've always been secretive. Never realising I'm on the same side.

And what will I say when you finally feel you can mention it? Not knowing I've already guessed. Will I ask my usual question?

Did you forget to tell me?

The same six words that haunted my own childhood and adolescence. Was I like you? I remember my father asking me this same question. And my sense of puzzlement. I'd told him everything, hadn't I? But he never felt that I had.

I'd ask his permission to go to a party or a school dance being held at night time. Dad's first question was always "What does your mother say?" So I'd make sure I spoke to her first.

Then, "What are the details?"

Somehow I always slipped up here. I'd tell him the how, when, where and why. Thinking I'd covered all the bases. But afterwards he'd hear bits and pieces from my sister. And always that third question. "Did you forget to tell me about …?"

There seemed to be a space between what I knew and what I was able to communicate. Try as I might, I never seemed to be able to shrink this space. At times, it seemed big enough to fall into. That scared me.

It made me question myself. Was I open with my friends? Was I honest with myself? Many's the time I chewed over these things in the small bedroom where I spent those years. Sometimes at night gazing out the window at the stars. The Southern Cross became a particular ally. Whatever else I might've forgotten to tell my parents, I spilled my whole heart to that wonderful configuration of stars. I lived in Australia then, taking for granted the wide blue skies and long days of sunlight. Just as I took my family for granted.

And I'd write it all in my diaries.

That's why I bought you a diary when I noticed you'd started writing. The first big "something" you forgot to mention. I overheard you reading a story to your younger sister one evening. "The Adventures Under the Cherry Tree" came your clear voice, amid excited noises of approval. I peeped in. Beth was lying in bed, under the sheets. You sat propped up, a big pillow at your back. In your hands there must've been thirty pages, yet you were only ten at the time.

"Did you forget to tell me you'd written a story?" I asked when you'd finished.

I'd been allowed to stay and listen to the fabulous things that'd taken place under that cherry tree. Mostly involving you and Beth finding abandoned puppies or kittens to adopt.

And always lots of yummy ice cream and sausage rolls and jam sponge, no doubt inspired by the mouth-watering treats in the Enid Blyton stories I read you at bedtime.

Then food was forgotten. You'd become interested in boys.

You were alternately dreamy-eyed and cranky, depending on whether a special "he" had noticed you at school that day. The phone became your extra limb, and you spent too many precious hours sitting at the computer, chatting to him online.

Still, you wrote in your diary every night.

Somehow I'd stopped writing in mine. Maybe there was too much going through my head? Or maybe I was just too wrecked by the time I finally got to bed and couldn't be bothered sitting up and writing?

Then life took another turn.

After some false starts, accompanied by an aftermath of tears and rage, Sam appeared on the scene. It was three months before I was found out you were seeing him.

Why did you wait so long to tell me about him?

And then, eighteen months later, the breakup.

Also discovered retrospectively. Did you forget to tell me that too?

I could've comforted you.

Did you inherit your father's stiff upper lip? Or do you suffer from my communication hiccups?

It was Christmas Day and I wondered why Sam didn't visit you. Admittedly, he lived an hour's drive away. But love usually finds a way, doesn't it? Especially when you're a teenager.

"Are you seeing Sam today?" I eventually asked.

"I saw him last night."

You'd spent Christmas Eve watching local fireworks with girlfriends. Had he tagged along? I was puzzled.

"What did he give you for Christmas?"

Your brown eyes flickered and you twisted a strand of dark hair through your fingers. Giving yourself time before answering. "He forgot to bring my present with him." The flatness in your voice provided my real answer.

You disappeared to the Boxing Day sales. That night, there was a parcel under the tree. In a sad charade, you opened it and showed me a pair of orange sandals "from Sam".

I let myself be convinced. We both found it easier to hold onto our illusions.

After New Year I set down a new ground rule. "I don't expect you to tell me everything. But what you do tell me needs to be the truth."

Your younger sister makes this complicated by constantly spilling the beans. Whenever there's a problem between the two of you, she lets slip something important.

Like yesterday.

"I'm going to get a tattoo," Beth said. "A quote, something poetic, right across the top of my leg."

"That'd hurt." My attempt to discourage her fell on deaf ears.

"No it wouldn't. Just ask Katie." And then she bit her lip.

I knew I shouldn't pry.

"What sort of tattoo has she got?"

And you described the small black cat on her inner hip.

The thought of the needles made me cringe. And I couldn't help wondering what happened to tattoos during pregnancy. Take your cat, for example. After the skin had been stretched taut all those months, what would it look like afterwards? A floppy old puma perhaps.

Maybe we'll find out in the not too distant future?

I've noticed you've hardly managed breakfast in weeks, and seem constantly tired.

How long will you wait before saying something? Three months? Four?

Surely you can see it's pointless? The sooner you say something, the easier it'll be to break the news.

Perhaps I need to speak out? Is that what you're hoping? I can't hold my tongue only to have Beth blurt everything out. Not over something this important.

I guess the father is Sam. But there were a few parties in January when we didn't see you until the following day…

My thoughts are interrupted. You've finally emerged from the doctor's surgery. I've sat here in the waiting room for the past twenty minutes, bracing myself.

"What's the news?" I ask.

Your eyes spill the beans before you can say the words.

"It's a false alarm," you whisper, hugging me tight. Forgetting you hadn't confided in me earlier.

We go for a celebratory coffee and chocolate muffin. Intense relief sweeps through me. I can't imagine how you must be feeling but am grateful to be sharing this moment.

"That was scary. But we'd have managed, if you'd had a

baby." I sip my latte. "I wish you felt you could tell me these things."

"I haven't been game to think about it, let alone talk about it," you say. "When my period didn't come, I freaked out."

"Just remember I'm here for you. You can tell me anything." I rest my hand on yours.

"You still don't get it, do you?" you say. "I didn't *forget* to tell you. I didn't want to worry you."

And something finally clicks into place in my brain.

The pieces of the jigsaw fit into place, forming a picture I hadn't expected.

You see, I still remember the pain I felt, seeing worry lines on my father's forehead, and knowing I'd caused them.

And the awful feelings of guilt when I heard him sigh over something silly I'd done – or something I'd forgotten to do. My stomach would feel hollow and sick.

I don't want you to feel that way.

Maybe it's time for me to simply let go of these six words? They're getting in our way.

As we walk to the bus stop, I go into the nearest newsagent and buy the biggest diary I can find – big enough to hold the hopes and joys and fears of motherhood.

All the Right Ingredients

Despite her circumstances, Rebecca felt herself relaxing as she began assembling ingredients for her mother's boiled fruitcake. Some things in life stayed the same, no matter how much else changed. It was a source of reassurance. The aroma of the currants and sultanas, simmering on the stove in melted butter, cinnamon and mixed spices always took her straight back to her childhood.

It was her earliest memory. Lying awake in bed the night before someone's birthday, breathing in the familiar smell of the boiled fruitcake being made. First the buttery spicy aromas as the fruit was heated on the stove. Then later, the house would be filled with the familiar cooking smells from the oven.

Rebecca was the youngest of six children, and birthdays seemed to come around quite frequently. The birthday girl or boy would be allowed to help decorate the cake next morning, stirring the icing sugar, melted butter and lemon juice with the big wooden spoon. Then, best of all, being allowed to lick the spoon once the cake was iced.

Next came the important task of adding decorations.

Which one of them had first thought of putting sweets on top of the cake, she wondered? Perhaps it was her older sister? Janet was eight years older than Rebecca, and liked colourful things. She always decorated her birthday cake with tiny pink, purple, red and green jellies. Rebecca preferred sprinkling hundreds and thousands onto the icing. Her brothers had jellybeans, and would eat half the packet when their mother wasn't looking. Sometimes the colours would seep into the icing, but no one minded. And there'd always be candles to blow out.

Best of all was making a magic wish. If it was your birthday, you closed your eyes and dipped your finger into the cake mixture before it went into the tin. "You can wish for anything in the whole world," Mum would say.

"Even something you know isn't possible?" Rebecca would sometimes whisper. Mum would smile knowingly and say that with love nothing is impossible.

Rebecca smiled for the first time today, as she remembered her mother's words. Now, more than ever, she hoped they were true.

But the peaceful feeling was fleeting.

As she looked for a knife to cut off a piece of butter to add to the saucepan, she recalled with awful clarity her visit to the doctor yesterday. His words etched into her brain. One word in particular. Cancer. A word that had dogged the women in her family for generations. Some had been lucky, others hadn't. Which group would she join? There was no way of knowing.

All she knew today was that she needed luck on her side. Making the cake had seemed the most logical thing to do, reconnecting with her childhood, showing faith in her destiny. There was a source of comfort in linking to those happy times.

Her two children were at school, and her husband at his office in the city. Rebecca worked for the government, in the educational system, and had taken time off when she discovered she needed tests. Being home, with so many question marks over her future, she found comfort in the simplest things. Making a pot of tea. Grinding coffee beans. Pottering in the garden. Watching the sun setting over the hills. Normal everyday activities she could no longer take for granted, so could appreciate properly for the first time.

She'd tell her husband about the diagnosis this evening, over a cup of tea and piece of cake. *I'll pour a little brandy into his cup,* she thought, remembering how her mother had sometimes done this when life was particularly difficult.

Over the years, the cake had shared many happy occasions as well as sad ones. It had presided over engagement parties, christenings, and family reunions. Any day that was special for the family.

Today was an important day too. She must treat it as such. Let it be part of a whole tradition. A tapestry of bright and dark moments in the journey of their family. It made her feel less alone to see it in that perspective.

She'd finish the cake now, and ice it in the evening after dinner, when it would have had time to cool. She'd bought lemons for the icing, and a packet of hundreds and thousands. Still her favourite.

She sifted the flour, beat the eggs, and gently folded these into the fruit mixture.

Before she finished, there was one last thing she needed to do. She couldn't help smiling as she closed her eyes and dipped a finger into the mixture. The familiar flavour and texture soothed her. Before she opened her eyes, she made her wish. It wasn't very different really to the wishes she'd made as a child. All she'd ever really wanted was to be part of a happy loving household. Now more than ever, she wanted to continue in her role.

There'd be changes. But that was just how it'd always been. Even for the cake.

Her mother's recipe had needed to evolve over the years, to take account of different people's allergies and health problems as they'd arisen. Sometimes the ingredients needed to be doubled when there were family reunions. Other times she'd halved the mixture when it was just for the two of them.

And then when her daughter had become intolerant to gluten, she'd needed to learn how to use gluten free alternatives such as rice flour and flours she'd never heard of before, such as quinoa. When her husband tried to lose weight, she'd reduced the amount of sugar and fruit, and added extra eggs so she could use less butter.

The recipe was always a work in progress.

Just as Rebecca had needed to be. It was no different now.

And it hadn't done either of them any harm, she thought with a smile, as she tasted the mixture.

Bargains

Carol kept quiet as she and Tony watched the program about hoarders. It was her favourite TV show but they always had a blazing row afterwards.

"Look at that woman's ridiculous collection of china angels," her husband muttered. "What a waste of a room."

The angels were beautiful. Carol would love to buy some, if the woman decided to reform her ways. They'd look lovely with her shelves of figurines…

The camera took them on a tour of the woman's house. She lived alone in a two-storey cottage in the countryside. Alone, but with thousands of china friends.

"Maybe it's time you decluttered?" Tony said as the credits came up. Just as he'd said last week. The woman had decided to part with an entire roomful of garden gnomes. Something to look out for on eBay.

"I'll sell figurines the day you clear out all the motor bike spare parts in the shed." She knew he'd never do that. Not in a million years.

But this time she was mistaken.

"It's a deal."

She didn't believe him, but he spent the entire afternoon taking photographs and cursing at the laptop. After dinner, she checked, just to make sure, and there they were. Fifty ads for spare parts, giving Tony's phone number.

Carol felt ambushed. A deal was a deal, she knew that.

"Who can I let go of?" she whispered. "I love all of you." She looked from her porcelain bride to the shelf of swans and the colourful set of circus characters.

In the end she couldn't choose. Closing her eyes, she let her hands select a dozen china figurines. Tony stood beside her, to make sure she kept her side of the bargain.

"This will do for a start," he said.

"Heartless man," Carol said under her breath. Pretending he couldn't hear.

"I can show you how to put up an ad," he offered.

But Carol took the laptop into the garden and sat under the mulberry tree. The basket of china sat on the grass beside her. Using the wooden outdoor table as background, she photographed each piece. Finally she typed out the ads. Rather than selling them as a collection, as Tony suggested, she made separate ads.

Next day they kept checking the laptop. Tony's motorbike spare parts had attracted a lot of interest overnight. Some of the bids exceeded his expectations. There were even offers from overseas buyers.

Tony couldn't help boasting.

"If you're so good at selling things, why don't you auction off the rest of the clutter in the shed," she said.

They were sitting in the kitchen having a cup of tea. Tony had the newspaper spread out in front of him.

"Only if you auction off some more of your stuff."

Before she could answer, Tony gave a surprised gasp. "That woman who hoarded her china is on the news." He pointed to the article and the photograph of the garden gnomes being loaded onto a truck. "Some of her gnomes are worth a minor fortune." He looked at Carol. "I wonder if any of your china is worth a lot?"

"Don't hold your breath," she said. "I've already checked. There aren't any bids yet."

Undeterred, Tony placed more ads. The shed was a treasure house of bibs and bobs that someone might find useful. He hadn't had much use for any of it in recent years, not since he'd retired.

"Your turn," he said over dinner.

They went through the same performance, photographing a dozen figurines and composing ads.

Still no results.

"Don't feel discouraged," Tony said the following week, as amounts of money appeared in their joint bank account. A garage had bought most of the bike parts. And someone was coming in the morning with a trailer to buy the ceramic pots that had been collecting dust.

Ignoring the smug expression on his face, Carol went online to check her own goods. As she anticipated, no one had placed any bids. She decided to place a few herself.

She didn't hear him come up behind her. And she didn't notice him looking over her shoulder. She was too absorbed in the screen.

"Isn't that one of your figurines?" he thundered.

Carol tried to scroll down the page but more of her ads appeared.

Tony was almost shaking with rage. "I did this in good faith."

"There's no need to go crook at me," she said sweetly. "I kept my part of the bargain."

"That's debatable." He rested his finger against one of her ads. "As if anybody would make a bid when the starting bid is $500."

Carol decided to wait until tomorrow before mentioning the garden gnomes she'd just won. They'd look lovely on the empty shelves in the shed.

For Your Ears Only

This teddy bear has seen better days. Her fur has worn a bit thin and her snout is lopsided. But she still has both eyes, unlike some of her contemporaries. Is it my imagination or have her eyes acquired a new understanding?

She seems to know how I feel.

Does she feel the same?

One minute loved and needed …

Now?

You've gone, leaving us both at home. The talked about "extra space" simply feels like emptiness.

In the recent topsy-turviness, she nearly ended up in a charity bag.

Heaven forbid.

I rescued her yesterday when your father wasn't looking. Horrified at the thought that she could be discarded after all these years.

Her name is Lisa. She only ever owned one dress but it was lovely. Soft white cotton with fine lace edging and embroidered flowers. The dress had belonged to your sister and I hadn't had the heart to give it away when she outgrew it.

Just as you've outgrown Lisa.

And home.

Not me, I know.

But you need extra space to fully develop into your own person. To find your niche in the world.

Just as I did, at your age.

And I know you'll find the things you need along the way. Just as you found Lisa.

She was given to your sister. One of many teddies and dolls. Everyone knows that little girls love to collect a family around them. But no one had realised that you felt the need for a friendly face beside you in bed.

You simply helped yourself, and were lucky to get away with it.

I wonder how you chose her name? How you decided that the pale beige bear was a "she"?

I simply noticed her beside you one night, and you said in a serious voice, "This is Lisa." As though you were introducing me to your best friend.

I started to give you a talk about not taking things, but there was a look in your eyes that silenced me. What did it really matter that you'd taken her? Your sister had more soft toys than she could hold and hadn't paid any attention to this one. Lisa was smaller than the others. Plain. Her absence wasn't even noticed. And you evidently felt the need of her company.

I gave you the dress and suggested it might fit her.

Did she stay in your bed when you had friends sleeping over or were you embarrassed? Did you hide her pretty dress when other boys came over to play marbles and fly kites?

I remember seeing you smuggle her into your backpack when you went on school camps.

I wonder what secrets and dreams Lisa has been privy to?

There's a gleam in her eyes. I think she knows more than me about certain things.

Just as a teddy bear should.

And it was a happy chance that just as you entered your teens, Mr Bean hit the world stage.

In our house he was idolised. Quoted. Imitated.

And of course he had a teddy bear.

Different to Lisa. His was brown, and had some rather bad experiences.

Lisa was spared those and was never in any danger of having her head snipped off with a pair of scissors.

But she gained a new street cred.

Boys could have teddies if Mr Bean had one. It was suddenly cool.

Lisa reappeared on your bed.

She was still there when your first girlfriend entered the scene. A girl with a big Snoopy toy.

More street cred.

A boy with a sensitive side.

Lisa became an unlikely asset.

She's proved very durable.

But not this time.

You left her on your bed, her head leaning comfortably on the pillow. Was that deliberate?

She was still there when I came to look at your room. After you'd moved into your share house.

We looked at each other. I thought she looked lonely all

by herself in a double bed. Just a few crumpled sheets and unwanted books for company.

Did she think I looked lonely too?

I brought her into my room. Made her comfortable on the pillow.

Once again, Lisa has been acquired. It seems to be her fate. And her furry ears are once more open to secrets and dreams. All those things that can really only be said to a discreet teddy bear.

Part II
The Language of Love

New Beginnings

I embarrass myself by referring to it as a wedding. And not just once. Three or four times.

Thank goodness it's my sister, Cheryl, I'm speaking to, and not someone else.

My mother's funeral. Hardly a celebration. So why am I calling it a wedding?

I ask Cheryl. She studied psychology at university.

"It's just the shock," she says, putting her arm around my shoulder. "You've been too busy organising everything for it to sink in."

"You're probably right," I agree. But I keep wondering. There's a niggling voice inside telling me that it's time for me to move forward. To get on with the rest of my life.

And the voice is Mum's.

Even today she's thinking of me, not of herself.

And it puts a whole new slant on the day. There's a little ray of sunshine amidst the tears.

I feel wrung out. Gutted. But there's something else happening today. Meeting friends and relatives I haven't seen for years, catching up on gossip, has buoyed me up. And perhaps there's an element of relief that Mum isn't suffering.

I can't tell my thoughts to anyone. They'd think I was heartless, that I hadn't cared.

And they'd be so far from the truth.

When Mum first received her diagnosis, I automatically asked her to move in with me. Just as automatically she graciously declined.

"Let me do this my way," she said. Her brown eyes held mine, and I recognised that determined look.

But I hesitated. She looked vulnerable, with her limp grey hair and tired smile. Was it time for me to mother her?

"But will you let me help?" I asked.

She smiled. "I'll let you know when I need help," she said. "You just get on with your life. That's the best thing you can do for me."

So, reluctantly, I did.

Until I visited her last week. I saw ants crawling in the sugar when I made tea. One of several tell-tale signs that she could no longer manage on her own. And that she'd been reluctant to put her hand up for help.

"Would you like to stay with me for a while?" I asked, handing her a cup of tea.

We gathered together her medicines, some clothes, her diary, and her blue handbag and camera. "I'll stay for a week or two, until I'm feeling stronger," she said.

I nodded, unable to trust my voice.

Neither of us admitted the time had already come to say goodbye.

And she'd quietly slipped away the following night. Her final trip home, to join my father.

That was last Friday. It seems so much longer ago than seven days. I've spent hours phoning everyone, and making arrangements.

And I've racked my heart for some words to say in the church.

We didn't have a eulogy at my father's funeral. His death was sudden, catching us unprepared and raw with shock. I've regretted this in recent years. So, much as I hate getting up in public to speak to other people, I've managed it in church today. In front of all these people. And I added some words about Dad, to make it up to him. Somehow it felt appropriate. And I know Mum would've approved.

Maybe that's partly why I'm relaxing now and thinking of the future. Maybe you can only do that when you've come to terms with things in your past that were unresolved? I'm not sure. But something in me, really deep inside me, is letting go.

I'm not the only one beginning to relax, now that the service is over. Cheryl's twins, Alexander and James, have been up to their eyeballs in mischief. James has spotted the morning tea laid out in the church hall. He has a tell-tale smudge of cream on his lips, and Alexander has chocolate icing smeared across the front of his new white shirt.

What did we expect of two boisterous eight-year-olds? Mum wouldn't have minded. Boys will be boys, she'd have said.

But the vicar's wife doesn't approve. It's written all over her face. Her lips are pursed together, and she's been following the boys with her thou-shalt-not eyes.

What real harm are they doing? Their antics have brought a smile to more than one face today, and that can't be a bad thing.

I'm feeling a bit detached as I stand here outside the church. I barely know some of the people signing the condolence book. Mum's quite a drawcard. There must be two or three hundred people here. There won't be a crowd like this when my turn comes, I can't help thinking. Not unless I get more involved with other people, the way Mum did.

There she goes again. Prodding me forward. Showing me the way.

My friend, Alan looks over at me and smiles. I instantly warm to him, as I've always done. We go back a long way. All the way back to my childhood. Thirty-five years. Where have they flown?

Alan walks up and shyly hugs me, kissing me softly on the cheek and holding me to him. I rest my head on his shoulder, and realise I'm tired. The last time we met was here, at this very church, six months ago. Alan lost his father to cancer at the beginning of the year so has some idea of how I'm feeling. That loose and floating sensation, a sort of no man's land, a place where things need to be redefined so you can move on.

Alan and I haven't seen each other since his father's funeral. This realisation hangs in the air between us.

"Let's make it somewhere happy next time," he whispers.

Alan's the son of Mum's best friend, Elsie. She walks over to us now and I feel a lump in my throat when I see how frail she's become in the last few months. I know how much she misses her husband.

Alan's arm is by his side again. I miss the warmth on my shoulders. The comfort, too short-lived. He's due to fly back to London on Monday. Back to the world of software design that keeps him in Armani suits. Suit, I should say. And he's wearing it today. He looks a far cry from the carefree, freckled boy I played cricket with in our backyard a lifetime ago.

I look down at my green tweed skirt and black cashmere jumper. I've done all right too. Nothing grand like Alan, but alright. I enjoy my job at the local newspaper. Not what I set out to do, but it's paying the bills.

Mum always said I'd write a book one day. She gave me a ream of paper for my last birthday to hurry me along. It's lying in the bottom drawer of my desk. Something else that hasn't come to fruition. Something else I've tried to ignore, the way I've kept hidden my feelings for Alan.

Everyone's heard on the grapevine that Alan and his wife have separated. I refuse to make myself a laughing stock by showing too much interest. We've been friends for as long as I can remember. Why throw that into jeopardy by wanting more? But I quietly admire the handsome figure he cuts in his elegant pinstripe suit, and am grateful for these few days he'll be here in this quiet little town.

The moment passes. Cheryl walks over and joins us. There's no time to wonder where else Alan and I could meet. And it's too late for me to offer any suggestions. Knowing my luck it'll end up being another funeral. Or perhaps a christening.

"Have you seen the boys?" Cheryl asks anxiously. She has that what-are-they-up-to-now look that seems to define motherhood. I wonder if I'll ever wear it?

"You don't want to know," Alan says with a smile. He points to the boys, who are sitting behind a tree in the church car park. Alexander is putting something into his mouth.

"No harm done," I say. But Cheryl shrugs, unconvinced.

Before she can reply, the vicar's wife herds us all into the church hall. The tables are groaning. There are plates of scones smothered in raspberry jam and whipped cream, rows of sandwiches cut into triangles and adorned with wilting parsley, coconut slices with chocolate icing, and a platter of hot sausage rolls.

The ladies' auxiliary has outdone themselves. All that's missing are the butterfly cupcakes. They were always Mum's speciality, and no one's had the heart to bake them for today.

I put a ham and asparagus sandwich onto a plate, together with a pumpkin scone, and walk over to the drinks table. Armed with a cup of milky tea I join Alan and Elsie on the far side of the room.

And before I realise what I'm saying, it's happened again.

"I'm glad the wedding's over," I say. "It's been such a long week."

Alan flashes me a look of wide-eyed surprise.

"Did you hear what you just said?" he asks.

I bite my lip, mortified.

But Elsie laughs and holds my hand.

"Your mother would've called that a Freudian slip," she says, her dark eyes twinkling for the first time today. Her gaze shifts to Alan. And she smiles to herself as she sips her tea.

I've always resisted Mum's attempts at matchmaking. Now it seems that Elsie has decided to take on her mantle.

By two o'clock we have finally said goodbye to Mum's friends and neighbours. The church hall has been cleaned. Mum's cousins have adjourned to Elsie's house for the afternoon before making their separate journeys home.

I'm sitting by the window in the kitchen, when a car pulls up outside. Alexander and James spill out, and race up to the front door.

"Let us in, Aunty Mary," they yell. "We're bored."

Someone's finger seems to have got stuck to my doorbell button.

I open the door and am gathered into a double bear hug before the boys rush inside.

Cheryl emerges from the car, with an armful of kitchen containers.

"The vicar's wife wanted us to share the leftovers," she says.

I take back any misgivings I might've had about Mrs Vicar.

Behind her, I can see another visitor. Alan's walking up the driveway. He's changed out of his Armani suit. Instead he's wearing faded denim jeans and a grey
T-shirt.

In his hands are a cricket bat and a battered red ball.

"Thought the boys might need to work off some of their energy," he says. "I knew I'd find them here."

Cheryl flashes him a grateful smile as she starts to load the fridge with plates of sandwiches and slices. "You're a treasure, Alan," she says.

Then she turns to me. "Can I leave them here for a while?" she asks. "There are a few people I want to catch up with at Elsie's. While I've got the chance."

I watch her drive off and then wander into the back garden.

Alan hands me the bat with a crooked smile. He nods at Alexander and James. "Better be on your toes, boys," he says. "Your Aunt Mary is a crack shot."

His fingers are touching mine as I take the bat.

"James can be keeper," he says. "And Alexander can bowl."

But it's me he's looking at while he talks. And I'm getting a different message entirely. It's got nothing to do with cricket.

"Where will you be?" I ask softly.

He hesitates. "I'll be fielding in the slips," he says. And then he winks. "The Freudian slip."

And as I stand to face the first ball from Alexander, I silently thank Mum for everything she's given me. The years of love. The years of being there for me. All the things she said, and the things she didn't say.

And especially for her efforts at matchmaking.

When You Wish upon a Star

Until two o'clock yesterday, my life was relatively normal. A bit boring, but my feet were on the ground.

One hour and one minute turned everything upside down. One hour of waiting followed by one minute of emotional storm. Today I can't right myself. Or even want to. I'm savouring every detail of that single minute.

I'm lying in the bath, up to my neck in white froth. I think the bubbles must've found their way into my brain. Usually a bath calms me. Today it's "bubble bubble, toil and trouble". Not helped by the dizzying aromatherapy blend assailing my senses. 'Desire', a potent combination of ylang ylang, patchouli, clary sage and rose.

This isn't a night for 'Tranquillity' or 'Sweet Dreams'. And last night wasn't for sleeping. Tonight I'm exploring that one minute. I'm going to a concert and staying behind to meet the singer. He made my blood run faster yesterday. And it's just been too long since I've felt this way.

Then there's the guilt factor. I'm a thirty-seven-year-old woman, it's Saturday evening, and all I can think of is the effect another man has had on me. My husband? He'll be home watching the soccer on television. If only life were that simple for me.

My hand is covered in bubbles, which hide my wedding ring. A band of gold I've worn for seven years. Covered now by bubbles of – desire? dissatisfaction? distraction?

All because of that one minute yesterday when the bubble of wedded bliss I'd been hiding in burst. And everything felt suddenly empty.

It'd been a last-minute decision, having my CD signed by the handsome singer. I'd heard on the radio that he'd be in a music store. And it was my rostered day off.

Since meeting him, my feet haven't touched the ground.

His photos hadn't done him justice, hadn't caught the sparkling ocean green of his eyes, or his incredible freshness and vitality. He was the most alive man I've ever met, and that meeting awoke something in me that I'm having trouble dealing with.

I stood in the queue that stretched around the music store like a drunken snake. Waiting for my turn. Feeling adolescent, standing there, my heart in my mouth.

The queue inched forward.

My turn finally came.

"Hello, how are you?" I melted in the heat of that familiar crooked smile.

A faint suggestion of shampoo and aftershave enveloped him. My senses were on full alert.

They seemed to be the only part of my body still functioning normally.

My legs turned to jelly, my palms grew damp, and my throat turned dry. As for my brain, it'd gone into meltdown when he smiled at me.

Somehow, he seemed to epitomise everything Daniel and I had allowed to slip away.

"Your music gives me so much pleasure," I managed, handing him my CD. It wasn't what I'd been rehearsing in the queue, but I couldn't help that. And at least I'd said something.

He gently kissed my cheek. "Thanks so much. Are you coming to our concert?"

I nodded. My voice was playing hide and seek again. And yet he was only a few years younger than me.

"I hope you enjoy the show," he said. "And I'll be staying back, in the foyer, for anyone who wants to say hello."

As he handed back the CD he'd signed, I felt the blood rushing to my cheeks as his fingers brushed against mine.

It was time for his next fan to have her moment.

I was on cloud nine. In no fit state to face going home to the breakfast dishes, the cat mewing crossly for food, or the unmade beds.

I went for a walk along the riverbank and sat down under a copper beech, staring into space. Eventually, I took out my newspaper and began to tackle the cryptic crossword. Trying to bully my brain into submission. But it wouldn't be bullied. The words skipped across the page, and my brain danced to a beat of its own. A bubble of rainbows, floating above my body.

As the sun caught the rippling surface of the river, my mind played with an image of me and the singer, sitting in a quiet corner of a restaurant, sipping champagne. By candlelight. Perhaps he'd sing me a song from his new CD.

The trouble is, the daydream won't go away. I prefer it to reality, and am confused by the battlefield my emotions have become. And by the gulf between how things are and how I'd like them to be. I'm sick of feeling ordinary. I want to feel special again. Why can't I feel that way with Daniel? Why has it been a total stranger who's awoken all these feelings in me?

The only part of the Cinderella story I relate to these days is the pumpkin. And perhaps the mice. I heard a few scurrying over the ceiling above our bed last night.

Forget the magic of falling in love, gossamer dresses and dancing the night away.

How did I let romance slip through my fingers, and down the kitchen sink?

Daniel and I seem to have fast-forwarded our way through the honeymoon stage of love, becoming an "old married couple" in a bare seven years.

How? Simply laziness, I'm ashamed to say. And I can see it's been as much my fault as Daniel's. My little black dresses and high heels gave way to aprons and sensible shoes as soon as I fell pregnant with Matilda. Almost as though I'd set up an image of motherhood for myself to slot into, without really thinking it through.

But can I reverse the process? Revive the passion? I've spent today chewing over this. But I keep getting distracting images in my mind.

During my lunch break I bought a black silk dress. I tried it on in the boutique and didn't want to take it off. It made me feel slinky and sexy again. A step in the right direction.

But is it too little too late?

I don't think Daniel's even noticed the effort I'm making with my appearance tonight. And why isn't he coming to the concert with me? I suggested a baby-sitter. It felt like a slap on the face with the proverbial wet fish when he said there was a good football match on TV.

And the fish has flopped about, flicking me again and again with its tail. There's been something secretive about Daniel. Is he really planning on watching football or does he have other plans? I said as much when we sat down for a cup of tea this afternoon and he couldn't look me in the eyes.

Not that I can talk. I'm harbouring my own guilty secret. My brain is no more rational at the moment than these floaty bubbles of 'Desire'.

A knock on the bathroom door drags me back to reality. And my guilt.

I'm lying here in candlelight. It's softer than the unforgiving electric light.

"You forgot your towel, Alison." Daniel quietly hangs my big green towel over the rail, closing the door behind him.

I sink back into the luxurious bubbles, inhaling the musky scent lingering on my skin and hair.

Daniel is so dependable, I feel guilty harbouring romantic images of another man. *It's only a daydream*, I tell my conscience. But I've also noticed the dirt on his trainers and grass stains on his old shorts. *No wonder you daydream*, says another part of my brain.

Maybe it's my mid-life crisis, arrived too early? Or maybe it's that Daniel and I just haven't seemed to gel again as a couple since Matilda was born. And I find myself yearning for the romance and excitement of our early years. Lately we've been too busy about the house and garden.

While I've been daydreaming today, Daniel has been spreading fertiliser under the fruit trees and digging the veggie patch. It's organic fertiliser and smells terrible. Even the dog has been avoiding him.

And I have to be honest, it's a real turn off. Looking at him, I've been asking myself what happened to the man I married. Is this tired grubby fellow the same man who cycled over to my house all those years ago with a bucket of pink roses over the handlebars? Who knelt down on one knee in the rain to ask me to marry him?

Where has the romance disappeared? The love songs on my new CD have brought an avalanche of memories flooding back into my mind. It's left me feeling dissatisfied and lost.

Is that why I'm having these daydreams?

The skin on my hands is wrinkly and furrowed. Time to dry myself. When I stand up in the bath, the bubbles cling to my skin. A wedding gown of bubbles, slowly sliding away and disappearing, to turn into ordinary water.

I slip into the rustling black silk dress and feel a million dollars. "That's the real me," I whisper to the mirror. Then bite my lip. The dress reminds me of the one I bought for my first date with Daniel.

Before I know it, I'm sitting in the concert hall, programme in my hand, enthralled. The hall is packed, mostly with women.

The last song sung, our hands are hot and sore from clapping. It's time to meet him again. I head to the ladies' room to freshen up. Unfortunately so do several hundred other women. Another queue, snaking out into the foyer and up the stairs. It's half past eleven. Daniel insisted he'll drive into the city to pick me up, although I've warned him it'll be a late night. Do I really want to spend the next hour queuing at the ladies' room?

Holding my programme with hands that have become clammy again, I head towards the lobby. A now familiar sight greets my unbelieving eyes. There's another queue of women. This time it's a python.

Even Cinderella wouldn't queue every time she wanted a few minutes with Prince Charming.

It's time to stop running away from reality.

There's only one man who loves me. One man I should be meeting tonight.

I phone home. There's no answer. So I walk outside, in case my phone's out of range.

Outside I blink away the tears when I see the familiar green Ford. Daniel is so dependable. More than I deserve tonight.

The car's sparkling, and so is he. I can't believe my eyes. He's wearing his good suit and his best white shirt – and the teddy bear tie I bought him that first Christmas.

For the second time in as many days, my throat is dry as I sit down beside him.

His finger gently traces the outline of my cheekbones, and his eyes have gone misty.

"Ready for a bit more adventure?" he asks.

And he drives a few more blocks and parks the car. He's brought me to the hotel where we came the night of our wedding.

At the desk the clerk hands him the key to the honeymoon suite.

"You looked so lovely tonight in your new dress," he says, much later. He smiles gently, stroking my hair. "You had me worried this afternoon. I thought you must've guessed my surprise when you asked what I was planning."

I sigh contentedly, as I snuggle into my husband's chest. Daniel mightn't have the looks to draw long queues of women. And he's the wrong side of forty. But he's like a fur-lined slipper on a cold winter's night. My slipper. Glass slippers belong in fairy tales, along with handsome princes.

Short-Sighted

You'd think that after working in an optometrist's shop for thirty years, I'd be expert at choosing frames.

But today nothing suits the face staring blankly back at me from the mirror.

The expression worries me. The mouth's in danger of settling into a permanently sad little twist. As though it's tasted life only to find it too salty or something.

Michelle, the young receptionist looks across with an encouraging smile. "Found anything yet, Jane?"

I shake my head.

People walk in here every day, looking a bit lost and bewildered. Sometimes they're on their own. The lucky ones have brought someone along to help them choose. It's always seemed one of life's ironies that to choose the best frames you need to be able to see clearly.

I remind myself of all the seemingly impossible-to-please faces that have stared back at me from this same mirror, as we've tried various colours and designs. And always, unexpectedly, that moment when we both realise we've found IT.

I have no intention of failing today - but if I offered an award for my most difficult customer, this one would top the list.

Why is that, I wonder? And struggle with the answers that spring to mind.

Perhaps more than any other single item we wear, our glasses define who we are.

Therefore it's only logical that to choose the right ones we need to *know* who we are and how we want the rest of the world to perceive us. And to feel comfortable with that.

But what happens when we're going through a period of change in our lives? It's not just adolescents who face the task of defining and re-defining themselves. My life's been turned upside down since my hormones went into meltdown. It's made me question almost everything I've been taking for granted.

The bell jingles. One of my regulars has entered the shop. I remember helping Jonathan choose his first pair of frames. He had an unruly mane of black curls back then. Now it's his eyebrows that threaten to become unruly. His hair has silvered at the sides and that mane is a distant memory. For both of us. I've always fancied him but have watched from the sidelines as he's become a husband, then a father, and a few years ago, a widower. The other week his son came in for his first pair of glasses. Seeing that familiar thick mane of black curls startled me. We'd joked about cloning. And he'd ended up deciding to try contact lenses, just to be different.

Now there's a thought. Contact lenses. Would they be a good option for …?

"I'm getting headaches." Jonathan interrupts my thoughts. "It must be time for another eye test."

His eyes look fine to me. Clear, hazel, intelligent. If only they didn't carry that look of sadness sometimes.

The appointments book is full for the next week but I squeeze him into an emergency slot.

"Would you like to look at frames today?" I remember how long it took him last time.

"I don't know if I can be bothered," he says.

His listlessness bothers me. "You take a seat and I'll show you some of our new designs."

Life has to go on, is what I'd like to say to him.

Perhaps I need the same advice myself?

He frowns at the thin rectangular frames with black mesh arms, although they make him look years younger. The ones with parallel gold strips along the arms are pronounced "intimidating". So as a joke I show him the Italian pair I ordered in for our younger customers. They have green frames and purple arms, and are decidedly funky.

"These would suit you," he says. And as I hold my breath, he gently positions them on my face, standing back to admire the result.

The intimacy of the gesture leaves me feeling flustered but with a warm glow deep inside.

His eyes hold mine and instead of the earlier sadness, there's a look of approval in them.

"Have a look in the mirror," he prompts. "Tell me what you think."

He's borrowed my usual words, and the twinkle in his eyes tells me it's deliberate.

I stare in disbelief at the face that beams back at me from the mirror. Such a different expression to earlier. This face has just sipped champagne not salt.

As for the eyes, they have a new confidence. The frames are perfect. There's no other word for them. Yet I hadn't even considered them earlier. I'd been trying on frames that were suitable for the various roles I played. Aunty Jane. Jane, the daughter, caring for her mother. Jane, the efficient optometrist's assistant. Why hadn't I realised my real customer was Jane, the woman?

When I finally drag my eyes away from the mirror, he's smiling at me.

"They look wonderful on you." Then he corrects himself. "No, it's you who looks wonderful." And he parades me in front of Michelle, who looks as though she's trying not to say "I told you so". She'd suggested I try these frames earlier.

"We should be finding frames for you, not me." I try to resume my air of professionalism.

It doesn't work.

"Maybe next week, after my appointment," he says. "Right now, I think you owe me a cup of coffee."

And as I sip my cappuccino in the café opposite, I see the world in a new light. Perhaps it's because I'm happy with the frames. More likely it's because of something Jonathan said.

"I'm glad you're going to be wearing glasses." He'd led me to a table in the far corner.

"Why do you say that?"

He gave me a quizzical look. "Perhaps now you'll be able to see what's right under your …." And he leaned over to kiss the tip of my nose.

And in that moment I'm grateful for all the circumstances that have led to this moment. Even my new short-sightedness.

Marilyn's Alter Ego

It's typical of Peter to have a thing about Marilyn Monroe, Tricia thought.

There he was, sitting opposite her at the kitchen table, sipping his morning coffee, raising his mug in silent salute to his idol, who smiled at him from the calendar, her skirt billowing around her shoulders. He should know better at his age. Seventy, for goodness sake. Old enough to know better.

Old enough to know that women and gravity weren't the best of bed mates over time, as she bore testimony. Was that Marilyn's big attraction? He never had to watch her beauty decline, the wonderful blonde hair become thin and lose its bounce, the famous legs get cellulite. She'd always be young and gorgeous. Timeless.

"It's her birthday tomorrow," he confided.

"And it's mine next week. You'd do well to remember that."

Last year he'd actually forgotten. Not Marilyn's special day, of course, but Tricia's. The one who'd put up with his moods and his sometimes tenuous grasp of reality all these years.

For what, she sometimes wondered? Security? A roof over her head? Surely it came at a cheaper price?

No, she loved him. Silly Peter, with his calendars and his hangups. He'd walked into her life one day at the supermarket where she worked, and that was it. Her life changed the moment he approached her checkout.

Love was blind.

And possibly silly as well.

Was it Marilyn taking him to hospital today? Sitting with him while he waited for the results of his tests? Going to the cafeteria to bring them both a cup of tea and a cheese sandwich, if the wait was too long? Did Marilyn care he was diabetic? That he might have a tumour?

Where are my thanks? Tricia thought. *I've spent my life watching my husband drool over a beautiful blonde. A cliché of male desire.*

"You'll have to hurry," she said. "The appointment's in half an hour. There might be heavy traffic."

Peter showed no sign of having heard her. He was gazing at Marilyn, the mug of coffee still at his lips, a faraway expression in his eyes.

Was it fear, she wondered? He'd had a good innings, of course, the biblical three score and ten years. But naturally he wanted more.

And so did she. A few tears welled into her eyes as she wondered how she'd cope if the tests came back positive. She averted her face, and became absorbed in washing the breakfast dishes.

"It'll be another false alarm," he said at last. "These young blokes and their tests. Enough to make anyone tear their hair out."

She didn't contradict him. Last time it hadn't been a false alarm. Just a lucky reprieve.

They'd caught the tumour in time, before it had time to propagate and do its worst in his delicate system.

Peter owed his life to the young bloke and his tests.

But he'd be the last to ever admit that.

She drove them to the hospital although it was only three blocks from their bungalow. It'd been raining heavily all night, and she didn't want him to slip again. Last time he'd been a bit wobbly after the tests and had tripped over his shoelaces, sprawling across the pavement, grazing his wrists and elbows badly. He'd looked like a child who'd fallen off a bicycle. He'd always retained his boyishness, part of him refusing to grow up. It was an endearing quality, but sometimes it strained her patience.

She held his arm, as they walked up the slope to the main hospital entrance. How she hated the signs to the oncology section. It was like a waking nightmare to trace and retrace her steps with him every four months. Waiting to hear if their worst fears had come true. Shaken and clumsy. It was so disempowering.

But the relief when the tests came back negative was breathtaking.

"It's dreary here," Peter said, looking around the waiting room. It was painted a light grey with a darker grey carpet.

"Surely they could find a more cheerful colour?" Tricia said.

This morning, in the waiting room, there was a young woman holding a baby. Tricia's heart stopped in her mouth. It was unthinkable that either of these could be at risk. She sighed audibly when an older woman joined them and the young woman squeezed her hand encouragingly. The woman looked across at Tricia with understanding in her eyes. Neither of them said anything.

They'd only been sitting there ten minutes when Dr Jacobs came to the doorway and called Peter.

Another doctor called the older woman.

Tricia caught the eye of the young mother and smiled.

"My mother's taken a photo of Clint Eastwood in with her for good luck," the young woman said. "I told her it was ridiculous, but she didn't care."

It seemed like a good opportunity to talk about the Marilyn Monroe calendars.

"At least Clint Eastwood is growing old like the rest of us," Tricia said. "My Peter seems to be in denial about age."

"Is that a bad thing?" the young woman asked. "Maybe it's what keeps him going?"

Tricia nodded. "He's come close to giving up a few times," she admitted. "Something seems to keep him going."

"My mum's the same."

"If this was a movie, they'd meet each other and fall in love," Tricia said. "You and I wouldn't matter. Just the power of attraction of two like souls. That's what the cameras would celebrate."

"Who are we to argue?"

"He forgot my birthday last year." Tricia surprised herself by admitting this to a total stranger. The words just tumbled out, needing to be said.

"Maybe he was too wrapped up in his own troubles?"

"He remembered Marilyn's."

They stopped talking as the older woman came out again. She looked overwhelmed. Tricia wondered what the news was for her. It was hard to tell.

Then she forgot all about her as Peter emerged.

"I'll live to celebrate Marilyn's birthday next year," he crowed in triumph.

Waves of emotion swept through Tricia's body. She felt her hands trembling as she hugged him in relief.

"What about those symptoms?" she asked. "And the tests?"

He looked sheepish. "Too much chocolate," he said, sounding much younger than his seventy years.

"Chocolate?" she echoed.

He didn't meet her eyes.

Instead of driving home, she headed to the nearby shopping mall, and steered him towards the boutique. The one where she'd seen the turquoise dress with charcoal beads on the bodice. Peter wasn't the only one who found temptations difficult to resist.

She sat him down on a wooden chair, and asked the assistant if she could try on the dress.

She was led to a small cubicle with an unforgiving mirror. Her fingers still trembling, she felt the silken material. Soft and lustrous, and probably not intended for a woman of her age. But she yearned for its beauty, and today felt she'd earned the right to wear it if only for a few moments.

To her surprise it fitted perfectly. It seemed to glide over her arthritic hips and sit gracefully over her full bosom.

Peter drew out his wallet as soon as he saw her. She peeped out of the dressing room area to catch his eye. No intention of actually buying the dress. She'd simply needed to feel womanly.

But he was at the counter paying for it, even as she started to protest.

"It's your birthday next week so no arguments," he said.

"Where would I wear a dress like this?" she asked weakly. She didn't want to take it off, but really, something sensible would surely be a better idea?

He gave a wicked smile. "I'm taking you to the movies next week on your birthday," he said "We're going to see *Gentlemen Prefer Blondes*."

"Don't you get enough of Marilyn with your darned calendars?"

"There's no such thing as enough of Marilyn," he chuckled. Then he reached over and held her hand, his eyes never leaving her face. "And that goes for you too."

It was as close as he'd come to a compliment lately.

Clutching the boutique bag with its precious contents, she walked back to the car with him. The sky had clouded over again, and the first drops of rain were falling, but neither of them noticed.

A Fresh Start

It'd be lovely to have someone waiting at home for me, Malcolm thought. *A friendly face.*

He'd only gone to look at these puppies from curiosity, the way he sometimes filled in time at the art gallery or browsing in bookshops. Since he'd lost Teresa three years ago, he'd avoided spending much time alone at home. The prospect of sitting in an armchair by the fire with a dog at his feet was appealing.

The pups were eight weeks old, with brown, melting eyes full of trust.

"Do you like any of the pups?" the woman asked. He noticed the name tag on her uniform. Janet. It suited her, he thought.

"They're beautiful, but I'm not sure I'd be a good dog owner."

Janet looked at him with curiosity. "A pup would have you trained in no time."

He couldn't help smiling at her words, and stood there undecided. Until now, he hadn't seriously contemplated owning a pup. But when he'd been buying milk, he'd noticed a sign with a photo, about a litter of pups out the back of the shop.

"Let me make tea while you decide," Janet said.

Malcolm sat at the wooden table watching the puppies. They were in a penned off area, the floor covered with newspaper. There were several toys but they were rolling around chewing at each other, too absorbed in their games of wrestling to need anything other than each other's company.

He looked around. It was cosy and welcoming, with floral curtains in bright pastels, colourful rugs and scatter cushions everywhere. *Almost bohemian*, he thought. In contrast to Janet, who had her long dark hair drawn back from her face in a tight plaited braid and wore a grey pinafore. *As though she's trying to hide her beauty*. She had an elegance and grace that had immediately impressed and attracted him. But her eyes seemed guarded. Had she been disappointed by life? Or was he being fanciful?

Sometimes he felt he couldn't rely on his impressions. His imagination seemed to provide details from nowhere. Perhaps that's why he enjoyed his job of literature teacher at the local high school?

Janet bustled about in the small kitchen, producing two mugs of milky tea and some chocolate cookies.

"I'm sorry to take up your time," Malcolm said, sipping the tea.

"My daughter's home now, so she can manage the shop." The earlier expression of guardedness returned at the mention of her daughter.

Malcolm would've liked to know more, but it was none of his business. There was something about this quietly spoken woman and her bohemian surroundings that intrigued him. And with the litter of puppies, it couldn't have been in stronger contrast to his own home with its uncluttered masculine style.

He'd lost his wife, and somehow the colour and vibrancy of his home had vanished at the same time, leaving him in a lifestyle he'd recently realised was too quiet and safe. Somehow these puppies were opening his eyes again to a whole new realm of experience. Something he'd been closing himself off from, through fear of being hurt.

As though I've created a situation in which there's nothing left to lose, he thought.

Was that why he didn't enjoy spending time alone at home?

He needed to change.

"What would I need, to look after a puppy?" He hoped he didn't sound foolish. The truth was he'd had few pets. There'd been a stray cat his parents had let him adopt. And goldfish, which seemed to die with alarming regularity.

Janet smiled. "To start with, you'd need lots of love and patience."

"I'm not sure I'd have enough of either. But I'm tempted to find out."

She looked at him with that same expression of curiosity again. "There's a booklet about puppies in one of this week's magazines. And I've got puppy food, feeding bowls, collars and leads." She paused. "They'd be cheaper at the supermarket."

"How much are the pups?" he asked.

Janet shrugged. "I'm giving them away. I just want to find good homes for them."

He looked around. She wasn't well off and the shop had to compete with the new supermarket. She must be a generous spirit, he decided.

There was a shout from the shop. Janet called out, "I'll be there in a minute." And looked at Malcolm, waiting for a decision.

He'd been watching one particular puppy, which seemed more curious than the others and slightly less boisterous. As he picked her up, she nestled into his chest, putting her white paw across his arm. He was captivated.

Am I crazy, he thought? This wasn't something to decide on the spur of the moment. But that's what had happened, the moment the puppy put her paw across his arm. There'd been a look of implicit trust and expectation on her face that he'd been unable to resist or disappoint.

"What will you call her?" Janet asked, as she put dry food into a shopping bag with the collar and bowl and magazine.

"A name? I'll have to get to know her first," he said vaguely.

*****

As he walked away, Janet's mind flooded with uncomfortable thoughts.

Why can't I be more like this man? Taking my time and giving things the right amount of thought. Able to act spontaneously.

She'd caught the tender look on his face when the puppy nestled into him. *A kind man*, she thought. But didn't allow her thoughts to dwell on him. She wasn't ready to learn to trust a man again. After Brian, she and Rose needed stability. But sometimes she felt lonely and wondered whether one day things would be different.

Her daughter had disappeared when she caught sight of Malcolm. Now she joined Janet.

"What was he doing here, Mum?"

"He was just a customer who wanted to look at the puppies."

Rose frowned.

Several customers approached the checkout with laden baskets of groceries, so they weren't able to continue the conversation. It was only later, when she was lying in bed that Janet remembered Rose's reaction and wondered what had caused it.

Rose had become volatile since hitting her teens. And recently she'd been angry.

I suppose she blames me for Brian leaving us, she thought. Her husband had simply not come home one night. He'd turned up several days later with an attractive young woman, and collected his things. He'd said their marriage was over, that he'd moved on.

How are you meant to explain that to an eleven-year-old, Janet thought? She didn't understand herself. Four years had gone by, and they'd managed well enough. She'd bought the shop, when they'd finally sold the family home. And now she was foster carer for a Border collie that had been heartlessly abandoned, when she was heavily pregnant. She'd read about her in the local newspaper. There was a deep satisfaction in supporting another female who'd been abandoned with her young.

*****

In the next room, Rose was also lying awake, going over names in her mind. Not for a puppy, but for herself. She'd decided to have her name legally changed when she was old enough. She hated the random way it seemed to have been chosen. And she hated her father for leaving them.

She tossed and turned most of the night until she finally dozed off. When her alarm went off next morning, she was having that same dream again, where she wandered empty streets calling to her father.

Her mother was already opening the shop. Rose grabbed a quick coffee and headed to school. Grateful he hadn't seen her yesterday.

First class was literature. Malcolm had brought a photo of the puppy.

"Today we're talking about names," he said. "I want you to look closely at this puppy. What name would best suit her?"

It was perhaps selfish of him, but he hadn't been able to come up with a name that felt right.

"Molly," suggested a boy in the front of the class.

There was a chorus of "No."

And so it went. They all participated except Rose.

"What do you think, Rose?" he asked.

She glared back at him. He couldn't help noticing how angry and hurt she seemed and wondered what had caused this.

She finally said, "If you want a random name, call her Janet."

Several students groaned.

Then someone suggested Lucy might suit the puppy. There was an unexpected silence.

Yes, thought Malcolm. *We've found her name.*

After class, he asked Rose, "What's your problem?"

She looked down. "I think it's a stupid way to name somebody."

"I don't understand why you find it upsetting."

"You'd understand if it'd happened to you."

He noticed tears on her cheeks.

"Tell me about it." He'd rather be late for his next class than leave this troubled girl just as she was talking about what was bothering her.

"My parents held a naming party when I was born," she said. "They invited their friends, and someone ended up suggesting Rose."

"Why does that upset you?"

"It's so random." She paused. "And they should've known. They should've tried harder themselves to come up with my name."

"Have you talked to your parents about this?"

She shrugged. "I don't know where Dad is, and Mum's hard to talk to."

"Would you like me to talk to your mother?"

"Maybe." She started to leave. "I've got another class now, Sir."

*****

After work, he phoned the veterinary clinic and was pleased they had an appointment available. He needed information about worming Lucy, and her injection schedule.

There were some familiar faces in the waiting room. Janet had the Border collie with her. Sitting beside her with a faraway look on her face was Rose. Her eyes were closed and she was listening to music on her iPhone.

Seeing them sitting together, the truth finally dawned on him. Janet must be Rose's mother. And he remembered that Rose had suggested the name Janet for his puppy.

At the risk of creating an awkward situation, he sat down beside Rose, and nodded to her mother. Janet looked more relaxed today. Her dark hair tumbled loosely onto her shoulders, and she wore a red hand knitted jumper with faded denim jeans. She looked amazing, if he was going to be completely honest with himself. It'd been a long time since he'd taken this much notice of a woman.

"I've decided to adopt Tess," Janet said, nodding to the Border collie. "I can't say goodbye to her now."

He nodded. "Lucy's already won me over, and it's only been a day."

"And you won't believe it. Rose wants one of the puppies."

"Why is that hard to believe?"

Janet's cheeks turned pink. "She hasn't been game to love anything since her father left us."

"There's a second chance for everybody," he said at last. "And we all need them."

Janet didn't look convinced. "What would you know about second chances?"

At that moment, the vet appeared and called her into the surgery.

Malcolm wondered how their conversation had suddenly touched on something so serious and personal.

They were with the vet nearly fifteen minutes. Rose gave him an awkward smile as they paid for the consultation.

"Would you like to join me and Rose for dinner?" Janet asked, as she was leaving. "Bring Lucy."

His own consultation took longer, but when he left, he

felt confident he could meet Lucy's needs for the foreseeable future.

As for meeting his own needs, his thoughts on that subject were changing too quickly for his comfort.

He checked the time. Janet was expecting him in a few minutes. He bought wildflowers from a nearby florist and as an afterthought, a few bottles of pear cider.

The meal was simple but delicious. Fish pie followed by apple and blueberry shortcake. Rose seemed more animated. No doubt the puppy she was holding explained that.

"Have you thought of a name for him?" Malcolm asked.

Rose blushed. "I'm sorry I was cranky in class."

"You weren't cranky," he replied. "You were trying to come to terms with your feelings."

"I think I'll wait until I know what I want to name my puppy. I'd hate to choose any name. It has to feel right."

Janet reached over and held her hand. "That's how I felt when you were born."

"Really?" Rose looked thoughtful. "You've never mentioned that before."

Malcolm poured cider into their glasses.

"Let's drink a toast." He raised his glass, looking from Janet to Rose, and then to the puppies playing on the carpet. "To waiting for that moment of certainty."

As he sipped the chilled cider, he realised in his heart that these new feelings he was experiencing also had a name.

Coffee with Bruce

Moira eyed the lanky man at the far table. He'd checked his phone a few times and had that self-consciously casual air she recognised. Clearly he was waiting for someone. Was this Bruce? Her friend Glenda had given her a rough description of him. But there was a world of difference between a few phrases and an actual man.

She'd asked for a photo. Why had Glenda been cagey? "I'm sure you'll know him when you see him," she'd told her. "You two are kindred spirits. It's about time you met."

She hadn't been on a blind date in years. Was it a mistake? Something she'd regret? Or was she just overreacting?

Why not just enjoy the occasion?

She turned her attention to the display cabinet of cakes and delicacies. All she'd agreed to do was meet him for coffee. She could be out of here in half an hour, if that was what she wanted. Enough time to do justice to the orange poppy seed cake.

She ordered a slice to go with her espresso, and made her way to his table.

His face gave him away, before he could even say hello.

An instant flicker of recognition in his eyes. Had Glenda shown him a photo of her? Why did the thought bother her?

"You must be Moira," he said, half rising from his chair. "I'm not sure why Glenda asked me to have coffee with you, but it's as good a morning as any other. For having coffee with a total stranger, I mean." He sat down again awkwardly, his chair scraping the tiled floor.

Something in Moira relaxed at his words. He wasn't any more comfortable about this than she was. Somehow it made her feel she could manage. Maybe even enjoy herself. She no longer felt at a disadvantage.

As Moira pulled out the chair opposite, she met his eyes. "I have to ask, Bruce, how did you recognise me?" It was a reasonable question, she thought. There were other single forty something women in the café. But only two other men, neither of whom could be described as lanky, and one of whom looked to be in his eighties.

So it hadn't really been hard for her to guess which one was Bruce. But what about him? How had he picked her out among the other women?

Bruce's eyes gave him away again and he half-smiled, almost guiltily. "I knew it had to be you, as soon as you walked into the café," he said. "There was a reluctance about your bearing that I recognised. I felt the same."

Moira sat down, feeling a bit puzzled. "Reluctance?" she echoed.

"Yes. You were giving out a why-am-I doing-this vibe." He nodded towards several customers entering the cafe. "Look at those women. They're obviously happy to be here. You can see in their faces how much they're looking forward to their coffee."

"But my face didn't say that?"

He shook his head, the half-smile lingering on his lips. "No, I'm afraid your face gave you away."

Her own earlier thoughts echoed back at her.

"Humour me, Bruce. We're both here because Glenda wanted us to meet. More likely than not, we won't be here again. So this is probably my only opportunity to ask you something." She felt awkward as she continued, trying to make her voice sound relaxed. "I suppose I'm curious how she described me. She wouldn't have said I'd look reluctant. So what did she say?"

He waited while their espressos and cake arrived at their table. To her surprise, he'd also ordered the orange poppy seed cake. And she could see from his expression that he'd noticed it too.

As the waitress moved to another table, he said, "Curious we both asked for orange cake and espressos. Of all the cakes in that cabinet we've chosen the same one."

"Yes. And the espressos. Not cappuccino or latte or affogato."

He broke off a piece of cake and put it into his mouth.

The simple movement aroused her in some way.

On a basic animal level, she felt she and Bruce were compatible. It intrigued her that Glenda had worked this out without ever seeing them together.

After washing the mouthful of cake down with a gulp of coffee, Bruce looked directly into Moira's eyes. Looking for something which apparently he found, as he continued where he'd left off. "Glenda said I'd know you by your manner. She described you as seeming both fragile and strong."

His words surprised her.

So Glenda hadn't mentioned her hair colour or clothes style or any of the things she might've expected her to say?

Fragile but strong? The description appealed. She looked at the other women in the café, trying to work out what their body language said about them.

"Strangely enough it was all I needed to know." He broke off another piece of the cake, scooping up the crumbs. "So how did she describe me?"

Moira hadn't been able to extract much from Glenda. Bruce was a loner, she'd said. Someone who felt comfortable in his own skin.

Moira had insisted on some physical detail. "Or I just won't meet him," she'd finally said.

So Glenda had offered the word "lanky".

"Lanky," she repeated.

"Is that all?" It was his turn to look puzzled.

Moira relented. "Plus the fact you're comfortable with who you are."

"Bloody psychologists." He laughed. "Anyone else would've gone about this differently."

Moira sipped her espresso. Enjoying Bruce's company despite herself. "At least she doesn't make a habit of it," she said. "You're the first person she's ever really wanted me to meet."

"Me too. Makes you wonder, doesn't it? I've known her nearly twenty years. She's making a late start if she wants to act as matchmaker for me."

"That long?" Moira couldn't keep the surprise from her voice. "I met her a few years ago." She wouldn't mention that she'd originally seen Moira as a client, after a relationship had failed. When her self-esteem had plummeted, Moira had helped her see the breakup in a more positive light. Shown her it was possible to move on.

She wondered how Glenda had met Bruce.

"Well, we can tick this meeting off today's list of jobs," Bruce said as he finished his coffee. "I'm assuming that's what you'd prefer? You don't seem terribly keen on being set up with me as a date. And I can't blame you."

Moira surprised herself by saying, "Why not order another coffee?"

"Maybe I will." His eyes held a flicker of something. Was it curiosity? Interest?

Moira wasn't sure. All she knew was that she didn't quite feel ready to say goodbye to him. Her curiosity wasn't yet satisfied.

She watched as he walked over to the counter to order more coffee. He was quite tall, maybe 6'2" or 6'3". The still-waters-run-deep type. She couldn't help wondering why a presentable forty-year-old man like Bruce was evidently unattached. He wasn't wearing any jewellery that would indicate a relationship, such as a ring. She'd checked his hands as he drank his coffee. A habit she'd acquired since being single again. Nice hands too, with short clipped nails.

"I ordered two espressos," he said, as he rejoined her.

She smiled, toying with the cake. "Tell me a bit about yourself."

"What's there to tell?" He looked around the café before meeting her eyes. "I've probably misspent most of my life. But I don't have any regrets. And I've managed to see a lot."

Moira leaned forward. "That sounds interesting."

"Which bit?"

She sipped her coffee, playing for time. Would she tell him the truth? Why not? In all likelihood they'd never meet again so there was nothing to lose. "I suppose *misspent* is the word that intrigued me."

"Perhaps it wasn't the right word. My life hasn't been intriguing, but that's a nice thought. I've lived a lot of my life without any real sense of purpose. Felt half-hearted about some of the jobs I've held, for example. Never really felt I was where I belonged." He paused. "Maybe I just haven't grown up yet?"

Moira chuckled. "You're right. That's not intriguing. But I can relate to it. I've often envied people with a strong sense of purpose."

Before she could say more, her phone rang. It was her boss, needing to see her urgently.

"Bother," she said. "I'll have to go now." Surprised how reluctant she felt. Disappointed even.

He seemed reluctant to end their conversation abruptly too. There was a question in his eyes.

She felt it reciprocated in her own.

Perhaps he'd noticed?

"We didn't finish our coffee," he said quietly. "I don't suppose..."

"The orange cake's very good," she said. "I wouldn't mind another slice. Perhaps tomorrow?"

The instant smile reached his eyes, causing them to light up again. He couldn't hide the pleasure in his voice. "A lanky man will be waiting for you here. Say at ten o'clock?"

Afternoons with Richard Gere

Was it a schoolgirl crush, as Norman suggested?
Did that capture how she felt about Richard Gere?
No, of course not.
Fifty-five-year-old women had outgrown crushes.
Hadn't they?
Yet here she was, spending her afternoons watching DVDs of *Pretty Woman*, *An Officer and a Gentleman* and every other movie he'd ever appeared in.

Jill simply couldn't get enough of him. She'd already gone to see *The Second Best Exotic Marigold Hotel* more times than she'd care to admit. And guilty creature that she was, she went with a different friend each time and even to different cinemas.

The day she lied to Norman, Jill realised she might have a problem.

"Where are you off to this time?" he'd asked. It was Saturday afternoon.

"The library," she'd said hastily

He'd got a funny look on his face. Puzzled and – could it be hurt?

It was only during the opening scenes of the movie that Jill remembered the library was closed on Saturday afternoons. The expression in his eyes haunted her during the movie, flaring during the scene where a male character notices his wife disappearing up a staircase with a man.

Norman thinks I'm having an affair, she thought with a pang.

She felt instantly guilty.

While one tiny part of her brain held an image of herself walking up a staircase with Richard Gere…

There was no one to turn to for advice. Today she'd gone to the cinema on her own. She'd run out of friends willing to accompany her. Some had already been twice.

There was only one solution. Telling Norman the truth. Well, part of the truth.

He was sitting in an armchair reading the sports pages when she arrived home.

Neither of them mentioned the library.

"I thought I'd make spaghetti bolognaise for dinner," she began.

She'd gone to the supermarket on the way home, stocking up on pasta, mince, mushrooms and so on. It was Norman's favourite meal.

Later as they sat down to eat, Norman finally spoke to her. "Lorraine phoned while you were out," he said. "She offered to see the new Marigold Hotel movie with you tomorrow."

A pause, while Jill collected her thoughts.

She was pleased, of course. But what else had Lorraine said? She didn't have long to wait.

"She'd been speaking to Diane and Lesley."

Jill's heart fell. She was outed.

"So you know?" she said simply.

"That doesn't explain why you lied to me," he said, the hurt look returning. "What if I'd needed you in a hurry?"

"I had my phone." It wasn't a lie. But she'd turned the phone off during the film, so its ringing wouldn't spoil any of the romantic scenes.

"That's not the point." The hurt look wasn't stopping Norman from eating his spaghetti bolognaise. His bowl was already half empty whereas she'd barely pecked at hers.

And then he'd referred to her having a schoolgirl crush.

"Your friends are talking about you behind your back," he added.

Jill left her dinner and walked out into the garden. Angry, upset and confused.

What was wrong with watching Richard Gere movies? If only Norman paid half as much attention to his fitness and appearance maybe she wouldn't need to look at Richard Gere? Her husband had become fairly careless since taking early retirement. Objecting if she wanted him to wear smarter clothes when they went out. Not listening properly.

She didn't hear him approach. Just felt an arm around her shoulders. Instinctively she nestled against him.

"Would you like me to take you to the movie next time?" he asked softly.

She nodded without speaking.

"And maybe I can try to be a bit more like Richard Gere? Would that help?"

It was hard not to smile. Norman's only similarity to Richard Gere was the white hair.

"I just want you to be more like yourself," she said.

Thinking of how he dressed. His general manners. His outlook recently.

"It's a deal," he said, leaning down to kiss her. "And there's something else." He paused. "Let's promise never to lie to each other again."

Jill felt the heat rise to her cheeks. Norman wasn't the only one who'd been at fault.

She rested a hand against the back of his head. "Even if I want to see the same movie a hundred times?"

"That's what I want."

Her lips met his. When they finally parted, she said, "That's what I want too."

It was a line from the film. But Norman wasn't to know that.

Maybe there was hope for them after all?

The Language of Love

Beatrice was surprised to find a box of love letters among her mother's personal possessions. And she was even more surprised to discover they'd been written by her father.

This was a side of him she hadn't seen during his lifetime. Or perhaps she'd been too young to notice? Too caught up in her own life and the struggles of growing up.

She and her husband had driven over to her parents' house to begin the enormous task of sifting through the papers, music, books, furniture and bric-a-brac produced by living in the same house for forty years. Anything that looked as though it might come in handy one day had been kept.

Beatrice had felt overwhelmed by emotion, and retreated to her mother's room to sit quietly with a cup of tea before starting her task. Paul followed, holding their baby son who was sucking his fist and whimpering.

"I never realised my father was such a romantic man at heart," she said. "He always seemed so practical. Gentle, of course, but …" She sipped her tea. "Did I just not see him as he really was?" she asked, when her husband didn't answer.

"There were seven of us children for my parents to look after. That wouldn't have left much time for romance, would it? Do you think having children changed him?"

"It certainly changed things between you and me," Paul said. "We've had to become very practical since Oscar was born, just to survive."

Practical. The word didn't sit very easily with Beatrice. She thought back to how carefree and adventurous her weekends had been like just two years ago. Drives into the countryside, picnics by waterfalls, moonlit walks along the seashore… It was a far cry from now. She'd spent last night pacing up and down the hall with her baby, wishing with all her heart that babies arrived with a complete set of teeth.

"Listen to this," she said, reading a few phrases from the letter in her hand. *Breathing in the beauty of your presence ….. a privilege to be allowed to hold your hand, to kiss you… the joy of loving you…*

And she couldn't help adding softly, "You've never said anything like that to me."

It was true. She and Paul had been high school sweethearts. Their first attempts at kissing had been fumbling about in a darkened cinema. Paul had been keen and desperate to go further, like any other seventeen-year-old boy in love. It was only now that Beatrice wondered whether she'd missed something. Had Paul ever felt privileged to hold her hand? To be with her? Perhaps. If he had, he certainly hadn't been able to express this feeling in a poetic way. It seemed to Beatrice in that moment as though they'd fast-forwarded through an experience better enjoyed at a slower pace. That old-fashioned concept of courtship.

"Would you like another cup of tea?" Paul asked.

Beatrice shook her head. All she wanted was to be alone with these beautiful letters. Some time to think about her mother and father as a young man and woman in love, rather than as her parents. Her father was a shy quiet man. She'd never realised he was capable of expressing his feelings in such a beautiful way.

And she'd never seen the special cards he'd made for her mother. Her favourite was the Valentine's card. She'd opened the envelope, surprised to see that it was handmade. Inside was another envelope, also handmade. And so on. The envelopes got so small she could barely open them without crushing the fine paper. Till she'd opened the final one to reveal the tiniest of cards with violets painted on the front and inside, scripted in fountain pen, the words *I love you*. It was the sweetest way of conveying this message that she could imagine. So much more meaningful than offering a bought card from a shop.

It was a depth of feeling she felt she'd missed out on. Her husband would never have had the idea of making a card like this for her. And to be honest, she wondered if she'd ever cared as deeply as this for him. It was an uncomfortable realisation.

Paul seemed to sense her mood. "I'll be in the garden if you need me for anything. The rose bushes need pruning, and I can separate the clumps of chrysanthemums," he said. "And I'll put Oscar in the pram. He'll enjoy watching the birds and the butterflies."

She nodded absently. Already rereading the letter. It'd been written on her mother's birthday in 1970. *A small gift to help to express the many things a husband thinks but does not say: like thank you and I love you.*

She remembered her father as someone who quietly worked in the background to ensure home and garden were well tended, all the while listening to his beloved Beethoven. He'd made all their cupboards, made their beds, painted the house – a real handyman, always busy on the latest project. He'd have given his life for his family and was never happier than when they were enjoying time together. Birthdays were special occasions, and every Christmas there'd been a big family reunion.

She'd never doubted his love. Had been surprised at times when she'd glimpsed its depth. But until today, she'd never realised how close was the bond that united her parents. Somehow she'd never thought of them as a romantic couple. Yet these letters could've come from a Cary Grant movie.

Reading them, she felt envious, if she was going to be honest with herself. And also just a little uncomfortable. *Should I be even reading these*, she wondered? Would her parents mind? She felt a twinge of guilt. The letters were never intended for her eyes, were they? But they were precious, and her mother must've realised that one day she'd be sitting here, reading them. Perhaps she'd meant her to? Wanted her to discover this treasure?

She felt this must be so. Why else would her mother have kept them in her dressing table, rather than locked away?

Her aunt had let them all know that her box of special letters and diaries was to be burnt unread after her death. They were kept in the locked compartment of her filing cabinet, and she'd included a statement to this effect in her will.

Beatrice's mother had made no such provision, and had never locked her own box of treasures away.

All Beatrice's instincts suggested she keep reading.

There must've been thirty letters. All tied together with delicate cream ribbon and kept in a chocolate box in an inner drawer of her mother's dressing table. Did the chocolate box hold memories too? Had they shared these on one of the picnics mentioned in the letters? She'd never know now. If only she'd talked to her mother about their courtship days. But then, her mother had never broached the subject herself, had she? And Beatrice had lost her father when she was too young to be able to talk about this with him.

She shivered and realised the sun was setting. It was five thirty. Where had the afternoon flown?

She was putting on her cardigan when there was a gentle knock on the door.

Paul was standing in the doorway, holding Oscar, who was fast asleep over his shoulder. He was wearing an apron, and looked pleased with himself.

"I've managed to put together a risotto I saw someone make on Master Chef the other night," he said proudly. "Pumpkin, spinach and leek, with chicken. Everything you like in the one recipe."

Beatrice was aware of a delicious aroma coming from the kitchen, and realised she was starving.

"That's nice of you," she said.

Paul's blue eyes grew misty and he looked vulnerable. "I do love you," he said. "I just have my own way of expressing it. And I'm not good with words."

So he'd guessed what she'd been thinking?

He looked tired now. She realised with a pang of guilt that she'd heard Oscar crying earlier. She'd literally left him holding the baby while she walked down memory lane, trying to glimpse what had existed between her parents.

Her father's words of love were poetic gems. But equally full of love were the actions of her Paul, who would never have those words. Paul couldn't write of his love, but it was expressed in everything he did for her.

Her heart felt full.

"You know how to put the right ingredients together to produce something beautiful," she said. "And I'm not just talking about dinner."

He drew her towards him in an awkward embrace. Oscar stirred between them, and began to gurgle happily.

We have our own language of love, she thought. *And it's right for us.*

Maybe one day she'd be able to talk about it to Oscar. Let him realise that his parents had also been a young man and woman in love.

Pieces of a Life

Adam was intrigued by the messages that appeared on his iPhone. This morning he was woken by a melody, and a reminder note had popped up on the screen. 6:30 *Monday, study pathology.*

At midday a message told him not to forget tennis practice at the university courts.

It was so interesting putting together an image of the previous owner of this phone. His mother had brought it to him last week, when he was still in hospital. "Won't someone miss it?" he'd asked. The phone was fairly new and had lots of apps and special features. It looked expensive. Too good to give away. But she'd assured him the phone was his to keep. Since then he'd received a variety of reminders from the phone. Apart from instructions to study various medical subjects, there'd been a message to collect contact lenses, mention of an upcoming anniversary, and a reminder not to forget Valentine's Day.

Was it February already? Where had the year flown?

There's no need for me to remember Valentine's Day, he

thought. That was just for people with someone special in their lives. He was living at home with his parents. His life at the moment certainly didn't hold any romance. Just an endless series of tests, medical procedures and changing of dressings since his motorbike accident.

How nice it'd be to be living the life of the original owner of this phone, he often thought, as the messages mapped out a life full of fun and love and purpose. So different to his own circumstances.

His only purpose at the moment was to become free of this plaster and the bandages, and to feel more like his old self. Whatever that was. Maybe he'd feel less jaded in a month's time or so? That was the opinion of his doctor, and he clung on to it.

And there was certainly no shortage of visitors to wile away the hours. He couldn't keep track of them all. Some he recognised, others he didn't. And sometimes he simply couldn't stay awake while they were there. The painkillers he'd been prescribed to make his life bearable also made him sleepy and unable to focus clearly.

Mostly, he was glad of the visitors. Especially Tess, the lovely blonde girl from next door who seemed to drop by most days. He often thought that when he was well again, he'd like to ask her out. Once the hair on his head had grown back, of course. They'd shaved it, so they could stitch a nasty gash at the back of his head. The mirror was a daily reminder that he looked a fright. Better to wait.

Besides, he wasn't really sure if he'd stand a chance with Tess. He seemed to have gotten off on the wrong footing. She told him she was studying to be a physiotherapist, and he'd said something about needing one of those in his life. He'd meant it as a joke, but she hadn't taken it well, becoming rather silent and a bit withdrawn after his remark.

"Why do you think Tess reacted like that when I said something about needing a physiotherapist?" he asked his mother after she left.

She smiled awkwardly. "Tess is in a difficult relationship at the moment," was all his mother would say. "Give her time."

He thought about the messages on his phone. Did physiotherapy students need to study pathology? Surely not? But maybe the phone had belonged to Tess? He had no way of knowing if it belonged to a male or female.

"Do you know who the phone used to belong to? Could it have been Tess's?"

"No, it wasn't Tess's phone. But she bought it for a med student she was in love with."

That explained Tess's reaction. But it didn't explain what happened the following week. Adam went to phone Tess, and as he started dialling her number, her name came up on the screen. No doubt the med student had listed her in his contacts but it still made him feel funny to see it like that. He lay down on his bed, unsure whether or not to wait for her to answer the call. He didn't need to decide, as it happened. Her phone went to voicemail, and that too felt odd.

But why should it? He had a strange sense of deja vu, and found it unnerving.

"Why should I feel weird listening to Tess's voicemail?" he asked his mother. "It doesn't make sense."

She was about to say something but thought better of it.

"You must've phoned her about something before, and forgotten about it. Then when you heard her recorded message, it triggered the memory. Nothing to worry about," she said.

The days passed. Weeks passed.

Adam's life started to take a more interesting aspect. The narrow confines imposed by his accident gradually widened and his life was no longer one-dimensional.

To his delight and surprise, Tess accepted his shy invitation to have dinner with him. It was a candlelit dinner at home, and his parents went out for the evening. Nothing grand, just gourmet pizzas, home delivered, with a bottle of cabernet sauvignon. But he felt comfortable in her company, and it was liberating to be able to date again, albeit within his present limitations.

There didn't seem any point trying to negotiate restaurants when he was in plaster.

The daily reminders kept appearing on his phone. He now knew how to turn them off, but he didn't actually do this. It was nice to patch together an image of the med student who'd been in love with Tess. Adam learnt that he'd played tennis, went to the gym regularly, and that they were going to celebrate their fifth anniversary of being together next month.

No wonder Tess sometimes looked so sad and lost in her own thoughts. Five years suggested a certain level of commitment and involvement.

As the day of the anniversary approached, and the phone kept reminding him of it, he decided to do something himself to cheer her up. But what would be appropriate? He didn't want to do anything that might upset her.

He asked his mother for ideas, and was surprised to see a few tears in her eyes. "Did you know the med student?" he asked her. Why hadn't he realised this earlier?

She nodded quietly. "They made a wonderful couple," she said. "Just perfect for each other."

"Do you think she could learn to love me like that?" he asked. Knowing that his feelings for her were no passing thing, but increasingly real and important.

"I'm certain of it." She wiped her eyes, and looked thoughtful. "You could buy her roses, of course."

"Is that what he used to do?" Adam asked.

She nodded again. "He'd always buy her a dozen red roses every anniversary."

"Then I'd like to do something different. Not remind her of him," he said. "Something to simply lift her spirits and show her she's important to me. Do you think she'd like a bottle of perfume or is it too soon?"

"I think she'd love perfume. And it's an appropriate gift, in the circumstances."

So the following day, Adam went shopping with his mother. She wheeled him through the department store to the perfume section. They were met by one dazzling display after another, with attractive girls asking if they'd like to smell the scent at their counters. Adam looked around, puzzled. It felt strangely familiar to be here. Then he caught sight of the Dior counter, and asked his mother to wheel him over to that. He reached out for the tester bottle of *Miss Dior*.

As he held the bottle to his nose, gently inhaling the sensual elegant scent, something happened inside him. It was a glimpse into another world. An illumination. A world where he was somebody else. Somebody who wasn't confined temporarily to a wheelchair. The pieces of the puzzle were coming together in a new and unexpected way that took his breath away. As memories flooded through him, his hands shook. His mother took the bottle from him, looking at him intently.

"Are you feeling alright?" she asked. "I was afraid you were going to drop the bottle."

He looked right into her eyes. "Everything's coming back to me, Mum," he said softly. "It's like I've been living in a dream all these weeks and now I'm finally waking up again."

She bit her lip, unable to speak.

And as she listened with her whole soul, he told her about his studies, his motorbike, and the lovely blonde girl who lived next door.

His phone beeped. And he knew this time that the med student who owned the phone, and the young man in the wheelchair, were one and the same person.

Paper Kisses

All I wanted was the real thing. A kiss from a boy who was in love with me. I didn't need all the romantic extras you see in the movies – French champagne, a dozen long stemmed red roses and expensive jewellery. I'd learnt that those things could camouflage a lie. It was simply true love I wanted. Nothing more and nothing less.

And I got off to a promising start.

At the age of five, when I was sitting under a large tree in the schoolyard, a blond boy called Christopher shyly asked if he could kiss my cheek. He was in my class and always sat in front of me. In those days of chalk and blackboards and summer holidays, a kiss under a tree wasn't a big deal. I let him, and kissed his cheek too. We decided it was our secret.

I was hardly about to tell my older brother, was I? William would only have laughed at me and said I was being silly.

My second kiss was eight years later, the wait more than compensated for by the fact that it was Keith, my first major crush. Like Christopher, he was blond with blue eyes. But this time there were complications.

It's not easy falling in love with your brother's best friend.

On the plus side, it meant seeing him quite often, something most of my friends would've killed for. Not that I could trust their judgment anymore. Not since my closest confidante, Dawn said she was in love with my brother. That discredited anything further she had to say on the subject, as far as I was concerned. If Dawn thought William was a heartthrob, I couldn't trust anything else that she might have to say on the subject of boys and love.

I knew William only too well. He was untidy, sometimes smelly, and only ever used soap to wash his hair. The floor in his bedroom was always covered with clutter – football boots, dirty socks and discarded clothes. Did he keep anything where it belonged? And why couldn't he use shampoo like the rest of the family?

William and romance? I don't think so. Dawn was making a mega mistake. But much to my chagrin, nothing I said had any effect on her. I could only conclude she was delusional. Whereas I, on the other hand, had found the real thing in Keith.

There was no denying the strong magnetic pull I felt whenever Keith was in my vicinity. By this stage I was reading all the Jane Austen novels so I was no newcomer to the concept of true love. I had all the symptoms. Elizabeth Bennett's feelings towards Mr Darcy were no different to what I felt for Keith. Although personally I thought Mr Wickham was appealing too, despite everything.

I felt my cheeks burn when Keith walked up our driveway. My hands would shake if I handed him a cup of tea. And I never seemed to be able to trust my voice when he was around. From the moment I met him, life felt embarrassing, exciting and totally unpredictable all at the same time.

It could only be love.

Any lingering doubts were quashed by the depth of my misery when his family moved away.

I poured my heartache into a diary. Not a proper diary, but a large notebook my father no longer wanted. An entire page was devoted to the goodbye kiss that summer's evening, when Keith walked up our driveway for the last time. My brother was out, so it was up to Mum and me to entertain him. I had the inspiration of showing him the parsley I'd grown in a pot under our leaking back tap.

Why I thought he'd be interested in parsley is beyond me now. My mother looked surprised. But as she was busy assembling ingredients for one of her famous spaghetti dinners, she was quite happy to see me wander downstairs with Keith.

Would she have been as happy if she'd seen him pull me towards him, behind the garden shed?

"Boys and study don't mix" was Mum's mantra.

I didn't agree with her. As I nestled into his arms, my heart bursting, I couldn't imagine life without him.

"Can't you stay?" I asked.

"I wish with all my heart that we weren't moving," he said, his blue eyes holding mine.

The kiss was gentle, soft and warm, and over too soon. I was lifting my face for another when my brother yelled out to Keith. We both leapt apart. I pretended Mum had sent me to pick parsley for the spaghetti she was cooking.

This second kiss was meant to remain a secret too. I knew William would only tease me if he found out, and Keith thought he'd disapprove of him kissing his sister.

But somehow my brother had guessed I kept a diary. I

still don't know how he found it because I kept it hidden behind boxes of photos at the bottom of the old dresser in the kitchen.

But find it he certainly did.

A week later when I retrieved it to reread what I'd written about the lingering goodbye kiss, there was a new entry written underneath mine.

"William read diary. Had a good laugh. He didn't kiss me goodbye."

I was furious he'd read it and knew my secret. But who could I tell? I couldn't even phone Dawn. She'd have only stuck up for William when clearly he'd been in the wrong.

I certainly couldn't admit to Mum that Keith had kissed me. She'd have felt upset with me.

I stopped writing in the diary.

And it was a while before I had eyes for any other boy. For at least a year Keith and I wrote to each other. I lived in hope his father would magically be transferred back here and life could return to normal.

This was when I learnt about paper kisses. The ones you write on letters and cards, interspersed with paper hugs. How real they can seem. Keith would sometimes send me a whole sheet of large ones. Once he sent me a photo of a clear blue sky full of white kisses made by the exhaust trails of jets. I framed the photo and kept it on my bedside table.

The longer he was gone, the more paper kisses arrived to sustain me and keep my love alive.

The first inkling they weren't designed to last forever came on the day when I accidentally spilt a glass of water over the letter I was reading. I hastily mopped it up but the damage was done. The paper was weak, and a whole section of kisses crumpled in my hand. I looked at them sadly, twisted out of shape, some broken. Perhaps it was an omen?

The next day the postman brought the letter I'd been secretly dreading all this time. The "I've found someone else" one.

No one could comfort me.

Dawn had ignored my advice and was now dating my brother. I hadn't found any other friend I felt I could really open my heart to. Everyone seemed lost in their own crush – and those who weren't in love wouldn't understand what I was going through.

I nursed my wounded heart, falling in love with Paul McCartney and David Beckham. I could love and admire them to my heart's content, without being in any danger of breaking my heart again. The walls of my bedroom were adorned with posters, I bought DVDs and magazines, and became absorbed in another paper world, one where my heart was safe.

I had other crushes, of course, but the years passed without anyone significant happening along. I was beginning to believe that was something that only happened once in a lifetime.

And of course in novels. Another paper world into which I still retreated.

But even I couldn't deny that Dawn and William were now an established couple. Their engagement shouldn't have come as such a shock to me. When Dawn asked me to be her bridesmaid, I experienced a new kind of happiness. In my excitement at having her as a prospective sister-in-law, I forgot about the fact she was delusional enough to be in love with my messy, happy-go-lucky brother. Instead I felt overjoyed and ridiculously proud.

As the date of their wedding approached, I wandered around in a daze, trying on bridesmaid dresses, helping Mum make the wedding cakes, and shopping endlessly with Dawn.

It was only a week before the wedding when I learnt Keith would be one of the guests. Dawn was asking my advice about where to seat everyone at the reception and showed me the list she'd drawn up. William hadn't mentioned Keith for years. I thought he was well and truly off the radar. But apparently I was mistaken.

"They work for the same company now," Dawn explained. She seemed as surprised as me that I hadn't been aware of their renewed friendship. "They stayed in touch via Facebook," she added.

No danger of paper kisses there. Cyber ones – were they any more reliable? Probably not. I wasn't planning to find out. At twenty-one I had my own plans and my own career. I had no intention of veering off course again, in pursuit of what-might-have-been.

Until the actual day of the wedding, that is. Seeing Keith in the flesh produced an array of physical symptoms that would've sent any sane young woman running in the opposite direction. When his blue eyes met mine in the church as I walked down the aisle in my finery, I found it difficult to breathe.

Don't be ridiculous, I kept scolding myself. And focused as well as I could on the ceremony. There was no avoiding the moment of truth, though, as he walked over to join me outside the church afterwards. I stood my ground. Ready to be friendly but not infatuated. That was eight years ago – and he was the one who'd ended our relationship. So why did my heart flutter and my knees feel weak as he approached? Until his eyes met mine, and then I began to relax.

He gave me a gentle hug and kissed my cheek, his eyes warm and appreciative.

He'd been good looking at seventeen. At twenty-five he was a knock out. But the sincerity and openness in his eyes suggested that he still wasn't aware of this.

I couldn't help noticing he wasn't wearing a ring.

"It's wonderful to see you again," he said, sounding as though he really meant it.

We said a few commonplace things and then I asked how he was. Trying to sound out subtlely whether he was in a relationship. What had happened to the someone he'd met, I wondered? Were they still together?

It was Keith who first mentioned our letters.

Would I mention the paper kisses? No. They'd been part of my first experience of love. They were something I'd left behind. Although the photo of the white kisses against the blue sky still sat on my bedside table as a reminder.

People were milling around us, talking and circulating. There wasn't much chance of a private conversation. Although I realised as soon as he walked over that there was nothing I'd like more. There was so much I wanted to talk to him about.

Was it closure I was seeking? Or was it something else?

I didn't have long to wonder. We were quickly swept along by the activities of the day. The photographer scooped me up, and then we all descended on the local hall, decked out with white satin ribbon and pink roses, with caterers and a band. I sat at the top table with the bridal party. Keith was at the back of the hall with the other boys from high school.

Forever a traditionalist, Dawn had insisted on a bridal waltz. I was lost in thought, watching them, when there was a gentle tap on my shoulder.

"Would you dance with me?" It was Keith.

For the second time in my life, I found myself in his arms. Whether it was the magic in the air, or the Johann Strauss melody the band was playing, I'm not sure. But with his arm around me, everything felt right in my world in a way it hadn't done in a very long time. I rested my head gently on his shoulder and let him lead me around the dance floor.

Finally, I mentioned his last letter. To my surprise his cheeks grew pink and a shadow crossed his eyes. "I'm sorry I told you a lie," he whispered. "I was trying to set you free. Give you a chance to meet someone else."

His words sank in.

"So there wasn't another girl?"

"There's never been anyone else," he said. "But you were only a teenager. It was too early for you to know your heart."

My heart soared at his words. Everything I'd told myself about not being ridiculous no longer seemed to matter. I felt I was where I belonged.

But the music ended. The dance was over. And one of the groomsmen came over to ask me for the next dance.

The magic moment was over.

Sanity prevailed.

Looking back, the rest of the evening is something of a blur. Champagne flowed, everyone was abuzz with friendliness and love, and I had more hugs and kisses than I could remember. William and Dawn set off for a honeymoon in Scotland, leaving the rest of us to return to our everyday lives.

Today hasn't been much different. I walked down the aisle in the same church, in another beautiful gown. White, this time. William and Dawn were there again, with their three-year-old daughter, who was my flower girl.

Keith is holding me in his arms again, as we waltz around the hall to the sounds of the band playing Strauss.

I'm a traditionalist too.

Flowers for Nancy

Everybody loved Nancy. Who could help themselves? A born party girl, she'd danced her way through life, enriching the lives of all who crossed her path.

Today they must find a way to say goodbye to her.

Today they must find a way to say goodbye to her.

Wayne swallowed hard, feeling the tears rising yet again. He held onto the bouquet of flowers and looked around the church. The pews were full. Young and old. All their lives touched by Nancy's love and vivacity.

As he watched, a tall auburn-haired man entered the church and quietly sat in the back pew. "I wondered if you'd come today," Wayne said under his breath.

He'd never met him. Perhaps he'd introduce himself after the service? Or perhaps not.

He was one of many people here who Wayne had never met.

His daughter squeezed his hand. "I thought Mum said no flowers," she whispered.

Her eyes held the watery look of loss as she nestled against his shoulder.

His precious Kathleen. The rose of the family, tall and elegant. Beside her was his son Jonathan who'd taken after Wayne's side of the family. Dark-haired, brown-eyed and five foot eight inches when he stood up straight. Everyone had said – not to his face, of course – that it wasn't fair for him to be shorter than his younger sister.

But life wasn't fair, was it? It was as capricious and unpredictable as the lovely girl Nancy had been when he'd first met her.

He'd gone along to a dance at the local hall one Saturday night. And there she was. The girl he'd spent his life dreaming of. They'd danced until the early hours, and she'd allowed him to walk her home. To kiss her soft lips. To meet her again the following night.

He'd given her a bunch of red roses that evening. Everyone knew red roses symbolised love and romance. Nancy had instantly held him tight. Their passion once kindled had never died out.

Over the years their love had burned and shone, sometimes brightly, sometimes more like glowing embers. Somehow able to withstand all the challenges they'd had to face in their thirty years together.

She'd been his wild rose.

He looked at the flowers in his hands, carefully chosen from the garden this morning. Could Nancy see them, he wondered? Red roses, of course. A few sprays of baby's breath. Forget-me-nots. And amongst them a white tulip.

"Mum meant bought flowers," he whispered. "She wanted the money to go to the hospice."

"When are you going to put them -?" Jonathan's voice trailed away.

In the centre aisle of the church sat the cream wicker coffin, unadorned.

"When it feels right," Wayne said.

There was a quiet hum of voices audible above the soft organ music. Restless shifting. The flicker of paper as people glanced through the order of service.

Several others had brought flowers, Wayne noticed. Nothing ostentatious that would appear to flout her wishes. But it was hard not to bring flowers for a woman like Nancy. He'd noticed someone holding a spray of lilac orchids. A perfect choice. Did they understand the symbolism or was it a lucky coincidence? Orchids – for love, thoughtfulness and femininity.

Nancy had a Victorian book of flowers and loved to read out their meanings when someone brought her a bouquet.

Wayne smiled as he remembered Kathleen running into the kitchen one day with a daffodil she'd picked for her mother. She was only ten-years-old, her long red hair held in plaits, already a tall and gangly girl.

"This is for you, Mum," she'd said breathlessly, offering it to her. Expecting Nancy's usual enthusiastic response.

But Nancy hadn't taken it. Instead she'd said, "Pick another, darling. One daffodil means misfortune. If you give me several, that means happiness."

So Kathleen had picked more daffodils and helped her arrange them in a vase.

Could Nancy see the lilac orchids?

Or the sweet peas he'd noticed someone holding? Sweet peas for goodbye.

There were noises and voices at the back of the church.

Wayne looked around. The minister was standing in the doorway. The service was about to begin.

As the organ slowly started to play Nancy's favourite hymn *How Great Thou Art*, Wayne rose to his feet with the other mourners. As the congregation began to sing, he gently placed the flowers on the coffin.

Red roses, signifying his love. Baby's breath, for everlasting happiness. Forget-me-nots for the girl who would always be in his heart. And amongst them the simple white tulip. Signifying forgiveness.

Everyone loved Nancy.

He hadn't been the only one.

Nancy thought she'd taken her secret to the grave with her.

But Wayne had guessed. Noticed the discrepancy in dates.

Perhaps he'd introduce himself to the man in the back pew after the service? It was time he met Kathleen's real father.

Holidaying with Harry

Lorna heard her bedroom door being gently opened, and knew it was Harry checking to see if she was awake.

She looked up.

"Would you like tea?" He was already showered and dressed, ready to head off on the day's adventures.

What would she be able to do today? She wasn't sure. It'd been a difficult night.

He came over to open the curtains. Leaves were being blown around in the garden outside. Another windy day.

Opening the curtains was Harry's way of stating that it was morning. She smiled as she remembered the early days of their marriage. He'd come in every morning with a cup of tea for her and open the curtains. When he was still making an effort. When they still had a marriage.

The gesture brought back unexpected fond memories. But she also remembered how these gestures had gradually stopped and their lives had drifted apart.

"Tea would be lovely," Lorna murmured. The bedclothes felt warm and comforting. She was reluctant to begin her day. Life seemed uphill.

She tried to manoeuvre herself into a sitting position and gasped in pain. Harry came over to help, propping two pillows at her back. Another thoughtful gesture. And one she was grateful for today.

As she waited for the tea, listening to the familiar sounds of Harry moving around in the kitchen, she looked out of the window. Her room had a lovely view of the front garden. Some brightly coloured birds had come to the birdbath. She always meant to learn the names of the different species.

Outside the kettle came to the boil and Harry reappeared with two cups of tea, sitting down beside her, legs sprawled out in front of him.

She didn't want to begin the day by sounding critical but his heavy shoes were on the white duvet.

"Put that blue towel under your shoes," she suggested. And was pleased when he didn't seem offended. There was a fine line between suggestion and criticism. She didn't always get it right. She knew he meant well but ...

She sighed as she sipped her tea.

Another day.

It was suddenly more important than ever to keep things on a friendly footing with Harry. And it was all her own fault.

Yesterday's accident rankled. She still couldn't believe what a stupid mistake she'd made. One she'd be paying for in the weeks to come, according to the local doctor.

One moment's inattention and now look at her. A badly twisted ankle, a heavily grazed knee and a torn shoulder muscle. All because she hadn't looked where she was going. They'd been talking when she'd missed her footing and her right foot had twisted into a ditch between the footpath and the tarmac of the road. Throwing out her arm to protect herself as she fell, she'd hyperextended her shoulder and torn a muscle. And her knee still felt hot and stinging beneath its bandage, especially when she bent it.

Harry had been able to borrow a wheelchair for the next few days. But then what would she do? How would she cope when she was back home again, living on her own?

Her life had suddenly become very complicated. She didn't relish being dependent on her ex-husband. And it didn't really suit him either. But what were they to do?

Being in rented holiday accommodation didn't help. She was conscious of how much it was costing. She'd have to make the most of the situation.

She and Harry had come here together for a fortnight's holiday, as neither of them had anyone else to travel with this year. It wasn't their first holiday together since separating, and probably wouldn't be their last. Something her friends found hard to understand. Yet it was perfectly logical. This apartment had two bedrooms and was very comfortable, better than either of them could have afforded on their own. There were definite advantages. And Lorna preferred it to travelling alone. That had lost its novelty quite quickly. And what if she'd come here on her own? How would she have coped with these injuries?

"I thought we might go to the Art Gallery this morning, if that suits you," he said.

It'd mean having him push her around the paintings in the wheelchair. He wouldn't know which ones she wanted to linger by and which didn't interest her. Did she want to go? Would it be churlish to say no? What were her options?

Lorna drank her tea, wondering how to reply.

"There's a café overlooking the lake," he added. "And a gift shop."

He knew she wanted to bring something back for their daughter. Brianna was studying art and design at university.

"Maybe," she said. "It sounds interesting."

She didn't want to stay in the apartment all day, looking out the window. No matter how pretty the birds were at the birdbath.

Lorna took her time eating the toast Harry brought to her, and accepted his offer of a second cup of tea. Trying to delay the inevitable moment when she needed his assistance getting bathed and dressed.

He seemed to understand.

"How are we going to manage this?" he asked.

She shrugged. "I can't stand up for a shower."

"No, of course not," he said. "Let me think." And then he disappeared and she could hear him on the balcony. What was he doing?

Harry reappeared in a few moments, holding a plastic chair.

"Now you can shower," he said, taking it into the bathroom. He half carried, half assisted her there, making sure she didn't slip on the tiles.

"I'll have to undress you," he said. "I don't think you should be using that shoulder."

She nodded.

His gentleness surprised her. And his concern for her feelings. If only he'd stayed this way when they were married. Somehow once Brianna had left home to go to university, things had deteriorated. They seemed to lose interest in each other.

Now for the first time she wondered if they'd both been feeling depressed.

"Would you like me to wash your hair?" Harry asked.

Lorna sighed with relief. She'd been wondering whether to ask.

As he worked shampoo into her hair, careful that none got near her eyes, she felt there'd been a change in their relationship. She was seeing a side of Harry that she hadn't seen since their early courting days. The considerate caring side. For the first time in recent years, she was seeing the man she originally felt in love with.

Here she was, sitting on a plastic chair in a shower recess, helpless and in pain. Yet somehow he'd managed to make her feel okay about it. Given her the help she needed while showing her respect.

The intimacy of the situation brought back memories, no doubt for him as well.

But she had to be realistic. Their marriage hadn't worked out. She hadn't regretted her decision for them to part and had felt pleased that their friendship had remained solid. That was a blessing. She had no intention of doing anything to put that in jeopardy. Yet he'd set her thinking along new lines. Awoken memories of their happy times together.

"What on earth would I have done without you here?" she said, as they drove off an hour later. Voicing her thoughts out loud. "What if I'd come on my own and then hurt myself?"

"You could've phoned me," he said simply. "I would've come."

She smiled. "Always my knight in shining armour." And

then regretted saying it, seeing the look of hope spring to his eyes.

But whatever he was thinking, he didn't say anything and the awkward moment passed.

She wasn't ready to explore the thoughts she'd had earlier in the shower, about whether it was still possible for them to have a romantic involvement again. She knew she was still in a state of shock from the fall and feeling vulnerable. That wasn't a good time to make any significant decisions.

She looked out the window of the car at the lovely views of the lake. At one particularly scenic spot he stopped the car.

"I just want to get a photo of this," he said. And winding his window down, he held up his iPhone to record the view, turning to capture the whole panorama.

"Would you like me to get a photo for you as well?" he offered.

And she'd handed him her phone.

The gallery was only ten minutes away and they were soon there.

Harry obligingly wheeled her inside and then slowly pushed her up and down the different viewing rooms.

Landscape art was the predominant theme, different painters bringing to life the wonderful mountains and lakes surrounding them. To Lorna's surprise they both chose the same print to buy to take back to their respective homes. The look on Harry's face spoke volumes, but again he held his peace. Not wishing to open up old wounds. They'd both moved on and managed to salvage a good friendship. Why put that at risk? Few couples they knew were even on speaking terms once they'd separated.

It'd been a series of little things that had led to Lorna's decision to live alone. Harry hadn't been unfaithful and neither had she. They'd simply grown apart in so many different ways that she'd finally chosen the path of least compromise. She'd fallen out of love with him. There was no longer any denying it. Bit by bit the little rituals that had held them together had gone. Harry had stopped bringing her tea in bed every morning. She often ate dinner alone, as he worked long hours.

Then he'd joined a golf club. What with practice, meetings and the social activities there, she'd barely seen him. And when he was home, she'd found some of his habits increasingly irritating. Separating had been her means of keeping things on a friendly basis. And it'd worked.

"You mentioned a café?" she said. They'd arrived back at the front of the gallery.

The café had an outdoor area and they chose a table at the far end with a wonderful view of the lake. A chilly wind caused Lorna to shiver. Harry gallantly draped his jacket around her shoulders. She could smell the scent of his aftershave, a masculine blend of cedar and citrus. It was the one she'd given him some years ago.

The scent brought back memories of happier times. For both of them.

"You gave this to me in Paris," he reminded her.

She nodded. It'd been an impulsive purchase, in the Galeries Lafayette.

And Harry had bought her a black cashmere cardigan, one she kept for special occasions.

A sigh escaped her lips.

Harry reached across the table and held her hand. "Those were the days, weren't they?"

She didn't answer, her mind travelling back to that time in Paris.

And to the evening, when Harry had proposed to her on a tourist boat on the Seine. The lights had sparkled their reflections on the inky waters of the famous river. And caused his eyes to sparkle with gold and green lights amid the blue. Her heart full of love and the romance of the setting, she'd accepted.

"What went wrong?" Harry asked, not for the first time. "We started off so well together."

"Do we really have to go over this again?" she asked wearily. "I find it sad."

"I blame myself," Harry said. "I was foolish to start taking you for granted. Letting things –" He didn't finish.

"Don't blame yourself," she said. Even though secretly she'd often blamed him for the decline in their relationship.

It'd been so gradual they'd barely noticed. Until one day she felt there was none of the magic left. What was the point in talking about this again now? It could only arouse unwanted emotions. Perhaps lead to unrealistic expectations on his part. There was no guarantee that things would be different if they tried again.

"There's never been anyone else." He was still holding her hand so she carefully withdrew hers. She didn't want to give him the wrong impression. Even though she'd enjoyed having his hand on hers.

"I know that," she said. "But we've done something not many couples manage to achieve. We now have a really good friendship. We can enjoy each other's company and even go on holidays together."

She didn't continue.

"Don't you ever want more?" he said softly.

They were both in their forties. Of course she wanted more. But she didn't want to lose what she'd managed to salvage either.

At that moment, their coffee arrived. Thankfully she didn't need to answer him.

Lorna busied herself stirring in a sachet of sugar. Aware that his eyes were on her.

When she finally raised hers, she was surprised to see a tear glistening on his cheek. She reached over and gently wiped it away. The movement hurt her shoulder and she gasped in pain.

"How could I have been so stupid?" she said, for the umpteenth time. Rubbing the sore area.

"These things happen." He looked out over the deep blue waters of the lake. "I hate to see you in pain."

She nodded in agreement. Only a few days ago she'd noticed that he'd cut himself shaving and had felt the same way. Wishing he wasn't hurt. These things still mattered.

But only because they were now living their separate lives and not having to deal with all the minutiae of living together, she reminded herself. Somehow things just hadn't turned out how they'd hoped when they'd been man and wife.

Lorna sipped her coffee, lost in thought. Wondering why this holiday was different to the others they'd gone on together since separating. She'd always managed to steer their conversation away from their feelings, focussing on things like the weather and what tourist attractions they might like to visit.

Was it the location, she wondered? They'd chosen a lakeside village. One they'd often talked about exploring. Last year they'd gone to London and spent their days sightseeing and shopping. The year before they'd gone on a cruise in the Mediterranean. Somehow the busier holidays had provided so much distraction that they hadn't had time to focus on what had gone wrong in their marriage.

Now there was no avoiding it, with this enforced intimacy.

"How will you manage back at home?" he asked.

She'd been wondering about this herself. "I won't be able to put any weight on my ankle for a while longer," she said. "I'd lose balance trying to shower."

Then there was driving the car. Buying groceries. Getting herself to all those appointments with her doctor, physiotherapist and so on.

Lorna closed her eyes. It was too hard to think about.

"There is a solution, you know." Harry was holding her hand again.

She looked into his eyes, knowing what he meant. The thought had occurred to her as well.

"You have a spare room," he went on. "I could take time off work to look after you."

"Would you mind?" she asked softly.

"Of course not," he said. "You're still my best friend and always will be."

"I can't make any promises," she said. Answering the question he'd dared not put into words.

His blue eyes had a tinge of gold and green in them today, she noticed.

"All I want is to help you," he said. "Let me make it up to you for all the things I didn't do when I had the chance."

She had to blink away a tear at his words. This was the first time he'd acknowledged that he'd changed. That he'd started taking her for granted.

That was how their relationship had ended. Could this damage be undone now? That was the big question on her mind.

Things were shifting. Somehow this accident had brought them together, forced a new kind of intimacy. Would this last once she'd recovered? There was no way of knowing unless she took the chance.

They were still holding hands. And she didn't want to let go. Not for now. Maybe not for ever. She'd give him the chance to make amends. Otherwise she'd spend the rest of her life wondering about it.

"You have the chance now," she said. "And so do I. Maybe if we both try harder, things will work out this time?"

Part III
Murder and Mystery

Learning to Fly

It happened three times before Lynne would admit to herself what was going on.

She was shrinking. Every time Bill made one of his veiled criticisms that made her feel small, she actually did get smaller.

But only if her hand was touching the new mouse pad.

Or mouse rug, as it was called.

She'd seen one at a friend's place and desperately wanted one of her own. "Your very own flying carpet," she'd said as she picked it up to admire. It was a perfect miniature of an ancient Persian rug, with tiny Minotaurs and swords worked into the green and brown design. *Perfect in every way*, Lynne thought, as she ordered one online.

If only it was big enough, she could fly away on it and escape from Bill.

Or if I was only small enough, she'd thought.

And now it was actually happening.

Part of her was scared. Another part was becoming increasingly excited.

There was nothing quite as alluring as the impossible.

It'd started Wednesday evening. She was at her computer reading *The Age* online, her hand resting on the tiny rug which had arrived in the mail that morning.

"It's recipes you should be reading," Bill complained. "I don't know what tonight's dessert was but it wasn't a plum pudding."

She'd felt her teeth start to grind as they often did. The pudding had been delicious. Her grandmother's special recipe. How dare he complain? He hadn't lifted a finger to help.

Angry words flooded into her mind but she said nothing.

But then as Bill continued speaking, a strange feeling began in her ears. A tingling itchy sensation that slowly deepened as it spread throughout the rest of her body.

She didn't think much of it at the time. Bill's bad behaviour often caused her unpleasant physical symptoms.

And when she had to tighten her belt by a notch on Thursday she felt pleased. Not putting two and two together.

Another belittling comment that night caused similar symptoms. But once again she was so involved in the heat of her emotions that her body's strange responses didn't really register on her consciousness.

However, tonight she had to admit something strange was happening.

When Lynne put her feet into her slippers, she could barely walk in them. It reminded her of childhood dressing up games when she'd been allowed to wear her mother's shoes.

She went into the bathroom, took off her pyjamas and tried to have a good look at herself in the mirror. Not easy for some reason. She tried standing on tiptoe. Even that wasn't enough so she climbed onto a small stool.

The sight that met her eyes caused her to gasp out loud. There was the evidence staring her in the face. Her body was barely half its normal size.

There was a resounding thump on the door. "What are you doing in there?"

She held her breath, waiting for the intense itching to begin. But this time she didn't get the sensation. And that's how she realised it only happened when her hand was on the mouse rug.

It might not be the flying carpet of her dreams but it did seem to possess strange powers.

Lynne turned off the lights and went to bed, hoping Bill hadn't noticed how small she'd become.

She needn't have worried. Bill had long ago ceased noticing her.

The following night she was prepared. She deliberately reheated the rest of the plum pudding to provoke him. Knowing how he'd react. Waiting in readiness.

"We used to be served muck like this at boarding school," he began, tipping his helping into the rubbish bin.

Lynne smiled, feeling oblivious to him for the first time in ages. In control, at last.

Later, when he was watching TV, she slipped into her study and sat at the computer. With one hand resting on the mouse rug, she carefully played Bill's comment which she'd recorded on her iPhone.

The itchy sensation began.

She kept playing and replaying his voice. Her body was a writhing mass of weird sensations. She wanted to scream from the itch. The symptoms were terrible. Then they slowly subsided. And she felt wonderful, a new strength surging through her veins. She felt invincible.

Opening her eyes, she marvelled at the mouse rug. She was standing on it now.

It's not small at all, she thought, gently touching the surface, admiring the pattern. Glorious shades of green and brown wools in a wonderfully intricate design. Far more detailed and subtle than she'd been able to see earlier.

She looked around. Her favourite coffee mug stood near the computer. It was a handmade terracotta mug her friend had brought back from Spain. It came up to her chin. As Lynne peered over the rim to inhale the aroma, the practicalities of her new situation began to dawn on her. How could she make coffee? What would she be able to eat? She sat down on the rug to think.

It was at that moment Bill entered the room.

"Where are you hiding?" he thundered, unbuckling his belt in a threatening way.

She flinched. He seemed like the ogre from *Jack and the Beanstalk*.

It took her a moment to realise he hadn't seen her. There was only one thing she could do. But would it work?

Holding tightly onto the fringed edging of the rug, she nudged her heels firmly against its flank.

"Up!" she silently urged.

The fringing began to move with graceful power and the rug slowly swirled upwards, taking Lynne with it. Using the fringing to steer, she circled the room, and then began to hover above Bill's head.

He swiped at the rug angrily but she kept it tantalisingly out of his reach.

As she steered it in arcs around the light, Bill climbed onto the desk, continuing to swipe with both hands. But even when he leaned up to his full height, he couldn't quite reach it. Cursing loudly, he unplugged the desk lamp and began hitting out with that.

Now Lynne was within reach. Sooner or later she'd be struck. There'd be no surviving that. But what could she do?

Attack was her only choice. She firmly guided the rug in a swift dive, and sped towards the backs of his knees.

The impact nearly caused her to topple off. She was so busy clinging on that she didn't notice Bill falling off the desk. Just heard the tremendous crash as he hit the floor. The whole room seemed to shake. Then the heavy metal lamp fell, landing on Bill's head.

Lynne froze in shock.

The rug gave a flourish to an invisible audience before gracefully landing on the desk.

Lynne felt stunned with shock, wondering what she should do. Perhaps she should escape and start a new life somewhere far away?

There were too many bad memories here.

She dug her heels once more into the rug's flank.

"Up," she said. Expecting it to fly.

But to her surprise it stayed where it was and began manoeuvring itself back into its usual position underneath the mouse.

As it did so, she began to experience more strange symptoms. A horrible bursting feeling. Bloating. Aches and pains. Lynne kept having to stretch her arms and legs to get comfortable.

She was rubbing her eyes when she caught sight of her reflection in the mirror. She rubbed her eyes again. Surely it couldn't be true?

But there she was. Back to her normal size. She wriggled her feet in the slippers. They were a perfect fit.

Had it all been a dream?

The thought crushed her. She climbed off the desk, wondering if she'd finally lost her marbles.

Then she looked down. Bill lay sprawled on the floor, the broken lamp lying on his head.

She hadn't dreamt this, thankfully.

Reluctantly she put a finger on his neck. Nothing.

Bill was indeed dead.

Lynne kissed the rug.

Then phoned the police.

The officer who arrived soon afterwards was familiar to her. He'd been to the house on several occasions, when neighbours had complained. Noticed her bruises. She'd always felt a bond of sympathy and support. Last month he'd handed her the address of a women's shelter, offering to help.

In a gentle voice he asked her what had happened.

She left one hand on the mouse rug as she spoke. It made her feel stronger.

"I'm not really sure, officer," she said. "I heard a loud crash and discovered my husband had fallen off the desk. When I checked, he was dead."

As he wrote in his notebook, she felt a curious tingling in her scalp. It was almost as though her hair had started to grow longer. Thickened. She looked at her hands and had to bite back her surprise. They looked so elegant, the blemishes dissolving to reveal perfect skin. The fingernails shiny.

The policeman was looking at her in a new way, admiration replacing the kindness in his eyes.

She noticed they were the same shades of green and brown as her mouse rug. And knew in that moment her future was secure.

The Poacher

Donald Thompkins just disappeared one day. Our village was alive with gossip. Had he run off with the beautiful blonde he'd been seen kissing near the common one evening? Or had he met a more sinister fate?

His wife seemed to think so. The very next day she took to wearing black clothing.

The police investigated. Posters were circulated. But in the end, married men disappeared now and again and were never traced.

I was just a young schoolboy. We started to tell stories about the Widow and her rambling house.

Most of the villagers saw her as a tragic figure. I held a different view, but was too scared to voice my opinion.

I didn't want to disappear too.

Things came to a head the night Billy Hodges and I decided to poach a rabbit or two from her garden. He'd made a cage-like contraption. We pretended to go to bed, slipped out, and met outside the Widow's house at eleven o'clock. There was a crescent moon that night, watching us through the gnarled yew trees.

Someone else had also been watching.

Billy set up his trap at the far end of the garden near the old stone well. We'd seen rabbits there before and knew there were a lot of baby ones around. We waited. And we waited. A fine mist seemed to seep through our clothes and chill us to the bone.

We were talking about giving up and going home when we heard the click, followed by a thump. The trap had actually worked. Inside, peering out at us, was a fat grey rabbit with long brown whiskers. For some reason, his whiskers reminded me of Donald Thompkins' bushy moustache.

As we were trying to bundle him into a hessian bag, we heard the crunch of footsteps. They got nearer.

"What'll we do?" I whispered. We both knew it could only be one person.

Billy's face was white. "You take the rabbit and run. I'll be behind you, with the trap. Meet you outside your place in ten minutes."

Billy didn't show up. I stayed outside my house in the freezing cold, trying to manage an unwieldy hessian bag. The rabbit wriggled and bumped. I nearly dropped him.

When the village hall chimed one o'clock, I gave up and went to bed. Leaving the rabbit in the bag at the bottom of my wardrobe. I didn't know what else to do with him. The cage we'd made was at Billy's house.

Everyone else had eaten their porridge and started doing chores by the time I woke up next morning.

For a moment it felt like a normal Saturday. Then Mum came in and said, "What are you and Billy planning today?"

My heart nose-dived as I remembered that Billy hadn't turned up at our rendezvous. Had he got home safely, I wondered?

"Nothing much," I mumbled.

After breakfast I went over to Billy's house. He wasn't there. His sister gave me the cage and told me everyone else was out looking for him.

By mid-afternoon the story was all over the village. Billy Hodges had run away from home last night.

His tearful mother sat at our kitchen table with Mum.

"He didn't even take a change of clothes," she sobbed.

Now I felt confused. Had Billy really run away? Or had the Widow done something to him? I kept telling myself that if something awful had happened, they'd find his body. And I couldn't help wondering if he'd felt too scared to go home. He was always getting into trouble and I didn't want to make things worse for him.

I couldn't sleep properly. What had the Widow done with Billy? Was he her slave? Had she killed him? Or was he a stowaway on a ship bound for the other side of the world? Would I ever find out the truth about that terrible night?

Thoughts of Billy haunted my every waking moment, and every night I dreamed about a rabbit. It always had Billy's eyes.

There were the usual investigations. The police came and questioned me about Billy, asking where he might've gone. Billy's mother appeared on national television, and local authorities organised searches of the surrounding countryside. In the end, it was concluded Billy had probably stowed away on a cargo ship or perhaps hidden on one of the trains to Newcastle. It wasn't unusual for young boys to seek adventure.

No one suggested the Widow might be responsible for Billy's disappearance. And I was too frightened to tell anyone what we'd done. I'd have been grounded for months if my mother knew I'd left the house after bedtime. And I'd have got a hiding.

I didn't want to go near the Widow's house after that.

I named the grey rabbit Tom, short for Thompkins. After all, I'd found him there and he reminded me of Donald. I was desperate to keep him as a pet, but after Mum discovered me giving him lettuce and carrots from our vegetable garden, she said I had to put him back where I found him. Otherwise she'd put him in a stew.

I couldn't bear that, so the following evening I set off alone for Widow Thompkins' house. I had a torch and a large stick, and wore my best running shoes. My heart was hammering in my chest and my palms were sweaty. But it had to be done. And it needed to be done at the end of the day when he had the best chance of taking care of himself. I'd noticed he was always active once the sun went down. Hopefully the Widow would be indoors having her supper.

I slipped through the broken palings at the same spot Billy and I had always used. The brambles scratched my arms and face but I daren't move about in the open. There was plenty of undergrowth to hide in.

The well stood where it always had, the stone covered in light green moss and dark grime.

Footsteps crunched on the dead leaves.

I lay behind a heavy lilac bush, face buried in rotting leaves.

An unnamed dread clutched my insides.

Was it my turn this evening?

She appeared beside the well. What was that strange gibberish she was chanting?

I had to take the risk and watch. For some reason I felt a bit safer. She hadn't come to the well on my account.

She seemed to be in a trance.

I inched closer, praying the rabbit wouldn't make a noise.

The moon peered out from behind the clouds. All I could think about was being back in the safety of my bedroom. I kissed the rabbit goodbye, patted him one last time, and put him on the grass.

The rabbit ran straight to the well, stared at the widow, and gave a piercing screech.

She swooped him up, and gave a strange cackle. "And where do you think you've been, Donald?" she said. "How did you manage to escape?"

The rabbit wriggled in her hands. As I watched, he bit her thumb. She screamed in pain and flung her hand about. "There's only one place for you now," she said in a husky voice. And dropped the hissing, growling rabbit over the side of the well. "Goodbye, Donald."

I sat crouched there as gentle rain started to fall. Rooted to the spot by my overactive imagination.

"Are you down the well too, Billy?" I whispered.

A small creature darted out from the undergrowth. Two brown eyes peered at me, under long floppy ears. It seemed to have Billy's cheeky grin.

It looked at me and then at the Widow, who was peering down the well. I knew immediately what it was trying to tell me.

I didn't give myself time to think. Just ran straight at her, pushing with all my might. She tried to turn around.

I grabbed her arm, collecting a scratch across my cheek. The little rabbit bit her ankle. She screamed and bent down. It was the opportunity I needed. One hard shove and she toppled in, clutching at the sides as she fell.

Her voice echoed in the darkness. It seemed ages before I heard the splash.

I peered over the side. Was the real Donald down there too, punished for being unfaithful? And the beautiful blonde he'd kissed? What had become of her? She wasn't a local so no one had suspected foul play when she wasn't seen again.

"I thought you'd never come." The voice behind me caused my hair to stand on end. A small squeaky voice that could only belong to one person.

I swung around.

The rabbit was looking at me. Slowly, as I watched, the ears grew shorter, the whiskers disappeared, and arms and legs formed.

I had Billy back.

Tears blurring my vision, I hugged him tightly to me.

"I thought you were dead," I sobbed. "What did she do to you?"

"When I was running away, I heard her chanting a spell. Next thing I knew, I was a rabbit."

"Why didn't you run away? Come and find me?"

He was shivering. "There seemed to be an invisible fence around the well. I couldn't get through it, no matter how hard I tried."

Then I thought of something. "Everyone's been looking for you. What are you going to say?"

Billy shrugged. "What did you tell them?"

"I didn't want to get you into trouble, so I just kept quiet.

They were saying you'd caught a train to Newcastle. I didn't know what to think."

Billy whistled. "Wow, that'd be fun."

"Don't even think about it, Billy."

"What's going to happen now?" he asked.

"Do you think I've killed her?" I whispered. "Will she become a rabbit too? Or something worse?"

"Do witches die?" he asked.

We both looked into the well. I half-expected to see her face. Or some frightening mutation that would have her eyes. A snake perhaps, or a toad.

But all I saw down there was grime and death.

The widow's screams seemed to echo up at me.

And the voice of Donald Thompkins.

Perhaps they'd find some kind of reconciliation?

Together again, at the bottom of the well.

Connie's Project

Connie decided to sew a model of everyone in the village, including the cats and dogs, and even the cranky postman.

"I need a project while I'm laid up with this wretched ankle," she told Martin. Last Christmas she'd enjoyed making a nativity scene for the mantelpiece. Now she had all the time in the world for something more ambitious. "Why did I have to break my ankle in the most boring place on earth?"

She threw her teacup across the room, and watched as it bounced off the carpet.

"Even cups don't break here," she complained. "Nothing ever happens."

She scowled as her husband retreated, picking up the offending teacup on his way. He'd left her the newspaper so she read her horoscope. Rubbish, as usual.

Yesterday they'd said she'd make a life-changing discovery. What she'd done was discover how slippery an icy footpath can be when you're not wearing sensible shoes. Five hours of pain later, she was home with a plastered leg, crutches and a foul temper. None of which was life changing.

What would they promise her today? She grunted as she read it out loud. "Inner peace will be yours, after a fiery encounter."

Surely this isn't a fiery encounter? she thought. Nothing fiery ever happened with Martin any more. He'd stopped arguing. Just as he'd stopped doing a lot of other things.

The box of material remnants from her sewing days was on the sofa beside her so she got to work.

Old Norton the postman would be first. She chose red for his face, and gave him small mean eyes. She even made a large satchel for the mail. That was the only reason anyone tolerated Norton.

When she'd finished she put it on the table, and checked the newspaper headlines. The usual disasters in countries she'd barely heard of. A plane crash. A car pile-up on the national highway. "Why don't they ever publish good news?" she said out loud. "Maybe there isn't any?"

Then she had another thought, and carefully read the paper cover to cover. "I just knew it," she told Martin when he brought her a lunch of egg mayonnaise sandwiches. "This village might as well not exist, as far as this newspaper is concerned. I can't remember ever seeing it mentioned."

Martin nodded. "It was your idea to move to the countryside, dear," he said. "I warned you it might get dull."

"You didn't warn me we'd be dull too," she said to his retreating figure.

She sewed Martin in pale beige woollen fabric, and didn't bother to sew on a mouth,

"It's not as if you ever have anything to say any more," she said to the doll, as she laid it next to the postman.

By the weekend she'd made her neighbour's annoying

dog, Joan from over the road, and the vicar. She decided to make Rev Graham's white collar separately, from a piece of elastic. "Just in case I feel like throttling you with it," she whispered to the doll. Rev Graham had visited her on Thursday to suggest she might like to spend this enforced rest by embroidering new cushions for the hard pews at church. She'd been pleased Martin was out. She wouldn't have to offer the vicar a cup of tea.

She left herself until last, for some reason. Maybe it was because she never knew what to wear? And she hadn't decided whether to make her leg normally or covered in plaster. And could she make crutches? They'd be tricky.

"I'll make myself look perfect," she sighed. And treated herself to a large piece of the chocolate cream sponge Joan had made her.

She used blue beads for her eyes, and fashioned a belted dress from a scrap of variegated silk she'd been saving. Then as a final touch, she pulled the belt in to give herself the tiny waist she'd always wanted.

"Maybe this feeling is the inner peace I was promised?" she wondered.

The thought buoyed her up all afternoon, as she attempted the jigsaw Martin had bought her. But there were 1000 pieces, far too many.

By five o'clock when her husband came home, she'd lost most of her good humour. Dozens of pieces of jigsaw lay on the carpet. All she'd managed to put together was a fire engine. The red pieces had been easy to spot.

"Wonder why there's never been a fire engine in the village?" Martin said. It was the longest sentence Connie remembered him saying in days. He continued to exercise this newly found skill by telling her he was off to play darts at the pub. He couldn't look her in the eyes as he handed her a bowl of reheated spaghetti leftover from last night.

Alone with only her boring handmade village to keep her company, Connie lost the last remaining shreds of her good humour. Perhaps also of her sanity?

She'd always been good at darts herself, and resented not being at the pub. She picked up the Norton doll and threw him into the fireplace. *A perfect aim*, she thought with satisfaction. And watched as the flames licked at the fabric. The vicar was next, but not before she'd managed to draw his white collar extra tight. She'd planned to spare the dog but he chose that unfortunate moment to start barking loudly so into the fire he went. By an odd coincidence he stopped barking as the flames engulfed him. The coincidence amused Connie. "I must have special powers," she chuckled.

She hesitated as she picked up the Joan-from-over-the-road doll. That chocolate cream sponge had been superb. But then she remembered noticing Joan help herself to a bunch of roses from her garden on the way out, thinking she couldn't be seen. Joan took longer to burn. She'd crafted her with more detail – a handbag, scarf, and even the cake.

Just as the brown felt cake caught fire, there was an explosion beside Connie. With terror in her eyes, she watched in silence as the real cake caught fire.

"Spontaneous combustion," she whispered. There'd been an article about it in the newspaper.

As she lost consciousness, she was dimly aware that the old bungalow was alight. She could hear sounds of chaos from outside. Sirens. Raised voices. What was happening?

It wasn't a mystery for long. To her amazement Connie

suddenly found herself above the village, looking down. Fires blazed everywhere. She recognised the post office, and Joan's house, and her own bungalow. All alight. Even the church where the vicar was meant to be conducting Evensong.

It was a breathtaking sight. Red and gold shimmery sparks lighting up the blackness of night. Spectacular.

"The village finally looks beautiful," she whispered happily.

Next morning, photos of the village fires were plastered all over the front pages of the national newspapers. "Spontaneous combustion" screamed the headlines. And in the paragraphs that followed a lot of questions were raised about what role Connie's fireplace might have had in the disaster.

Unfortunately Connie wasn't alive to see them, so in the end she missed out on experiencing the promised inner peace.

One Missed Call

My phone vibrates into life in my jeans pocket. The name I see on the tiny screen chills my blood. Then my temperature rises to fever pitch.

The name I read is Timothy. My husband.

Or he was, until yesterday.

I go to push the picture of a green phone to make contact with my caller. The line goes dead. No one's there.

'One missed call' pops up on the screen.

One missed husband.

One Timothy, who didn't come home from work last night. Whose dinner, overcooked from being kept warm too long, was finally fed to my golden retriever this morning. She didn't realise what a sad excuse for beef in Guinness it was, or that the dumplings had once been fresh and springy.

I'd lain awake for hours, wondering why he hadn't at least phoned. It'd felt so ironic. Being married to a telecommunications expert and unable to make phone contact with him. Him with his state-of-the-art phone that could take photos and post them on Instagram. All the bells and whistles. I must've dialled his number a dozen times before midnight. Not to mention the text messages I sent.

After midnight, I'd stopped trying. Just lay in bed staring in disbelief at the ceiling, my thoughts whirring about my head like the ceiling fan.

As they are still whirring. Unable to slow down or focus.

I pour water into the kettle and hunt in the cupboard for the jar of instant coffee. I measure two teaspoons of the brown granules into my biggest mug. There's a chip on the handle. I hadn't noticed it before.

Now my senses are on alert. I'm more aware than I've felt in a long time. The kettle comes to the boil and clicks itself off. The steaming water swirls into the mug, creating a satisfying froth.

I sip the bitter liquid. Relent, and add a heaped spoonful of sugar. My diet can wait until tomorrow. Or next week. Or next year. Sugar's good for shock. I stir in a second spoonful. It's only as I drain the last mouthfuls of the strong brew that I realise what I have to do.

Timothy's phone is the only clue I have to the mystery of last night. Slowly I tap in his number and listen for the ringing sound. Cold beads of perspiration break out on my forehead.

A voice answers. The voice I've been wanting to hear. A voice I never thought I'd track down.

"It's Laura. You forgot to take your new laptop," I say. "And I still owe you $5000."

The voice hesitates. I can sense his greed. Sense it overriding his caution.

"Can you bring them to me?" he asks, after a long heart beat pause. His voice sounds muffled now, unfamiliar. He's attempting disguise. Too late.

I listen keenly, trying to work out where he is. There are background noises. Female voices, and a dull roar that could be traffic. Is he in a hotel? Or a café perhaps? Is he with the woman whose voice I can hear?

I'm going to find out. No matter what it takes. And it'll have to be now. This chance won't come again. There's much more than wounded pride at stake here. And $5000 would be a cheap way of sorting this out once and for all. I'd have offered $20,000 if I'd had my wits about me. Maybe even more. The sum was irrelevant.

I'll just have to hope and pray that $5000 will be a sufficient lure. On top of the laptop.

A lifetime of expecting the worst of someone stands me in good stead. Yes, I'll bring them. I smile in relief as I name a landmark. "I'll bring the money and the laptop, and meet you on the old bridge by the docks," I suggest. "I can make it in fifteen minutes."

The bridge Timothy should've crossed late yesterday afternoon, on his way home from work. I'm adding my own irony to this sorry situation.

Within minutes I'm revving up the old Ford and heading towards the docks. It's early morning. There's only the odd jogger about and the first of the day's commuters.

When I'm nearly there, I pull over to the side of the road. I tap in his phone number again. Has he kept his word? Will he be there, waiting for me? As I've been waiting?

I hope his waiting hurts as much as mine has.

The voice crackles over the phone. "How much longer will you be? I haven't got all day."

"Nearly there," I soothe. "I had to stop by the bank to withdraw the money."

I can almost feel his smile of satisfaction at the prospect of pocketing this unexpected windfall.

When I arrive at the bridge, he's waiting by the side of the road.

As I approach, he steps out to flag me down. Does he worry I mightn't recognise him?

I stiffen. There's a gun in his hand. It's aimed at me.

My foot pushes savagely against the accelerator and the car lurches awkwardly forward. It gathers speed. The dull thud doesn't register on my brain straightaway.

I glance up into the rear vision mirror. The grey-suited puppet has bounced off the car into the road. It isn't moving.

Quickly I reverse. It takes only a moment. The phone is in his hand.

Timothy's phone. I grab the phone and quickly drive off. Another glance in the rear vision mirror reassures me. There's no one else about yet.

Later I'll make an anonymous call to the police. Let them know there's a body. I'll use the public phone booth in a side street near my office.

And they'll scratch their heads.

Just as they scratched them last night when they found Timothy's body on the bridge.

Minus his phone.

Golden Opportunity

Sue gazed outside at the fallen branches on the lawn, the only sign of the violent storm of an hour ago. "What a weird day it's been," she said. "No internet, no phone and no electricity. This is what it must've been like in the old days, Jacob."

"Yes, the so called good old days, before we all had an armoury of gadgets to protect us from the natural rhythms of life." Her husband put his arms around her waist.

"What's made you so lyrical all of a sudden?" she said.

"It's kind of romantic, isn't it?" he said. "No TV blaring away, no emails to answer, no responsibilities. Just the two of us, and the night."

Then all of a sudden, Jacob became matter of fact. "You realise what this means, don't you?"

Sue, who was snuggling against him, looked puzzled. "We'll have an early night and hope power's restored by morning."

"Aren't you forgetting something?" He indicated the quiet dark street. Nobody in sight.

"I can't see anything."

"Exactly," said Jacob. "And what can you hear?"

Sue shrugged. "Nothing, I suppose." As she spoke, next door's dog started barking loudly, as it'd done several times already this evening. "Well, people's pets seem to be disturbed. They sense things aren't normal."

"And who's come outside to see what the dog's barking about?"

A gleam of understanding lit up Sue's eyes. "Now I know where this is heading. Are you thinking what I think you are?"

"It's a golden opportunity. Just think – nobody's security system is working and nobody's paying any attention to the dogs. Plus no street lights."

As he spoke, next door's Mercedes revved up, and their new neighbour drove off into the night.

"What are we waiting for?" Jacob said, fossicking about with a torch, trying to find his toolkit. "Did you hear Gordon bragging about the gold necklace his wife inherited?"

"She told me about that too," Sue said. "A bit careless of her, I thought at the time."

"Maybe, but with that security system, why would they have to worry about being careless?"

Sue grinned. "Except when there's no power."

"Just think how lovely that necklace will look on you," Jacob said. "We'll wait till we're renting our next house, of course."

Sue sighed. "I've always wanted a real classic piece."

"Get a move on," Jacob said. "They might've just gone to the shops for a bottle of milk or something."

With practised ease, they kept out of sight, slipping through a side gate into their neighbour's back garden.

Jacob produced a deft metal tool, and within seconds they were inside.

"Whereabouts did he say the necklace was kept?" Sue asked.

Jacob pointed up the staircase towards the bedrooms. "Not even in a safe. Rich people aren't always the smartest, are they, love?"

They bounded up the stairs silently in their socks, pausing now and again to listen. But the house was silent and empty. There was nobody home, and the alarm system wasn't functioning. What a golden opportunity. One that Jacob had been waiting for since renting in this exclusive neighbourhood.

Upstairs, in the master bedroom, things weren't so easy. It was a mess - clothes thrown everywhere, opened bottles of cosmetics lying about, magazines. And the dressing table was barely visible under a clutter of jewellery and scarves and photographs. Where would she have left her valuable pieces? The stuff on show was all imitation.

The sound of a car in the street outside caused the two to start in alarm. Disappointed, they slipped back downstairs and out the back window, closing it carefully after them.

Back home, hearts pounding, they sat in the darkness together to catch their breath. Their plan had seemed perfect. How could they have known the necklace wouldn't be where Gordon had said it was?

"Might as well go to bed, love," Jacob said.

"Did you leave the bedroom window open?" Sue said, puzzled.

"Of course not," Jacob said. "We always -"

He stopped, suddenly alert. "What's been going on here?"

Sue followed his gaze. Their bedroom was in a state of chaos. Boxes opened, clothes strewn about. Sue shrieked in alarm. "My pearls? My diamond studs?"

Frantically she opened her jewellery box. It was empty. Every decent piece was gone.

She turned to Jacob, furious. "You idiot," she screamed. "This is all your fault."

"It was a golden opportunity," he protested.

"Yes," she said. "For somebody to rob *us*."

Eat up, Colin

Colin was wearing his irritating smug look. One of the many reasons she'd left him for another man last year. "It's too late to put in an application for the job, Wendy. Last Friday was the deadline," he said.

"But I was on holidays when you advertised my job," she said. "How was I supposed to submit an application when I was in Spain?" She didn't add "with Jim". Colin was only too aware that she'd moved on to someone else.

Obviously, this opportunity to get back at her had been too hard for him to resist. Wendy hated having to work for her ex-husband but whenever she applied for other jobs, he gave her a poor reference. She felt trapped.

Colin took a sip from the bottle of diet cola that lived on his desk. "It's not my fault. If you were good enough for the job, you'd have been smart enough to get an application in. That's all there is to it."

Which was nonsense. Wendy wasn't psychic. The job had been advertised internally, not online. How was she supposed to know?

It wasn't hard to see what he was up to. Colin planned to give the job – *her* job – to his new girlfriend, Vivian.

"I'd appreciate it if you could reconsider your decision," she said, in as polite a voice as she could muster.

Wendy stared out the window. This was the only part of the job she'd miss - the view of the river as it meandered through the city. She loved watching the boats unhurriedly going about their business.

The office was on the tenth floor and this entire wall seemed to be one long picture window. If only the window opened, Wendy thought, she could just push Colin out. She loved accountancy and knew she did a good job for the company's clients. But it was getting hard to stay sane in this toxic environment. Especially now that Colin's girlfriend was working in the same office.

Vivian looked up from her desk in the opposite corner. "I told you he wouldn't let you put in a late application." She bit into a chocolate caramel bar. "You should've brought him back a present from Spain."

Perhaps that's what Vivian would've done.

"I see you've brought in our usual Monday treat," Wendy said. There was a large plastic container on Vivian's desk. "What did you make this time?"

"I thought Colin might enjoy sushi. I have to be careful because he's on the Hollywood diet this month." She smiled smugly. Colin had been trying to improve his image since dating a younger woman, and Vivian liked to let Wendy know he was making an effort for her.

"Shouldn't the sushi be in the fridge?" Wendy said.

"It won't matter. We're having it for lunch and I only made it this morning. The air-conditioning's cold enough to keep it fresh," she said. "Since when are you an expert on cooking anyway?"

Vivian had earned a reputation in the office as resident chef. Despite existing mostly on junk food, each Monday she'd bring in something healthy and delicious she'd cooked.

Wendy turned on her computer and groaned at the mass of unread emails in her inbox. Hadn't anyone done any work here while she'd been in Spain? Vivian had been paid higher duties to cover for her, but didn't seem to have done anything. Wendy started with the most urgent emails, and called some of her regular clients to reassure them. The morning sped by.

The phone on her desk rang. It was her lover. Jim had brought her a bunch of roses and was waiting downstairs in the foyer. Wendy hurried outside, hoping Colin wouldn't notice that she was gone for five minutes. But the moment she came back, the bunch of red roses in her hand, he was standing by her desk.

"Wasting company time again, Wendy?" he said. "Wasn't your holiday long enough?"

She hastily put the roses into a glass vase. There was a packet of white powder with them.

"What's that powder?" Colin laughed. "I thought I knew all your bad habits. Seems I was wrong."

Wendy adjusted the roses. "This powder keeps the roses fresh for longer. The florists all recommend it." Something Colin might've known if he'd ever bothered to buy her flowers.

"Do it in your own time. Not while I'm paying you good money to work," he said roughly.

Wendy slipped the sachet of powder into her skirt pocket.

It'd been good of Jim to think of her today. He was busy himself. Jim was a warden at the city jail.

Colin was still standing beside her. "I think you'd better work through your lunch break today," he said. "You've got a lot of catching up to do."

Just then Vivian came over. "Time for your Monday treat, Colin." She held out a plate of the sushi.

Wendy looked at the rolls of seaweed, with its inner layers of avocado and chicken. She was grateful she'd brought sandwiches today. The thought of the sushi not being refrigerated turned her stomach.

Colin helped himself to a roll. "Delicious," he beamed. "Up to your usual standard."

Vivian put the plate on Wendy's desk and walked over to the kettle to make coffee. "Would you like a hot drink, Colin?" she asked.

"No thanks. Wendy can get my cola." And he smiled at her in an irritating way.

Wendy made her way into Colin's office, returning a few moments later with the diet cola. She felt almost light-hearted. The holiday must've done her some good. It'd certainly helped clear her head. She and Jim had talked long and hard about her work situation. She no longer felt helpless when her ex-husband and his girlfriend bullied her today.

Colin had almost emptied the plate. Wendy excused herself and made some coffee. She brought over a fresh cup for Vivian.

"The sushi is making me very thirsty," Colin said. "You'll have to use less salt next time." He drained the bottle of cola. "Unless you want to kill me."

Wendy smiled as she sipped her coffee.

It didn't escape Colin's notice. "Since Vivian went to the trouble of cooking lunch, I think it's only fair if you clean up, Wendy. Just don't take your time about it." And he went back into his office.

Wendy filled the sink in the staff room with hot water and added a squirt of detergent. She'd make sure the dishes were sparkling clean today.

There was one piece of sushi remaining on the plate. Wendy opened it out to examine how it'd been made. She could see the white grains of salt. She added more, and then carefully wrapped it up again, before putting it into the fridge. Someone might want it later, she thought. She washed the coffee cups, and even washed the cola bottle before putting it into the recycling bin.

Back at her desk she casually said, "I wonder if Colin's still feeling thirsty?"

Vivian looked up. "I'll see if he wants another cola."

A few moments later, Wendy heard a piercing scream. She rushed into Colin's office to find her ex-husband slumped over his desk. Vivian was standing beside him, whimpering.

"What have you done to him?" Wendy asked. And she dialled the emergency services number.

The ambulance officers declared Colin to be dead. They were clearly not satisfied. Within minutes, the police arrived.

"Did he eat anything out of the ordinary?" an officer asked. "It looks like a case of poisoning."

"Vivian made sushi for him," Wendy explained. "But she didn't eat any herself."

The two policemen exchanged glances. "Did she now? That's an odd thing to do. Is any of the sushi left?"

Wendy handed them the plate from the fridge.

Next day the policemen returned to the office. Grains of arsenic had been discovered inside the sushi. Vivian was arrested.

"I haven't done anything," she protested. "Tell them I'm innocent, Wendy."

Wendy shrugged. "I'd like to be able to help you, Vivian. But I've just remembered what Colin said when he ate the sushi."

"You'll have to tell us everything he said," said the taller policeman. "It might be important evidence." And he produced a notebook and pen.

Wendy turned to the policeman. "He said Vivian was trying to kill him."

"But he was only joking," Vivian said.

"He's dead. That's not a joke," the policeman said. "And we have evidence that someone poisoned him." He clamped a pair of handcuffs on Vivian's wrists and led her away.

When they left, Wendy looked around the empty office. How peaceful it seemed. She had plenty of work to do, but first she'd need to place advertisements for new staff. She'd need someone to replace Vivian, and a good accountant to take on her old job. As senior accountant, she'd be working in Colin's office from now on, of course.

She put her hand into her skirt pocket. Her fingers found the empty sachet. She'd have to throw it away. One of those bins on the pavement a few blocks away would do. No one would think to look there. Just as no one had thought to look in the empty cola bottle. But she'd cleaned it with hot soapy water anyway, just in case.

Some months later, Wendy found herself with some spare time. The new accountant was efficient and had quickly got on top of the job.

Wendy decided to visit Jim at the jail. It was a Monday. She found him at his desk eating a spinach and ricotta lasagne. There was a side salad of baby spinach leaves, cubes of roasted pumpkin, cherry tomatoes and toasted pine nuts, with pomegranate dressing. "That looks appetising," she said. "You never used to eat this well."

Jim grinned. "And it's all thanks to you. We've put Vivian on kitchen duties, just as you suggested."

An Open and Shut Case

Detective Veronica Alton looked around the bungalow. No signs of forced entry. Nothing disturbed. Had the victim known her assailant? It seemed so.

"It should've been an open and shut case," she said.

The victim was Dorothy Chambers, an elderly woman who lived with her nephew, Nicholas Jones. A neighbour, Thomas Johnson, had reported several disturbances lately. Loud arguments that had caused the dog to bark.

Detective Kurt Adams nodded. "We'll never crack Jones's alibi."

Dorothy had been stabbed with a knife from her own kitchen in the early hours of the morning. Scene of crime officers had found nothing to indicate the presence of a third party. But they'd taken copies of fingerprints found on two wine glasses.

Nicholas Jones faced them now. "I couldn't sleep so I'd taken the dog for a long walk," he repeated. His story hadn't varied.

"Where did you walk?" Detective Kurt asked.

"It was dark and I had a lot on my mind. I didn't take any notice where I was going."

"And you didn't return for nearly two hours?" Detective Veronica looked at him in disbelief.

Nicholas was overweight and breathed heavily. She wasn't convinced but how could she prove otherwise? An officer at headquarters had tracked Nicholas's phone. It confirmed his story that he'd gone out for two hours.

"I believe you're inheriting this house?" she said. "Plus a large share portfolio."

He met her gaze. "I wasn't here so you need to start looking for the real killer. You don't need to look further than next door."

"Why is that?"

"Thomas Johnson was infatuated with my aunt for years," he said. "Last weekend she told him she'd never marry him. He's been upset ever since, coming over every day."

The two detectives exchanged glances. This put a different perspective on the situation. As they went outside, a black Labrador appeared. The blue checked jacket on his back gave him a friendly appearance but the loud barking belied this.

Next door they faced Thomas Johnson. He was yawning as he opened the door. Inside the house was untidy. Several empty wine bottles lay on the floor.

"Where were you at one o'clock this morning?" Detective Veronica asked.

"I was asleep in bed," he said. "Why do you want to know?"

"Can anyone verify that?"

The suspect shook his head. "What's going on?"

"Your neighbour was murdered," she said. "We have to establish everyone's whereabouts."

"Which neighbour?"

At the news, he slumped into an armchair, head in his hands. When he looked up again, there were tears in his eyes. "It's that nephew you should be talking to," he said. "He ordered a Ferrari last week. How can he afford that on his clerk's salary?"

"Did you hear any suspicious sounds coming from next door?" Detective Veronica asked.

"Nothing. Everything was quiet. Otherwise it would've woken me up. I'm a light sleeper."

Outside again, the detectives conferred.

"The nephew has motive, means and opportunity, but his alibi is watertight," began Detective Kurt.

"The neighbour might've got in if Nicholas had left the door unlocked," Detective Veronica said. "Thwarted love is a strong motive. If Nicholas and the dog were out, he had opportunity."

It was hard to talk above the dog's barking.

Detective Kurt bent down to pat the dog. The padded jacket was almost a miniature of one he owned, complete with pockets and zip.

"We thought it was an open and shut case," he said. "Maybe it is?"

Nicholas appeared in the doorway, and called to the Labrador.

Detective Kurt faced him. "You're under arrest for the murder of your aunt."

Veronica looked enquiringly at Kurt.

"We found it hard to believe this man could walk for two hours, and I bet we were right," he said. "But the dog? No problem."

"What about his phone? Headquarters checked it out."

Kurt bent down and put his own phone in the pocket on the dog's jacket. "Simple," he said. "Nicholas put his phone in this pocket and let the dog out the gate to wander the neighbourhood, giving himself a watertight alibi." He put the handcuffs on their suspect while he was talking. "Had the dog been home, it would've barked and woken Thomas, who's a light sleeper."

"Well done," Veronica said. Then she turned to Nicholas. "Since you enjoy walking so much, you can walk back to the station with Detective Adams. It's only three kilometres. The road's hilly but that's nothing for a seasoned walker, is it?"

Death Comes Silently

Detective Liz Ferguson stepped through the rubble of overturned furniture and books, making her way to the oak desk, where Professor Julian Stone sat slumped, a revolver in his right hand.

"He's finally found out what happens after death," she commented wryly. "I read his latest book, *Beyond the Grave*. It seemed to ask more questions than it answered."

Sergeant Hansen wasn't sure whether to smile. He carefully withdrew the gun and inspected it. "Why would he use a silencer when he lives here by himself?" he observed, putting it into an evidence bag and handing it to a scene of crime officer. "The nearest neighbours are miles away."

"He certainly wasn't by himself last night, by the look of this room," said Ferguson. "What were they looking for, I wonder?"

Hansen shrugged. "His next manuscript perhaps?"

"That book was a best seller. He must've been wealthy," she said. "Let's see what his housekeeper Emma Jones has to say. Isn't she the one who found the body?"

"Surely you don't suspect murder? He's obviously shot himself."

"I'm keeping an open mind, and suggest you do the same," Ferguson said, as the body was removed on a stretcher. "Just because he was interested in death doesn't mean he'd want to take his own life. Someone might've arranged this to look like suicide."

She stopped speaking as the housekeeper was led into the room.

Emma regarded the detectives with watery eyes. "Why would he do this? It doesn't make sense," she sobbed. "He was on the point of exposing a well-known medium."

Ferguson leant forward. "Go on."

"He was watching one of those programs on TV yesterday afternoon, where psychics compete against one another. He pointed to one and said he was a fraud. That he could prove it."

"Do you remember who?"

"I certainly do. It was his nephew, Kris Mathieson," she said. "He phoned him after the show. They had a furious argument."

"Did you happen to overhear anything?" Hansen asked.

"Something about changing his will," she said. "The Professor told him he was going to leave everything to me, since his only living relative was a fraud."

Ferguson looked around at the wood-panelled room, and the breathtaking ocean views through the library window. Someone was going to inherit a fortune. It certainly gave both Mathieson and Jones a solid motive.

"Did he say how he could prove Mathieson was a fraud?" she asked. "Did he have any evidence?"

"There was something on the show yesterday. He got

excited and tried to explain it to me," she shrugged. "It was all above my head."

Ferguson could barely contain her excitement. "Try to remember anything he said. Whether you understand it or not."

"It was the jewellery. Each psychic had to hold a gold bracelet and describe the owner." Emma paused. "The professor kept saying the bracelet was Maggie's and he could prove it. But who is Maggie? And what would it prove?"

The name Maggie rang a bell. Ferguson remembered a reference to her in *Beyond the Grave*.

There was a copy lying on the professor's desk. She picked it up and immediately noticed bookmarks.

Fingers trembling with anticipation, she flicked through the pages. On page 298 she found what she was looking for. It was a full-page photo of a young woman, Maggie Sanderson. A twisted rose gold bracelet adorned her wrist. This must be the one the physic had been asked to talk about.

Some handwriting caught her eye. In the margin the professor had jotted down a phone number.

Ferguson dialled the number, while Hansen looked on, a puzzled expression on his face.

No response. When it went to voicemail, she left a message.

"Have you heard of Scott Barnes?" she asked Hansen.

He shook his head.

But Emma gasped. "Scott Barnes is the compere of that psychic show the professor was watching."

Finally, a connection. If Professor Stone had shown this photo to Barnes, his nephew could be proven to be a fraud.

So what possible motive would he have to commit suicide?

She waited with interest for the arrival of the psychic. How could he explain this?

It was half an hour later when Kris Mathieson was escorted into the library. He was a tall angular man. "What on earth's happened in here?" he said, looking around at the upheaval, his face distraught. "And why did Uncle Anders shoot himself?"

"Perhaps you'd like to tell us why you were arguing with the deceased yesterday?" Ferguson had no intention of revealing what she already knew.

"A difference of opinion," he said. "One professional to another. He disapproved of my methods, but I managed to persuade him that I'm legit."

"How did you do that?" she asked. "I understand he'd watched you on TV during the afternoon."

Mathieson blinked at the reference to TV. His eye fell on the copy of his uncle's book sitting on the desk.

Finally he said, "I offered to come over and explain. He said it wouldn't be necessary."

"And where were you between seven and nine o'clock last night?" Her tone had hardened.

"I was watching the news on TV, and catching up with emails," he said.

Hansen noted this down. "Can anyone verify that?"

"No. How was I to know I'd need an alibi?" He turned to the housekeeper. "Where were you? Sucking up to him again, trying to get him to change his will?"

"Where is the will?" Ferguson said, looking from one to the other.

"It's supposed to be in the top drawer of the desk." The woman wiped her eyes, and glared accusingly at Mathieson. "Why don't you use your psychic powers to find it? Isn't finding things one of your tricks on TV?"

Mathieson frowned. "Don't belittle my profession," he said. "Have you told them you're living here now? Housekeeper? I don't think you've been limiting yourself to cooking and cleaning."

Ferguson turned to Elizabeth. "You didn't mention that you lived here?"

She folded her hands and then unfolded them. "Nobody asked me."

"Has it occurred to either of you that he didn't actually change his will last night?" Ferguson said. "He would've needed to organise it with his lawyer, line up witnesses and so on."

"Well, why would he say he had?" Mathieson said.

"Think about it," Ferguson said. "He set a trap and you walked right into it. All he had to do was mention the will."

She turned to the housekeeper. "And you fell for it too, didn't you?"

"We're not getting anywhere with the will," Hansen commented. "We might need to try a new line of enquiry."

"On the contrary, our murderer has already given themselves away." Ferguson looked from one suspect to the other. "Are you going to own up?"

Neither spoke.

She turned to the housekeeper. "You came in here early this morning looking for his will. That's when you found him, isn't it? But you didn't see him straight away. You were too busy ransacking his things."

Elizabeth Jones sobbed. "He was dead. I thought he'd killed himself," she said. "He told me last night he'd changed his will." She looked accusingly at Mathieson. "I wanted to find it before he had a chance to destroy it."

"That doesn't implicate me," Mathieson said. "You could easily have killed him last night and then pretended to discover his body this morning."

"On the contrary. You implicated yourself the moment you walked into the library. You couldn't conceal your surprise at seeing the mess. It was tidy when you left, wasn't it?" Ferguson said. "Did you know he bookmarked the photo of Maggie Sanderson? And he wrote down the contact details for the TV producer too." She paused. "He deliberately left the evidence that you're a fraud somewhere he knew it'd be found. I think he realised you might try to kill him."

The colour drained from Mathieson's face. He didn't respond.

"And you're the only one who'd need to use a silencer," she continued. "You didn't want Elizabeth Jones to hear the shot and discover you here."

As she applied the handcuffs, she added, "You didn't see this coming, did you? Then again, you wouldn't. You're a fraud and your uncle's been able to prove it, even from beyond the grave."

Jumping to Conclusions

Lucy Richardson lay on the rocks, enjoying the last warmth of the sun. Her day off was drawing to a close. Tomorrow she'd be back in uniform, at the local police station.

A wet nose on her hand, and a soft whine told her Jess, her golden retriever, was ready to go home.

Lucy looked around. Cold foam lashed her legs. The rocky promontory where she'd been lying with her book was being buffeted by an icy breeze that'd sprung from nowhere. The tide was rushing in. Time to head to safety. Fishermen had disappeared from these rocks.

Jess growled, tugging at her. Lucy gathered her book and car keys, and scrambled to her feet. It was impossible to go back the way she'd come. That part of the beach was underwater.

Blow it, I'll have to climb up the cliff pathway, she thought.

Jess shot ahead, growling. What was the matter with her this afternoon?

Then Lucy's ears picked up two voices raised in anger.

She made her way carefully over the slippery rock to the

base of the cliff. She couldn't hear the voices now. Jess was in a state. Hair raised along her back, on full alert. In her mouth was an old towelling cap.

Lucy laughed. "Is this what all the growling is about? You must've got very bored to find this exciting."

Then she stopped laughing. There was blood on the cap.

As she looked up the face of the cliff, two figures came into view. A man and a woman, standing at the very top. At first Lucy thought they were embracing. Then an icy fist grabbed her heart. They were struggling against each other, screaming. She started to climb up the narrow path that led to the top of the cliff.

"Be careful!" Lucy yelled. But the wind carried her voice away and no one heard.

She tested her feet on sturdy-looking clumps of grass, continuing the harrowing climb upwards. If only there were more substantial things to hold onto. Further up she noticed some young saplings jutting out from the cliff face at an impossible angle. She'd feel safer there.

She'd grasped the saplings a few moments later and paused to catch her breath. Jess was whining.

Lucy looked up. As if in slow motion the man tumbled over the side of the cliff, and bounced sickeningly off a rock. As she watched in horror, he fell towards her. She stretched out and grabbed as he reached the saplings.

The heavy weight slumped beside her, held fast by a sturdy branch.

Lucy's heart pounded. With trembling fingers she felt for a pulse.

He groaned heavily. Blood oozed from an ugly cut on his head, and his skin was a deathly blue-white. He needed immediate medical attention.

Lucy delved into her jeans pocket and started tapping numbers into her phone. *Blast, I'm out of range.*

He stirred and opened his eyes.

"I'll get help," Lucy said. "You need to be in hospital."

She flinched as he grasped her hand. He was cold and clammy. She must hurry.

"Wait," he whispered.

"There's no time," said Lucy. "What's your name?"

"Peter Strahan," came the faint reply. Lucy leant closer to hear his next words. "Tell them Charlotte pushed me."

She gasped. "Was Charlotte the woman at the top of the cliff?"

He slowly nodded.

"And she pushed you deliberately?"

"Yes," he said. "She's killed me."

Tears filled Lucy's eyes as she held the cold hand. Then he slowly opened his hand. He was holding a gold wedding ring.

"Charlotte's ring," he said. "I grabbed her hand as she pushed me."

His voice had become weak and his face was grey.

"Make sure she pays for this." And he slumped into unconsciousness.

Lucy's muscles had turned to jelly. How she made it to the top of the cliff she never knew. But at last she stood shakily at the top.

She tried her phone again.

"Dolphin Rocks Police Station," came the voice of her partner, Sergeant Greg Walker. "Greg, I need help," she gasped. "Cliff path. Man injured."

"Get a hold of yourself, Lucy. Start again and give me all the details."

When she got to the name, Greg's voice changed. "Peter Strahan? That can't be right."

Lucy looked inside the towelling cap. "That's definitely his name."

"Can't be," said Greg slowly. "He fell off the cliff last year and died."

Lucy's legs gave way and she slumped to a sitting position, rocking on her heels. Which was how Greg found her when he arrived five minutes later in the squad car.

"Where is he?" Greg asked.

Together they walked to the edge of the cliff and peered down. There was nobody there. Just the saplings jutting out halfway down.

"He must've fallen again," whispered Lucy.

Greg put his arm around her. She was shaking and could barely talk.

"Whatever happened here, it wasn't Peter Strahan you saw," Greg said. "And there's nobody here now."

"He said Charlotte pushed him."

"Charlotte Strahan? She was in bed with his best friend at the time. Rock solid alibi."

Lucy opened her hand. There was the ring. She looked inside and saw initials engraved there P.S. – B.M. 1995. "Would this convince you to re-open the case? What's her wedding ring doing here?"

Greg examined the ring. There were traces of blood and skin on it. He carefully put the ring into a clear plastic bag.

"Handled this case myself," he said. "Chap fell over the cliff." He kept shaking his head. "A year ago today."

A Deadly Dull New Year's Eve

Mark looked dispirited. "It's New Year's Eve, we should be out partying," he said. "No one warned me that this place would be so damn boring."

"Sshhh, lower your voice," said April. "We don't need any more trouble from Herself. Not after what happened last time."

The one they all feared had made it very clear there'd be no more wild parties here. Not since they'd all disgraced themselves at Halloween. There'd been photos of them in the national newspapers, and several magazines had run features about it, referring to their behaviour as "a new phenomenon". Ridiculous. All they'd done was let their hair down like everyone else. Why all the fuss?

"I can't believe we've been grounded at our age," said Jonathan. "You'd think at sixty-four the rules could be relaxed."

April nodded. From the day she first arrived here, she'd fancied Jonathan. If only she could spend more time with him. And move closer. She'd had to be on her best behaviour since ill health had led to Mark joining her here. Her husband was always complaining. Whereas Jonathan was far more laid back. It'd been so much easier to talk to Jonathan when Mark was only visiting her on Sunday afternoons.

The thought irritated her. "Move over, Mark, you're squashing me," she said.

"How can I move? They've put me here, and you know as well as I do that I can't change that."

April sighed. It was true. She'd never imagined that a person could feel so utterly disempowered. You couldn't even decide who you'd be next to. Naturally everyone assumed a wife would want to be with her husband. But that wasn't always the case, was it?

As for having fun, that was against the rules.

It'd been dreadfully boring since Halloween. All those lectures about proper behaviour. Setting a good example to the younger ones. Not drawing unfavourable attention to this place. They'd certainly had bad press in recent months but that wasn't April's fault, was it?

"I like your idea of a New Year's Eve party," said Jonathan. "Would we organise a secret party here? Or would it be more fun to gatecrash someone else's?"

April's eyes lit up. She'd always loved New Year's Eve parties. The prospect of kissing a handsome stranger at midnight still caused her a shiver of excitement. And who knows? That man could even be Jonathan if she played her cards right…

"Let's gatecrash a party," she whispered excitedly. "A really big fancy dress party where we wouldn't be noticed among the crowd. Maybe Sydney Harbour, so we could see the fireworks?"

"Yes, it was a mistake to try to organise something here

at Halloween," said Mark. "But I'd only just arrived and was still learning the ropes. And it'd seemed like a good place to congregate."

"Wasn't it fun?" giggled April.

"You certainly attracted a lot of attention in that long white dress," said Jonathan. "I wasn't expecting you to be in a wedding gown."

She hadn't actually mentioned to him back then that she had a husband.

"It was all I had," said April. She'd been very impressed by the tailored black velvet jacket and grey flannels Jonathan had worn. A bit old-fashioned but still quite sexy, in a Cary Grant kind of way.

And the freedom they'd felt that night had been breathtaking. If only that group of Goths hadn't arrived to spoil their fun. All hell had broken loose when they'd gatecrashed the party, trying to join in the revelry. There'd been photographers and journalists. Even the police.

The sudden sound of a disembodied voice caused them all to stop talking. What was going on?

"Is someone else joining us?" whispered April, as quietly as she could. "I think I recognise that voice."

Mark nudged her. "Isn't that your cousin Sarah? What's she doing here? Surely she's too young to be put in a place like this."

A pale figure appeared. "April? Mark?" she said tentatively. "Anyone got any plans for New Year's?"

One by one, the ghosts drifted across the graveyard to her side. A newcomer – better still, someone they knew. Always cause for celebration. Especially on New Year's Eve, when the rest of the world was partying, and they'd been feeling left out.

A Terrible Eavesdropper

When Linda saw her daughter's face, she knew something had to be done. And quickly. Kim had tried to conceal the bruise with makeup but it only made it more obvious to her mother. Especially as Kim didn't normally wear makeup.

"What's he done this time?" she said tightly.

"He overheard me phoning Molly," Kim began. "We talked about him."

"So he's an eavesdropper now?"

Kim shrugged. "He's always listened in. I'm usually more careful. I didn't realise he'd come home."

Linda could imagine the scene. Ronan creeping silently into the house, hearing her voice, positioning himself to listen. She shuddered. What kind of low life did that? And how on earth could she protect her daughter, when Kim didn't seem to have the strength left to defend herself or walk out?

So he was an eavesdropper? Well, maybe that was the chink in his armour?

She poured tea, a plan forming. Looking at her daughter's

lost expression, she realised she'd have to manage on her own.

After the visit Linda went online. It wasn't difficult to track down what she needed.

A week later she was ready to put her idea into action.

Heart pounding, she dialled her daughter's number. Knowing Ronan would be home watching football.

"I've decided to keep your grandmother's jewellery at home," she began. The valuables had always been held in a bank deposit box.

"Are you sure they'd be safe?" Kim asked.

In the background Linda could hear Ronan saying, "Would *what* be safe?"

"I brought it all home today," she said. Hating having to lie to Kim. But what were her options? Allow Ronan to continue the way he was?

"Maybe just keep a few rings there?" Kim suggested. "Take the diamond necklace and gold chains back to the bank tomorrow."

This time she didn't hear Ronan. He must be too busy listening.

"They'll be safe," she said. "I'm storing them in an old biscuit tin in the pantry."

"A biscuit tin in the pantry?" Kim echoed. "That doesn't sound safe."

"Thieves wouldn't think to look there."

At ten o'clock she turned off the lights and went upstairs. She knew she wouldn't sleep. Sitting up, her back propped against two pillows, she quietly waited.

She must've dozed because suddenly she was alert. She opened her eyes, ears straining. And then she heard the sound of a downstairs window being slowly opened. Movements. She held her breath, wishing she'd locked her bedroom door. Was it too late? Was she safe?

Her breath came in shallow gasps. She dared not move. And then in the still of the night came a terrible scream. Linda didn't move a muscle. Not until she heard a crashing sound later.

Then she phoned the police, describing what she'd heard. The patrol car arrived ten minutes later. It was only when she heard a knock on her front door that she ventured downstairs.

"The scream came from my kitchen," she said.

"Sounds like a burglar." The officer was about Kim's age, with kind eyes. If only her daughter had found a nice man like him.

"You stay here while we check it out," said his partner. Linda hadn't expected a female officer.

Linda watched them walk through to the kitchen. She could hear their voices but not make out what they were saying. *Now I'm the eavesdropper*, she thought wryly.

The female officer returned. "You've had an intruder," she began.

Linda shuddered. A genuine shudder, not a feigned one. The idea of Ronan creeping around in her kitchen in the middle of the night was indeed frightening.

Then the policewoman phoned for an ambulance.

"Is he injured?" Linda's voice was barely audible.

"I'm afraid he's dead."

Linda's shoulders sagged. The burden was lifted. Her daughter could be free.

"Dead?" she said, her knees buckling.

The officer with the gentle eyes dashed forward to grab her as she slipped down to the floor.

The sky was beginning to lighten by the time everything was over. Linda watched the police cars drive away. She finally had the house to herself again.

Slipping into the pantry, she picked up the old biscuit tin from the floor. It was empty now. There was only one thing left to do. She phoned a pest control company. The whole house would need to be fumigated. She wasn't taking any chances.

To her relief they could do the job right away.

Next she booked to stay a few days in a posh hotel in the city.

When she came home on Friday, it'd be safe to give everything a good clean.

She wondered if she'd find the funnel-web spider's body.

.

Which Ones Are Real?

Penelope Everett-Barnes adjusted the sparkling diamond clasp on her peacock blue evening gown. She'd had her dressmaker design it especially for tonight's gala ball, and Rupert had given her a ridiculously large diamond. Did a woman ever have a more understanding husband?

Everyone who was anyone would be there, and tomorrow's newspapers would carry coloured photos of the better-known guests. Penelope wanted to stun the photographers and steal the limelight. As she usually did. What better way than to wear this bright skimpy gown, and use a real diamond on the strap around her right shoulder?

"Will you be wearing your diamond and sapphire pendant tonight?" Rupert had quietly entered her dressing room, her black leather jewellery box in his hands. "Or would that be overkill?"

"A girl can't wear too many diamonds," she purred.

As he carefully placed the pendant around her neck, she admired yet again their reflection in the mirror. Her dark good looks and his more mature handsome profile. They suited each other to perfection.

A jaguar and a silver fox. That was the caption from last month's ball. She'd worn a black satin sheath dress, Rupert had been in a white evening suit.

What caption will adorn tomorrow's photo, she thought?

Rupert glanced at the newspaper strewn on the bed. A headline caught his eye.

"Listen to this," he said, reading the article to her. "Police fear an organised gang of jewellery thieves will be at tonight's gala ball, masquerading as guests."

Penelope bit her lip. "What should we do, darling? Do you think we'll be safe?"

Rupert held her face gently in his hands and looked into her eyes. "You and your diamonds are always safe when I'm around."

"But what about…?"

He touched her lips gently with his index finger. "You'll get wrinkles if you frown. Trust me, there won't be any problems."

She sank gratefully into his arms, and nestled against his strong warm chest. He was her rock, her castle. And she needed him. Magazine editors had called him other things like sugar daddy and worse. But she knew his heart was hers. They made a good team.

Without another worry, she gathered her mink jacket and gold clutch purse, and set out for the ball, determined to enjoy herself.

They arrived at the same time as a patrol car of police officers in full regalia. A visible presence, meant to deter thieves, no doubt.

For a moment Penelope felt upstaged, but then as light bulbs flashed around her, she realised their uniforms would look sensational as background for her dress. And it'd guarantee front page coverage, which she always craved.

She was a bit annoyed when Rupert led her quickly inside, but after several glasses of champagne she'd forgiven him.

Even though he'd left her to her own devices for a while, as he often did at these functions. He'd seen an old friend the other side of the room, and gone over to chat.

"You're in safe company," he'd said, indicating the group of officers.

Several of the police officers were good looking. She enjoyed flirting with them.

"Will you protect me and my diamonds from these terrible thieves?" she simpered, to one particularly handsome officer.

He gallantly held her hand and kissed it. "With my life, princess."

The band played for the first waltz. "Will you dance with me?" she asked.

He hesitated. "Policemen aren't supposed to dance when they're on duty," he said. "But I guess it'd help me protect you if we stayed close together, wouldn't it?"

She led him onto the dance floor. As he swept her around the room in his arms, she began to feel seriously tempted. What had begun as a bit of fun was now something more dangerous.

There were times when she missed the thrill of being with a man her own age…

As he held her close, and led her across the ballroom floor, she felt as though she was dancing on air. Maybe it was the last glass of champagne, or maybe it was the lights glinting off the chandeliers, but she suddenly felt faint, and staggered against him.

"Where's Rupert?" she whispered. "I don't feel well."

"Let me look after you," the officer said, leading her outside onto a private balcony. "Some fresh air will make you feel better. It's crowded in there."

She looked into his eyes, which were a dark brown, and saw admiration and concern. What harm could there be?

There was a velvet chaise lounge in one corner. The perfect place to rest and gather herself. The officer's arm around her shoulders felt warm and protective. And it was a relief to be in this dimly lit alcove, overlooking the garden. It'd felt too bright and noisy inside. Champagne didn't normally affect her like this but she'd felt strange just now.

"Perhaps you could bring me a cup of coffee?" She smiled into his lovely eyes.

"Your wish is my command," he said, and withdrew.

Minutes passed.

It's taking him a long time, she thought. Without his arm around her, and his warm hand on her shoulder, she was beginning to feel cold.

She was just wondering whether to go inside and find him, when Rupert appeared. He looked anxious.

"Where on earth have you been?" he asked. "I've been looking everywhere for you."

His face was pale and he was breathless. It made him look older, she realised with a pang. And wondered again why it was taking the young officer such a long time to bring her coffee.

She became aware of a commotion inside the ballroom.

"What's going on?" she asked. "I came outside because I was feeling faint."

"So you haven't heard what's happened?" he said.

"Go on," she said.

"The thieves have struck. Several women have been robbed of their jewellery. Mostly diamonds. One woman even had a diamond ring taken from her finger without realising it."

"That's ridiculous," Penelope said. "I don't see how it's possible."

Rupert drew her into his arms.

"Not all thieves look like criminals," he said. "Will you ever forgive me? I left you with them."

Penelope's heart quickened and her hand flew to her neck. The diamond and sapphire pendant was missing.

She remembered the handsome officer and how nice it'd felt to have his warm hand on her shoulders.

As she stood up, her dress slipped and she had to clutch it to prevent it falling down. The diamond clasp that held the strap was also gone.

Her diamonds and her hopes both taken cruelly away from her.

Next morning her photo was on the front page of the national newspapers.

Tears came to her eyes as she sat up in bed, reading the article. The photo was taken as she arrived, surrounded by the officers.

Except they weren't really officers. They were the notorious gang of jewellery thieves and had stolen a police car. By the time the real police were rescued, the robbers had completed their job and escaped.

She looked guiltily at Rupert. "Will you ever forgive me?" she said.

"Everyone deserves a second chance," he said gallantly.

"But what about the diamonds? You went to so much trouble to get them for me."

He smiled, as he handed her a brown paper bag. "Even diamonds deserve a second chance," he said. "I couldn't risk the real ones last night so I had paste ones made up. That's what he stole."

She held up the diamond and sapphire pendant, and the large diamond clasp. And found it hard to tell the difference. The ones she'd worn to the ball had looked so real.

"Why didn't you tell me?" she said.

"You wouldn't have enjoyed yourself if you'd known you were wearing fake jewellery," he said. "I wanted you to sparkle and look dazzling."

"I sound shallow, when you put it like that."

"Never mind," he said. "It's all worked out for the best. The real police were so busy taking your statement they forgot to search everyone."

"Surely you don't mean…" Her eyes lit up.

"Hold out your hand, my love," he said. And carefully slid a diamond ring onto her finger.

"You wicked man!" she said gleefully. "I didn't think you'd be game to steal anything when there was a well-known gang of jewel thieves around."

"It was the perfect opportunity for me," he said. "Who would ever suspect the husband of one of the victims?"

Going to the Show

As the clock struck midnight Christine felt a surge of energy tingle through her legs. They twitched.

The full moon lit up her bedroom, the crutches and wheelchair silhouetted against the wall.

It's the painkillers I took last night, Christine thought, and rolled over. When she'd googled them yesterday, there'd been several accounts of these drugs causing strange hallucinations for some people. What she was experiencing must be some kind of dream state like the ones she'd read about.

But whatever it was, her legs wouldn't stop. It felt glorious.
I feel strong enough to go out, she realised.

Beside her, Joe lay sprawled out, snoring. She wouldn't disturb him. And anyway, this was her special time, best enjoyed alone. Something she'd hoped for and not believed possible. There'd been no movement in her legs since the car accident fifteen years ago. Just a heavy leaden sensation that kept her mostly housebound in the ground floor apartment where they lived.

The street outside was strangely empty, lit only by the

moon as Christine slowly ventured out, one step at a time. How her heart danced with enormous delight and relief at this unexpected freedom. Standing in her white long nightie, barefoot, without any thought of danger, she breathed in the cool night air and looked up at the glorious stars. She was in heaven, and planned to make the most of it.

Without any conscious thought, she walked to the showground. Assuming the surge of energy would be permanent, not just a momentary gift.

The show was being held at the county showground on the edge of town, over a mile from their apartment. It'd featured on the evening news, with close up footage of the sheep and calves and the show dogs. Watching with Joe, she'd felt sad at missing out, as the annual show had always been a highlight before the accident. As it was for many people, going by the scenes of bustling crowds and the hordes of school children.

But Joe hadn't been able to face the uphill task of taking her there this year. He'd grown a bit jaded from the burden of his responsibilities.

Entering the showground, she glided through the stalls until she found the sheep lying in thick fresh straw. Beside one sheep lay a newborn lamb, its clear eyes and soft fluffy wool melting Christine's heart as she sat down on the straw beside it. Time seemed to stand still as she absorbed the peaceful surroundings. There were several other lambs lying on straw. None of them seemed in the least disturbed by her presence. The stall was dimly lit by the moon. Nobody was about.

What a contrast to the scenes on the TV news where the

sheep had appeared to her to be stressed. Now they were enjoying the absence of crowds as much as Christine.

Feeling a heady mix of elation and freedom, she floated on air all the way home. Free of her usual restrictions and pain. If only tonight could last forever.

As she approached the apartment building, she noticed Joe standing outside on the pavement in his dressing gown. His hair was sticking out and the way he frantically looked up and down the street caused her to feel ashamed and guilty. He must be worried sick about her, assuming she'd been abducted or worse.

The sudden shrill of a siren pierced the stillness. Had he phoned the police?

No. An ambulance sped around the corner, lights flashing, pulling up beside Joe. Two paramedics emerged and hurried inside.

Quietly Christine followed them into the building, to their apartment.

As she entered her bedroom, where they were gathered, she noticed the wheelchair and crutches against the wall. All looked normal.

Except for the peaceful woman wearing a white nightie, who lay on the bed. At first Christine thought she was asleep. But then she noticed she wasn't breathing.

One of the paramedics bent to gently remove a piece of straw from the woman's hand.

Who Is My Visitor?

The young doctor took my hand in his. "You've been hallucinating, Phyllis," he said. "Not surprising after the anaesthetic you had for the operation."

His words nearly convinced me.

Then I noticed an older nurse listening in to our conversation. The look that crossed her face convinced me otherwise.

The woman with the large wicker basket was no figment of my imagination.

She'd sat by my bedside for the past forty-eight hours. Held my hand while I was in that muddled painful no-man's land. Would I have made it without her? That's one of those things I'll never really know for sure.

Had the older nurse seen her there with me? It wasn't exactly something she could mention in passing to the doctor, when he did his morning rounds. Especially now that he'd dismissed it as hallucination.

There was an opportunity to speak with her when the morning tea trolley arrived. With a broken collarbone, as well as my broken elbow and hip, I certainly qualified for the assistance of a nurse. My bones were held in position by pins at the moment. There was virtually nothing I could do for myself. And with my only son and his family holidaying overseas, I was reliant on the nurses for everything.

"Tell me about your visitor, Phyllis," the older nurse began. She spoke very quietly so she wouldn't be overheard. And she didn't look directly at me, just quietly poured milk into my tea and stirred in sugar. It was as though she was pretending, even to herself, that this conversation wasn't taking place.

Part of me wanted to believe the doctor. Close my eyes and pretend nothing had happened. Cling on to my rational self. But my curiosity was too great. I wanted to know who this woman was and why she'd spent those forty-eight hours holding my hand and offering comfort. I'd read about the spirits of retired nurses, walking the corridors of hospitals, still wearing their old uniforms. Sometimes centuries later.

But the woman with the large wicker basket didn't look like a nurse, and she'd been wearing a long blue floral skirt with a mismatched pink cardigan and a pretty embroidered white cotton shirt. There'd been a distinctive brooch on her cardigan, two bluebirds linked by a bar of gold bearing the name Nancy, written in fine script. Her shoes were what we used to call clodhoppers when I was a child. Stout sensible black shoes that laced up and had thick soles and heels. My grandmother used to wear a similar pair. But her name wasn't Nancy and she didn't in any way resemble this woman.

And how on earth had I seen her so clearly when I'd been unconscious the whole while? I'd even noticed a faint scent of lavender and the freshness that clothes have after drying in the sunshine instead of a clothes dryer. Evidently part of me had been in better shape than these broken bones. But which part, exactly?

And what would I say to the nurse?

She was quietly helping me sip the milky tea. I could feel her expectation.

"The first thing I noticed about her was the large wicker basket she was carrying," I began. "I got the impression that she didn't go anywhere without it."

The nurse nodded, her blue eyes lighting up at this detail.

"Was she on her own?" she asked.

"Yes, she sat on my bed and held my hand, talking to me," I said. A sudden memory returned. She too had blue eyes, and I'd noticed that she'd powdered her face lightly and applied a muted red lipstick. The cosmetics had a gentle scent which reminded me of visiting my grandmother and being allowed to apply her makeup as a child. When I looked at the nurse's makeup it occurred to me how much styles had changed over the years. The rosy pink cheeks of my visitor were quite unsophisticated by comparison with the subtle shading created by modern foundations and blushers.

"Did she bring you anything?" the nurse asked.

I could feel the tension in her body as she said this, and wondered why she set so much store by my answer.

I closed my eyes for a moment. Her words had awakened another memory. My visitor had peeled a mandarin and slowly fed me the segments. My mouth had felt parched. I'd had difficulty swallowing. But somehow the moist fleshy fruit had soothed my tongue and the subtle sweetness had whetted my appetite for more. I'd absorbed the nourishment like a dry pot plant gratefully soaking up water.

I sipped the tea, remembering. "Try to eat this, Phyllis," the woman had said. It occurred to me now that she'd known my name. At the time it'd felt quite natural but now it made me feel strange. I already felt very disempowered, being unable to take even basic care of myself. To add to this brought further discomfort.

There were many more questions in the nurse's eyes but as I finished my tea, a male nurse wheeled in a blue plastic contraption and announced that he was here to give me a wash.

I gazed imploringly at the old nurse. "I've never been bathed by a man before."

She shrugged sympathetically, a helpless look in her eyes. I could sense that there were ways in which she too felt disempowered. What could she do? It was out of her jurisdiction. But I couldn't help noticing that she'd crossed her fingers. This puzzled me a bit, seeming almost childlike.

The male nurse drew the curtains around my bed.

"This is one of your fantasies, isn't it?" he said cheerfully. "Being bathed by a man."

I could've thumped him. "Not a man like you" is what I wanted to say. Had George Clooney wheeled that contraption over to my bed and drawn the curtains I might've felt differently.

But this nurse was no George Clooney. Not even his plain younger brother, if such a man exists. No, he was just terribly ordinary, with an overly familiar air about him that grated. And too much aftershave.

I closed my eyes. This was an ordeal I wanted as little part of as possible. The loss of dignity weighed heavily on me, increasing my feelings of helplessness.

And that was when I saw her again. Still wearing her blue floral skirt and pink cardigan. She winked at me as she fiddled with the settings on his contraption. I no longer felt disempowered. I had an ally. And she seemed to know what she was doing.

He cursed softly when his contraption failed to start. Before I knew it, the curtains were being opened again and he was asking the older nurse to freshen me up with a wet washer instead. He was still cursing at the machine as he wheeled it away.

The nurse smiled at his departing figure. "That'll be Nancy's doing," she whispered. "I was hoping she'd spare you."

Whoever Nancy was, I felt very grateful to her at that moment for preserving my privacy from the male nurse.

And I was intrigued by this older nurse who seemed to have some kind of connection with Nancy. Who was she?

I read her name tag, trying not to be too obvious. Linda somebody. Well, it wasn't Nancy. Had I expected it to be? Was I still suffering from the side effects of the anaesthetic, as the young doctor had said? Would I wake up tomorrow, and this would all feel like a dream? Maybe. But right now my curiosity was aroused. "Who is Nancy?" I whispered. "You obviously know a lot more about her than I do."

Linda looked thoughtful. "I almost envy you, having met her. I've just had a glimpse of her, one day when I was doing my rounds."

"Go on," I prompted.

"There's not much to tell," she continued. "Several women have told me about her. Always describing the same hat and the same clothes."

"And the mandarin?" I asked.

She nodded.

"Anything else?"

She looked awkward. What didn't she want to tell me? Did Nancy only appear to women who were dying? My heart ached at the thought. I was only sixty-four, and had too much to live for. I'd overheard the doctor saying one of my lungs had collapsed and the other sounded 'crackly', whatever that meant. And he'd said I wasn't 'out of the woods' yet.

"Tell me what you know," I said. "I think I deserve that."

Her cheeks reddened and she couldn't look me in the eye. She seemed afraid of being overheard, and I could hardly blame her. What would her colleagues have thought?

"Perhaps it's a good time for me to make your bed?" she said brightly, as a younger nurse came into the ward. "I'll get some help moving you into an armchair."

Five painful minutes later I was sitting a bit too upright in the hospital's idea of an armchair, a sheet across my knees, watching Linda make my bed. The younger nurse was writing up someone's chart at the far end of the room.

Linda began by carefully removing the sheets, holding them in such an odd way that I had to wonder what she was up to. It looked as though she'd caught a big spider or something.

With a quick glance to make sure her young colleague wasn't watching, she brought the crumpled sheets over to show me.

The burst of orange colour stunned me, as she opened them.

A mandarin.

She peeled it and fed it to me, segment by segment.

Something about the gesture struck a chord.

"Surely you're not Nancy?" I asked. It didn't make any sense at all.

She shook her head.

"I think it's my aunt," she said softly. "She fell pregnant when she was only a young girl, and the baby was taken from her to be adopted."

"Did she have the baby here, in this hospital?"

Linda nodded. "In this very room. This used to be the maternity wing in those days."

"Does she visit male patients as well?" I wanted to know.

"No, it's always a woman, always someone the same age her daughter would be."

"She doesn't know their name?"

"I can't really answer that," she said. "In those days young unmarried mothers weren't told very much at all. It must've been terrible for them."

I nodded in agreement, my brain working quickly.

I was due to go to a rehab unit the following day. This would be my last night in the orthopaedic ward.

I had a good look around me, taking in the details of the windows, the old pressed metal ceiling. So familiar in my dreams and yet so unfamiliar in reality.

When Linda resumed her rounds, I quietly waited for my visitor. I knew in my heart that Nancy would accompany me to rehab. And then back to my home.

Finally reunited with her daughter.

Could I tell the old nurse? She deserved to know, but I needed to get my head around it first. Adjust to this longed-for discovery, before meeting new cousins and other relatives.

For the moment, my birth certificate held all I needed to know. Before she'd died, the woman I'd called my mother had told me that she'd retained the name I'd been given at my birth. Phyllis Nancy.

Her Husband's Secret

Tiffany stumbled upon Donald's secret identity almost by chance. He'd always been a creature of habit. Lunching at the same café every day. Driving home from work along the exact same route. Holidaying in the same seaside resort.

You could set your watch by him.

Now it seemed he'd achieved the impossible. He was also doing this *somewhere else*.

The letter in her hand was addressed to Frank Lambert.

What made her suspicious, she couldn't say afterwards. But she'd noticed subtle changes in his behaviour recently. Uncharacteristic mistakes and things left unexplained. Donald was that rare individual who organised his wardrobe with military precision, shirts arranged by colour, no sock missing its partner. Yet she'd searched the house without finding his blue checked shirt. It puzzled her. And the other day he'd mentioned a new exhibit at the Art Gallery. When he noticed her blank expression, he'd quickly changed the subject.

When this letter arrived, it felt as though something clicked into place in Tiffany's brain. Something was going on. But what? How could she find out? Would she open the letter?

The name Frank Lambert rang a bell. She'd heard it recently – or had she seen something on Facebook? She couldn't recall. All she knew as she looked at the letter was that it felt like the missing piece of a puzzle.

"Impossible," said part of her brain. "Have a Scotch and forget it."

"That explains everything," said another part of her brain.

Which would she listen to?

It was ten to six. Donald would be nearly home. She had less than a minute to decide.

Quickly she grabbed her handbag, placed the letter exactly where she'd found it, and ran out the door. She'd reached the bus shelter and hidden behind it as his grey Ford swung into their street.

She'd pretend she'd caught the later bus. At least she wasn't predictable like him. It'd pass unnoticed.

As she watched Donald arriving home, Tiffany felt a new sense of detachment.

Who was this man she'd lived with for the past ten years? It was like watching someone she no longer knew.

Just because of that letter.

Which she hadn't even opened.

I should've had the Scotch, she thought. Shivering.

And she should've read the letter.

Minutes passed. Lights went on inside the house. He'd have turned on the kettle and settled in front of the TV.

Finally the next bus drew in. Several passengers spilled out onto the footpath. Tiffany joined them.

Inside, Donald offered her a cup of tea. The mail was on the kitchen table. Gas bill. Junk mail. A postcard. Conspicuous by its absence was the letter addressed to Frank Lambert.

Tiffany's heart fell. The fact that it was missing confirmed her suspicions. Why had he hidden it?

She went through the motions that evening. Cooking sausages, mashing potatoes, frying onions. Her mind buzzing the whole time.

Finally she excused herself.

Next morning she pretended to sleep in. By half past seven she knew Donald would be heading to the bank where he worked. She logged into Facebook but couldn't find any clues about Frank Lambert there.

"What did I expect?" she muttered.

She carefully searched the living room but the letter wasn't there. She even ventured into the forbidden realm of Donald's study. Nothing.

There weren't many options left. Today was Thursday. That meant he'd be working late.

Then the penny dropped. What if he'd been lying? What if he did something else on Thursdays?

Tiffany phoned her office, saying she had a migraine.

She'd follow Donald to find out.

Stuck in a traffic jam half an hour later, she already regretted this decision. But she needed to know.

A thoroughly boring day ensued.

Donald's car was in its usual parking space at the rear of the bank.

At precisely nine o'clock, the bank opened.

At half past twelve he emerged, crossed the street, and went to the café opposite.

No doubt he'd order his usual steak sandwich and light ale.

After he'd returned to the bank, she spent the afternoon in the café, ordering the occasional espresso. At five o'clock, he left the bank. Abandoning her coffee, she followed. He was on foot. She'd have to be careful.

Three blocks away he stopped outside an apartment building. Intrigued, Tiffany watched him let himself in.

Trust Donald to choose somewhere like this. He didn't need to drive here so there was a clean paper trail. No extra mileage on the car and no extra petrol costs. You had to credit him, he was clever.

Someone else approached the apartments. A young man wearing a black leather jacket. She followed him inside, giving a friendly nod. She'd seen people get into buildings this way on TV. The secret was to act normally.

It worked.

She noticed the lift had stopped at the eighth floor. That's where she'd begin.

A loud argument could be heard as the lift doors opened on the eighth floor. Donald's voice unmistakable.

"How did you get this address?" he shouted.

A woman whimpered something unintelligible.

The sound of a slap.

Tiffany gasped. Donald had never struck her. Had never seemed capable of violence.

"I don't know what you're talking about, Frank," the woman sobbed.

Tiffany had heard enough.

Moments later a door opened onto the corridor. A blonde in a floral dressing gown appeared. Her long hair was dishevelled. She rushed inside the lift, holding her face. The doors closed, leaving Tiffany alone in the corridor.

Frozen with fear lest Donald aka Frank should suddenly appear.

Where was he? What was he doing? Would he hit her too, if he saw her?

She quietly moved to the open doorway and peered in. Donald had his back to her. He sipped a Scotch, the letter in his hand. From his position on the balcony he watched the pavement below. Watching for the blonde?

Her speed surprised Tiffany. Arms outstretched she hurtled through the room, using every ounce of her strength to push against Donald.

The impact winded her. And was ineffectual.

As he turned, the sneer on his face changed to one of shocked disbelief.

"Your secret's out," Tiffany said.

His hands moved towards her. The fire of menace in his eyes.

She didn't wait. One hard blow caught him off-guard. As she jerked one of his legs up, realisation turned to terror in his eyes.

"No," he screamed, falling backwards over the railing. She deftly snatched the letter from his flailing hands.

The temptation to watch was overwhelming but she must get away quickly.

Running up the stairs in the fire escape, she entered the lift on the eleventh floor, hoping to avoid any connection with the commotion on the eighth floor. There were several tenants in the lift. Nobody seemed aware there'd been a calamity.

It was a different story on the ground floor when the lift doors opened.

Screams. Rushing figures. Urgent voices on phones.

Tiffany quietly slipped out and walked to the bank, heart pounding. Making herself walk at normal speed, the letter in her pocket the only evidence linking her to the crime.

Donald's car sat in the car park. It was half past five.

She must go home. Pretend everything was normal. But first she sat in her car and finally read the letter. To her surprise, it was a bank statement. In Frank Lambert's name. She read through his expenses. Restaurants, cinemas and the art gallery. It must've been easy for him to set up this account without anyone knowing, siphoning off part of his pay. But somehow he'd made a mistake. The letter had come to their address. Typical of Donald, he'd blamed the woman. But more likely he was the culprit.

No wonder he'd been angry. This letter exposed his deceptions.

As she drove home, she tore off tiny pieces of the letter, dropping them out the window. Thinking ridiculously of the bread trail in *Hansel and Gretel*.

As it was Thursday, Donald would normally arrive home at eleven o'clock. She must stick to her own usual pattern. Dinner, TV, phone her mother, and in bed by ten. She'd be accountable for her actions later.

As she lay in bed, wondering when to report him missing, the front doorbell rang. For one awful moment she wondered if he could've survived the fall. Reported her to the police. Or worse, come back to exact his own revenge.

Heart pounding, she wrapped herself in a towelling robe and padded outside.

Two policewomen stood on the front landing.

She looked from one to the other in stunned silence. The younger asked if they could come inside.

"There's been an accident," the older officer began. And told her of Donald's fall.

"I'm afraid we'll need you to identify his body."

Tiffany's first sensation was one of relief. She was careful not to show that. But she was puzzled. Why were the police here? Wasn't it someone called Frank Lambert who'd been killed? That's what eyewitnesses from the apartments would've said. Shouldn't the blonde be the one doing this, identifying Frank?

How had they traced Donald so quickly?

She wasn't left to wonder for long.

"He's my bank manager," the younger officer said. "I recognised him immediately."

Neither of them used the name Frank Lambert.

And of course Tiffany couldn't.

The shock she felt was genuine. This wasn't what she'd expected.

Her distress at identifying him was also genuine. The police were satisfied it was an accident. Even the insurance company rubberstamped her payout.

Almost too easy, Tiffany thought, as she stood by his coffin at the crematorium a week later. Unexpectedly she'd become wealthy.

The first jarring note came when the blonde approached her at Donald's wake.

"I know what you did," she said. "Give me half the insurance payout and you'll never see me again."

"Who are you?" she asked coldly. What she really wanted to know was what the woman had seen. Whether anyone else had seen anything.

"Have it your way," the woman said. "I'll see you in court."

Was this a serious threat? What evidence could she possibly have?

Or was she bluffing? She must surely be as shocked as Tiffany to discover Frank aka Donald had been living two separate lives?

Whatever, the woman needed to be silenced. Otherwise she'd contact her again. And again.

Tiffany wasn't prepared to part with the money. She was his wife, after all. But she couldn't contemplate cold-blooded murder either.

Luckily there were options other than killing her. That was the beauty of her new wealth.

Inspired by her husband's actions, she bought a seaside villa and adopted the name Camilla Parkinson. A four-hour session at the local hairdresser transformed her into a brunette with short curly hair.

Sometimes Donald was right. It was easier to simply become someone else.

Family Matters

I didn't really expect Kath to go through with it. It's one thing to talk about killing your husband. Quite another to do it.

There's no doubt he had it coming to him. He'd been impossible to live with. And I should know. He was my kid brother. The bane of my life until he got married. Josh turned bad living habits into an art form. Put him within coo-ee of a bar and there was bound to be trouble. He'd served time for some of the things he'd got up to while under the influence of a beer or ten. And all he'd managed to learn while he was inside was how to get into even worse trouble. He'd also acquired a gambling habit. He'd place a bet on a grasshopper race if it was on offer. And not hesitate to write I.O.U.s he'd never be able to repay.

It was easy to understand why Kath had run out of patience.

Still, I'd miss him. Blood's thicker than water, and all that.

"How did you manage to make it look like suicide?" I asked.

Had Josh told her this himself, I wondered? That was the sort of advice he spouted from time to time. Too often when there were kids around, or gentle older folk. We assumed he'd heard it in prison, but who knows? He didn't keep very nice company at the best of times. Me and Kath excepted, of course.

Kath sipped her chardonnay. We were sitting in the local pub. There was a private courtyard area so we didn't have to worry about being overheard.

"I knew there had to be a note left behind," she said. "Something handwritten that contains an explanation and a goodbye." There was a faraway look in her eyes. Had she looked like this when she'd …?

I wouldn't allow my mind to go there.

"You mean Josh actually wrote the suicide note himself?" I asked. This was too hard to believe. I'd assumed until now that Kath must've forged it.

She nodded, still seemingly miles away. Perhaps murdering someone did this to you? Put you in limbo so you were no longer part of everyday reality?

"But Josh wouldn't have done that," I protested. "That's out of character."

Had she held a gun to his head, I wondered? But even under those circumstances, I couldn't imagine him doing it.

She looked me fairly in the eyes. I felt a shiver travel from my neck vertebrae down to my tail, rattling all the way. This was a new side to Kath. Something terrible that Josh had unleashed. We'd let her reach breaking point, and were experiencing the results.

"The trick was to get him to write it," she said. "It didn't matter if he meant it or not, just that he wrote something that would convince the police."

Her words chilled me.

They also aroused memories of murder mysteries I'd watched on TV involving these notes. Sometimes there'd be a letter and the murderer would've torn off the 'Dear somebody' part, or the address or something. And perhaps the date as well. So it meant something different when it was found. Had Kath done this? Looking at her now, she seemed capable of it.

"How did you manage that?" I asked. She'd got me curious now. Perhaps I'd joined her in this weird time warp she inhabited?

She smiled. I could've sworn she looked pleased with herself. She had that I've-done- something-clever look. The sort goody-goodies used to get at school when they got top marks in a maths test.

"We played a game of Cluedo," she said at last. "You know, Professor Plum in the kitchen with a leaden pipe. That sort of stuff. I told Josh it'd be fun to act it out."

"I'm not getting this," I said. "It doesn't explain why he'd write a note."

"I knew he was getting a bit bored. He always hated having to keep any sort of rules. Even in a board game." She paused for a moment. "I wasn't surprised when he tried to cheat."

"And?" I prompted.

"Cheats don't prosper," she blurted out.

After this chilling conversation I'm not really sure why I accepted her invitation to dinner and a game of Cluedo.

Lightning doesn't strike twice in the same place, I reasoned. And to be honest, I was curious. I needed to know exactly what had happened to Josh and why nothing was done about it. How had Kath managed to convince the police of her innocence? And that Josh hadn't been murdered 'by person or persons unknown', as they say in the murder mysteries on TV.

So I turned up at my brother's bungalow the following night armed with a bottle of merlot and an overactive imagination.

She'd roasted a duck and made blueberry cheesecake for dessert. I hadn't expected such a lavish meal. Was she celebrating her new freedom, I wondered? Dinner parties had been few and far between, what with his unpredictable behaviour and everything. But it didn't feel right to be here in these circumstances.

After coffee, Kath produced the game of Cluedo.

"The easiest way to show you what happened would be if I pretend to be Josh," she began, "And we can act it out."

This was becoming weird. But it was fascinating. And something made me agree.

As I watched, she slurred her voice and put on Josh's denim jacket. "I'm sick of this game. I never win."

I could certainly imagine him saying that. He'd been the same when we were kids.

She shuffled through the game cards. "Silly game, it's all murder," she said, in Josh's tones. "What if someone committed suicide and it had nothing to do with Mrs Peacock or Professor Plum or any of these suspects?"

I sat forward in my chair, absorbed.

She looked at me expectantly, willing me to join in. So I tried to pretend I was Kath and to speak in her Liverpool accent. "You'd have to write a note, and leave it somewhere the police would find it," I said. "Otherwise it'd be just another murder, and Professor Plum and everybody else would still be the suspects."

There was a nod. "Well, hand me a pen and some paper."

I handed over a pen. As I watched, unable to speak, the words were written. Different ones this time, of course. Out of respect for my feelings. But just as clear in their meaning. Kath read the letter out to me, slurring her voice to imitate Josh. "That should convince them," she said.

"What happens next?" I asked. "Where are the weapons?"

Silently a rope, a revolver and a lead pipe were produced. They'd been hidden behind books on the bookcase. No wonder they hadn't been discovered. Who'd think to look behind a huge dictionary for a gun? I couldn't help wondering how long Kath had been planning this. She seemed awfully well prepared.

My hands felt cold and clammy.

This had been a trap, cleverly set. And Josh had been too drunk and too trusting to realise.

Had I made the same mistake?

Was I to be her next victim?

Maybe Kath had developed a taste for murder? The once-is-not-enough mania I'd read about. Would she end up as a serial killer?

But she looked innocent enough as she handed me the revolver. "It's even loaded," she said. "And the rope is thick enough to use. Everything's real."

This was too much for me. Something inside me snapped.

As she said the word 'real', I fired the trigger. She had a look of utter disbelief in her eyes as she slumped forward. Dead.

It wasn't hard to wipe away my fingerprints and put the weapon in her hand.

The note was still on the table.

In her own handwriting.

There was no need to feign shock as I dialled emergency services.

"My sister-in-law just shot herself," I told the police when they arrived. "She hasn't been the same since her husband took his life last weekend."

One of them made me a cup of tea.

"She couldn't bear being in the house on her own," I said. "That's why I joined her for dinner this evening."

The older policeman had attended the original death and nodded. "Yes, she seemed very distressed," he said. "But why would she bring out the game of Cluedo after what happened?"

"I have no idea," I said. "I'd gone to the bathroom, and ran back when I heard the shot."

It took a while for the scene of crime officers to do their work. But just as last weekend, the handwritten note paved the way to a 'case closed'.

It was around midnight when the older policeman offered to drive me home. "This has been quite an ordeal for you," he said. There was a note of sympathy in his voice.

As I washed off my makeup in my own bathroom, I looked at my eyes. Had they changed? Did they have that chilling faraway look?

Not that I could tell.

I felt relieved as I lay down in bed. I didn't blame Kath for what she'd done. But I couldn't let her get away with it, could I? After all, he was my kid brother. And you know what they say. Blood's thicker than water.

Messenger

Would I mention the ghost in the corridor?

I wasn't sure. This was my first visit to a psychic.

Perhaps they all had one? The way you often saw a sleek cat at a vet's clinic.

But it'd still been unnerving, seeing it dangling there. It was a wispy cloudy thing and kept changing. A woman's face would appear and then disappear. And I had to somehow walk through it.

In the end, I'd simply closed my eyes and pretended it wasn't there. Nothing terrible had happened, just a vague sensation of movement and energy, hard to describe. I wasn't looking forward to a repeat performance, after the session. Or perhaps I'd feel differently then?

"I met your ghost," I began.

Veronica smiled. "Which one? I hope you weren't frightened. We only attract happy spirits around here."

I sat in the armchair opposite her, wondering what to expect. My mind was full of doubts. Why had I really come? And why hadn't I been able to talk to Ben about this?

I had questions and no answers. None that I could face anyway.

Veronica was wearing a flimsy colourful caftan, which reminded me of a dress my mother had worn in the 1970s. There was a photo, which I kept on my bedside table.

"What is it you want to know, Sophie?" she asked softly.

I jumped. How did she know my real name? I'd make the booking under the name, Jan Summers. Being overly cautious, wanting to make sure Ben didn't find out. He'd be angry if he knew I was here 'wasting' our money. But it was my money. I was the one with a job. Not that I could say that. He was trigger-happy, too many moods and not enough self-control. Only yesterday he'd thrown a plate in my direction.

Something about Veronica's deep blue eyes made me relax again. They were awakening memories. I felt able to talk to her.

The sorry tale of my relationship poured out despite all my resolves. I'd come to learn something, not to be the one doing all the talking. What had come over me today?

Veronica didn't seem to notice anything amiss. She sat quietly nodding, a faraway look in her eyes. I felt a positive energy flowing from her and was glad I'd come.

When I finished talking, she said, "You realise you have to leave him, don't you? Things will only get worse if you stay."

"Do I have the strength to do that?"

A soft smile lit up her face. "You know you do, Sophie. That's why you have a suitcase full of your clothes sitting in your car outside. The blue Nissan."

My heart fluttered with excitement. Veronica was evidently the real thing. How else could she know this?

"Where could I go?" I had no idea where my future lay. That suitcase had been in my car for several days.

The blue of her eyes intensified and as I looked into them, I felt my resolve strengthening.

"You'd be safe in your mother's cabin," she replied. "Ben doesn't know about it, and it's sitting unoccupied." As it had, for the past twenty years.

"Are you sure?"

"The door key is under the big geranium pot plant," she said. "It hasn't rusted."

There were voices in the corridor outside. Veronica seemed uneasy.

Was this my cue to leave?

I checked my watch. It must've stopped. It still read ten o'clock.

A woman entered the room.

I looked at Veronica for an explanation but she was no longer there.

The woman came over and introduced herself.

"I'm Veronica. You must be Jan. I'm sorry I'm running late."

I opened my mouth to speak but nothing came out.

Behind the real Veronica, I noticed the woman I'd been speaking with. She'd become a cloudy apparition.

"I've changed my mind," I said, making an undignified exit.

"I hope it wasn't the ghost in the corridor that put you off," the woman began.

As I drove to my mother's cabin, I was aware of a loving energy in the car.

"Thank you, Mum," I whispered, as I opened the door for us both to enter.

Death Claims His Prize

There were four Deaths at the party.

Well, what had Fiona expected? It was Halloween after all.

The one with ginger hair was obviously Anthony. Surely he could've worn a wig tonight? Or a black beanie. Such a dead giveaway, she chuckled. He wouldn't even make the short list in their competition.

And who said Death was male? The blonde Death in heels would be Cindy. Her long flowing black gown and white makeup looked quite creepy, and she'd painted her fingernails a brilliant blue.

Who was the dark-haired one in the corner? Maybe a friend of a friend? The invitation had been open.

She knew the short one was Willow. Not content with the usual black cloak and ghostly features, she'd opted for blood-splattered shoes and what looked like her grandmother's walking stick. Incongruous, but it actually worked. She was the most adventurous Death, as well as the youngest and shortest.

It'd be hard to pick a winner.

She walked over to the newcomer. What did he look like under that black outfit? He was probably the tallest person in the room. A true alpha male. She had a weakness for those. Especially if they had an air of mystery about them, as this one did.

"Welcome to the party, Death," she said breezily, holding out her hand in greeting.

There was a flicker of surprise in his dark eyes. He didn't take her proffered hand.

As she withdrew it, she couldn't help feeling relieved. She'd belatedly noticed he had pale almost bluish skin, so fine you could almost see his bones. The makeup was terrific. It must've taken hours to achieve that effect.

Handing him a beer, she moved on.

The young lads from over the road were doing a great job playing guitar and singing the list she'd provided. *Highway to Hell, Don't Fear the Reaper, Creep, Deal with the Devil.* They'd dressed as zombies for the occasion, in swathes of blood-splattered bandages. They'd perform lighter pieces once the fun part of the evening began, when prizes would be awarded for the best costumes.

She looked down at her own outfit. Could she beat Death? The skeleton suit had been sitting at the back of a charity shop, dusty and forgotten. How could she pass it by? And being shabby and dusty only added to its authenticity. It'd cost her less than the price of a cup of coffee.

She recognised some of the costumes here from browsing through shops yesterday. That vampire outfit Kelly was wearing cost $50 per day to hire. Hopefully Kelly would take out one of the prizes, to make it worth her while.

Mind you, Death had cast his eye in her direction more

than once tonight. *She probably already feels she's got her money's worth*, Fiona thought. He seemed such a tall impressive man and quiet. Easy to be with. So long as you could overlook that pale skin. Maybe Kelly would like to help him wash the blue makeup off?

She'd have lots of competition. Death was a party animal. Every time she looked he was somewhere else.

There was a tap on her shoulder. A giggle. "Your skull's back to front," Willow said, laughing. "I'll help you readjust it."

Fiona felt ridiculous. How had she not noticed? Skeletons were meant to know where their bones belonged. No wonder Death had wandered away after she'd introduced herself.

Where was he now?

A loud cry came from the far corner where Kelly was gathered with friends. Fiona saw someone lifting the front of her vampire sleeve to check her pulse. A zombie shrieked and pointed to blood coming out of Kelly's eyes. She seemed motionless.

"This is a wind-up," Fiona said to Willow. "She told me she's desperate to win."

But Willow began to shake. "I think she's dead."

"Don't be ridiculous," Fiona said. "I'll bet she's just bought that red ink actors use when they've been shot."

As she rushed over to see what was going on, Death smiled at her. His eyes were bright, but there was an iciness in his features.

Fiona decided she wasn't interested in him.

He isn't a party animal after all, she thought, as he turned to leave. It was still only nine o'clock.

Kelly lay on the floor. Fiona realised something was seriously wrong. Her friend had no pulse. Her hands were icy and her eyes looked like the eyes of fish she'd seen in the supermarket, staring blankly back at her. Except these ones left thin trails of blood down her cheek. She noticed a red splatter on her hand and recoiled. This wasn't ink, it was real blood.

She looked across the room.

Death was leaving through the door. Her stomach lurched. The door was closed.

Rushing outside she saw him disappearing among the trees, a translucent blonde Vampire by his side.

Death by Misadventure?

George Carmichael stared gloomily around the hospital ward. A sense of humour would come in handy, but his was nowhere to be found. Beside him on a tiny set of bedside drawers were the obligatory flowers and grapes. In his hands was a paperback whodunit. But his eyes glazed over whenever he tried to read it. He should be the one out there solving crimes, not stuck here with his legs in plaster, swallowing painkillers. And his pride.

"Idiot," he kept muttering to himself.

Chief Inspectors were meant to be fit enough to chase criminals and capture them. All he'd been trying to do was improve his fitness. A recent case involving the disappearance of Cecilia Armstrong had shown him that his lifestyle had finally caught up with him. He'd had to run several hundred metres. It'd left him exhausted and out of breath, something he wouldn't have tolerated in his junior colleagues. Cycling to work had seemed the logical way to improve his fitness.

If one more friend suggested he'd have been better off buying an exercise bike rather than a bicycle, he wouldn't be responsible for his actions.

Voices in the corridor interrupted his thoughts. Was that Cecilia?

His spirits lifted as she entered the ward and walked over to his bed. Their lips brushed. She couldn't conceal the concern in her eyes but he was grateful she didn't voice her worries. It was bad enough being here without having to cope with other people's reactions.

"How's my patient today?" she asked.

He tried to raise a smile. "Things could be better," he said. "But I'm happy to see you here."

"I've brought you something," she said.

His heart sank momentarily. Then came a wave of guilt. No doubt she'd brought him flowers from her garden. And he'd have to look up the small volume he now kept with him. Flowers and their meanings had become part of his life once he and Cecilia had become involved. Initially it'd felt romantic, a secret language. That first time she'd given him gladioli and daffodils. When he'd checked their meanings, he'd discovered that gladioli signified strength of character. Then he'd checked daffodils. Secret desire. The potential to communicate this way had excited him.

Now after seven months he often thought with nostalgia to the days when he could simply buy a woman a dozen red roses, knowing they'd let her know his feelings.

But instead of producing some significant flowers, she handed him what looked like an old engagement diary. His interest was finally aroused.

"What's this?" he asked.

"Something to occupy that brain of yours," she said. "You look as though you're dying of boredom."

"That's an accurate diagnosis," he said, finally smiling.

He opened the diary and immediately understood. The opening page contained the name Henry Paxton, with details of his phone number and address.

"There hasn't been an opportunity," he began.

She patted his hand. "I know that. But now you've got compulsory time off, I thought you might be able to shed some light on Henry's death for me."

Cecilia's brother-in-law had died five years earlier, when he'd gone out in a fishing boat one evening. He'd never returned. The coroner had concluded his death was due to misadventure. Naturally the police had accepted the findings. They had more urgent things to attend to than a man rowing out on a lake and drowning. There'd been a gangland murder the same day that Henry's body was discovered. That killing had occupied most of their resources.

Cecilia firmly believed that Henry's difficult daughter Jasmine was involved in his death. There were inconsistencies and odd coincidences that in her opinion warranted a closer examination. There was the fact that his boat needed repair. His personal fears for his safety. Warnings he'd received, with flowers left on his front doorstep each morning. Flowers that Henry knew signified death and danger. Like Cecilia, Henry had made a study of the ancient language of flowers. Clearly the flowers could only have been left for him to discover by someone who knew him well.

However, despite Cecilia's protestations, there was simply no firm evidence of any foul play. Nothing to convert her suspicions into something that might stand up in court. The fact that Jasmine benefitted from Henry's death was not by itself sufficient to warrant further investigation. Consequently, she had been unable to persuade the police to continue their enquiries. Henry's death was officially recorded as an accident.

Now, five years later, Cecilia had asked George to look into it. She needed closure.

And his newly discovered feelings towards her had contributed to his interest in shedding any light on the events of that night.

When Cecilia herself had disappeared seven months ago, and he'd investigated the case, it'd come to light that Joseph, the secret love child of Cecilia and Henry, had left the flowers as a warning.

But why Joseph believed his father to be in danger had never been discovered. He'd simply told his half-sister Jasmine that their father had been afraid of her. It'd been said in the heat of the moment, with bullets flying seconds later. And it was only now that George had the time to ponder why. He realised he needed to talk with Joseph as soon as possible.

Would Joseph be mentioned in this diary, he wondered? Or had Henry discreetly omitted any reference to him?

He looked up at Cecilia. "I'll browse through this. I assume it was his last diary?"

"Yes, it was never examined by the police."

"There was no reason for them to look further once the coroner established that Henry's death was an accident," he said. "But if it makes you feel better, I'll read this."

After Cecilia had left, and the nurse had checked his blood pressure and temperature, he opened the diary. He'd expected it to consist simply of appointments but Henry had written in comments as well. Until September 12. After that date, there were only appointments pencilled in.

George suddenly felt sorry for this man. For the first time he found himself wondering what had really happened to him on that fateful evening.

He flicked through the pages leading up to Henry's death. Fairly mundane jottings about a dentist appointment, having his car serviced and paying his gardener. And then something caught his eye. On September 6 he'd written "Jasmine has ordered a Lamborghini!!" and he'd underlined it.

George looked up in surprise. He knew she'd bought one, of course. Who could miss her bright yellow Lamborghini? But he'd assumed she'd made the purchase after her father's death and once she'd received her inheritance. But according to this, she'd ordered it on September 6. How had she intended paying for it?

His interest was piqued.

Maybe there'd be other discrepancies as well? But would he find enough to overturn the coroner's verdict? He very much doubted it. Not after all this time. If there'd been foul play, surely any scent had well and truly grown cold?

He was about to close the diary but then decided to look at September 12. Cecilia had said something about Henry having plans to meet someone on the evening of his death.

There it was. Pencilled in for September 12 was an 8:00 p.m. appointment with M. H. Who was that, George wondered?

He turned to the end of the diary. His own diary had a space at the back for frequently called numbers and addresses.

To his relief he found several pages of names and contact details in Henry's.

There was only one possibility. Havers and Smythe. That sounded like a firm of lawyers? He'd have to find out. Perhaps Havers was the mysterious M.H.?

He decided to start at the beginning of the diary and work his way through methodically. That way he wouldn't miss anything, and he might be able to discern patterns. Or something that seemed out of the ordinary.

"I've got nothing better to do," he said softly to himself.

He felt too curious to put the diary down. His mind buzzed with possible scenarios and questions. All because of that appointment with M.H.

If Henry had arranged a private appointment at home with his lawyer, it must've been about something significant. What if he'd decided to disinherit Jasmine? That'd certainly provide a strong motive. George didn't feel greed was enough, even though he'd investigated many deaths where it was the overriding motive. Having a motive wasn't enough. There needed to be an urgency as well. That was his experience.

Now it appeared there may well have been urgency as well as motive, if Cecilia's suspicions were correct. If Jasmine knew Henry had arranged to change his will at 8 o'clock on the evening of September 12, that gave her an overwhelming motive to kill him beforehand. Especially as she'd ordered the Lamborghini.

The appointment also gave credence to Cecilia's doubts that Henry would've voluntarily gone fishing at seven o'clock when he was meeting someone an hour later. Judging by the entries in the diary Henry was a man who planned in advance rather than acted on the spur of the moment. Appointments were written down well into November and December.

After Cecilia had gone, George lay staring at the ceiling. Something had been bothering him for a while now and he couldn't quite put his finger on it. Something he remembered that didn't seem to fit in with the facts. He knew it'd come to him eventually but for the moment it was out of his grasp.

He fell into an uneasy sleep. When he awoke, he felt disoriented. It took a few moments to realise with a sinking heart that he was in hospital. Voices in the corridor announced another visitor. It was his Sergeant, Timothy Dawson. No doubt bearing more grapes.

Indeed, such was the case. Muscatels this time.

Dawson must've sensed his mood because when the nurse had left, he winked. "I thought you might need something for the pain, Sir," he said. "Something like this." And lifting out the bunch of grapes, he drew out a small bottle of Scotch. "I thought it best to hide it."

"That's it," George said, sitting up excitedly. "What did you just say?"

Dawson looked puzzled. "I thought you might need something like this."

"Something like this," echoed George. "Yes, that's it."

Dawson didn't attempt to disguise his confusion.

"The gun," George said. And then he finally noticed Dawson's expression. "Let me explain," he began. "You remember the case when Cecilia Armstrong was kidnapped?"

And he described the moment when Cecilia had come out of concealment in the cottage holding a gun. The moment had stayed in his mind.

"She held up the gun and asked Jasmine whether she'd held a gun to Henry's head. *Like this one* were her words."

"I'm not following you." Dawson absentmindedly helped himself to a few grapes.

George had become quite animated. "Don't you see? Maybe the gun originally belonged to Cecilia's sister? She may have inherited it from their father. In which case, surely Jasmine would know about it."

"Why would Jasmine necessarily know about the gun when she didn't live in the house?"

"Maybe you're right. We can't be sure. But we can't assume she didn't know about it either. This is just what Cecilia suspects." He was silent for a moment. "And the gun may have no bearing on the drowning."

He resolved to talk to Cecilia about this as soon as possible.

Dawson's eyes were beginning to glaze over. "Is there anything else I can do for you, Sir?" he enquired politely.

"Yes. Could you dig out the old file on Henry Paxton's drowning? The date was 12 September, 2014."

When Dawson left, George dialled Cecilia's number. There was no response.

He was rereading Henry's diary when she entered the room. His heart lifted.

"I have to talk to you about the gun," he began, as she leant over to kiss him.

She smiled. "That's more like it. What do you need to know?"

"Was it originally your sister's?"

"Yes," she said. "But Henry was the one interested in it. He often got it out to polish and oil."

"So Jasmine knew he had a gun?"

"She must've."

"I need to know for sure. Can you remember any occasion when Henry had the gun out while Jasmine was in the same room?"

Cecilia frowned, lost in thought. Finally she nodded. "Yes. There was one afternoon when I visited Henry. We were discussing how we could help Joseph. I remember he was polishing the gun at the time," she said. "Jasmine suddenly barged in on us and we had to stop our conversation. She must've seen it then."

"Good. Now think carefully. This might be important," he said. "Did Henry keep it loaded?"

"Of course not," she said. "He wasn't sure how reliable it was. Don't forget, it was an old gun that had belonged to my father."

George nodded. "Did you ever put bullets in it?"

She shook her head. "I think I can see where this is leading."

"Exactly," he said. "If Henry didn't put bullets in, and you didn't, then who did? That day in the cottage when you confronted Jasmine with the gun, it was loaded. We know that for a fact. It was fired twice, if you remember."

"How could I ever forget?" she said. "When she tackled me and wrested the gun out of my hand, it went off. Poor Joseph. His arm took weeks to heal."

"You haven't answered my question," he said. "Who put the bullets in the gun?"

"It must've been Jasmine," she said. "It was loaded when I brought it back from Henry's after his death. But how does that help us?"

"Don't you see?" he said. "If we have the remaining bullets examined, there may be fingerprints."

"After all this time?" she said. "Surely there'd be no trace of fingerprints after five years?"

"It's not out of the question," he said. "So long as you haven't touched them too."

She shook her head. "But surely the gun and bullets have already been checked? Wouldn't that have been done at the time?"

"It should've been. And perhaps it was. But since the gun was never actually linked to Henry's death by the police, it may well not have gone to the lab. After all, it wasn't fired on the night when Henry drowned."

"What about after it was fired in Joseph's cottage that day?" she said. "That shouldn't be hard to check. It was only seven months ago."

"I'll have to follow this up with the lab." Excusing himself, he phoned Dawson. "There's something I need you to do for me," he began. "I need a gun checked by the lab. And see whether anyone's already done this, will you? Cecilia will bring it into the station."

He looked up at her questioningly.

"This afternoon would suit me," she said.

"And there's something else, Dawson," he added. "I want Jasmine Paxton's finances investigated. See whether she could afford to buy a brand-new Lamborghini in September 2012."

There was a pause.

"Yes, I said Lamborghini. She ordered one on 6 September 2012. I want to know whether she had the money to pay for it. Or whether she'd applied for a loan."

"Maybe she had a sugar daddy?" Cecilia said, when he'd finished the call. "She certainly attracts a lot of male attention."

He remembered the red mini skirt and black stilettos. Cecilia might be right.

"Would anyone have known about that?" he asked.

"If someone had visited her at the house, I suppose it might be in Henry's diary?"

"I didn't notice any regular male visitors," he said. "I don't suppose you know who M.H. is?"

"That'll be Michael Havers, our family lawyer."

"That's who Henry was expecting at the house on the evening of September 12."

She raised an eyebrow. "I'd forgotten that."

George had a sudden thought. "Could Michael Havers be Jasmine's sugar daddy?"

"Good heavens, no," she said. "Michael and Jasmine?" And she laughed. "You'll have to cast your net wider. It isn't Michael. He's gay."

There was so much groundwork to cover, George thought, once he was on his own again. So much to unravel. Where would he start?

He felt there were still vital pieces missing from the puzzle. Was it too late for him to pick up the scent again? Five years was a long time.

His thoughts kept chasing each other.

What if the meeting Henry had arranged with M.H. had nothing to do with Jasmine? What other possibilities were there? He knew he had to keep his mind open at this stage of his investigation.

And if Jasmine meant to kill Henry, in order to prevent him from changing his will, would she really have left it so late? Only one hour between his fishing trip and the appointment he was destined never to keep. That was simply cutting it too fine. He couldn't believe she wouldn't have attempted something sooner.

Unless of course she'd only just learned of Henry's intentions?

Was he clutching at straws, hoping to find fingerprints on the bullets after all this time?

Yes. But straws were all that he had.

The arrival of a nurse and the painful beginning of physiotherapy exercises left him with little time or energy that day. He was making excellent progress, he was told. But it didn't feel like it, not with his body screaming out in pain afterwards.

It was several days later when he phoned Joseph asking him to come to the hospital.

He was well enough now to be wheeled to the main cafeteria. It made a nice change. And his body seemed to be finally responding to the physiotherapy.

Leaning back in his chair, admiring the view of the small lake in the hospital grounds, George felt himself beginning to relax. This certainly beat looking out at the car park from his bed.

He drew the diary out of his pocket.

"Do you mind if I ask you some questions about Henry?" he began. "And you might be able to fill me in on a few things concerning Michael Havers."

At his words Joseph's face became a mask. He automatically reached up to run his fingers through his hair.

"Is there something wrong?" George asked.

The young man didn't meet his gaze. Instead he looked around the cafeteria, as though collecting his thoughts.

"Of course not," he finally answered. "What would you like to know about Henry?"

George noted that he hadn't mentioned Havers. He might be Cecilia's son but that didn't stop alarm bells ringing in his detective's mind. Nobody was out of contention when it came to murder investigations. The perpetrator often turned out to be a member of the victim's family. George had learned that very early in his career.

He decided to push the advantage. "Let's start with Michael Havers, shall we? What can you tell me about him?"

Joseph paused just a bit too long. "What do you want to know?"

His cautious manner convinced George to pursue this line of questioning. "Let's start with your relationship with him," he said.

And was rewarded by an audible gasp. "How did you know about that?"

"I didn't," George said, startled by this admission. "Go on. You need to tell me everything now."

Joseph's shoulders drooped. "Nobody knew. Especially my mother." He leaned forward. "She doesn't know I'm gay. And I'm hoping you won't have to tell her."

"So it's over now? Your relationship with Michael Havers?" He couldn't make any promises about what Cecilia would find out.

"We broke up not long after my father's death. But recently we've started seeing each other again."

"Did your father know you were involved with his lawyer?"

He looked down. "Nobody knew we were seeing each other," he said. "Michael's a very private person. And I didn't want to upset my parents."

"Can you be sure nobody had guessed?" He watched the young man struggling to find words.

"What about Jasmine?"

His words had hit a nerve. "I don't think so," Joseph said at last. "Michael said not to worry about Jasmine."

"Did he now? And what else did Michael say? Did you know Henry had arranged to see him that evening?"

He nodded. "Yes, Michael was worried he might've found out about us."

A dark shadow crossed the young man's face. George could see him struggling with a new thought.

"You can see the implications, can't you?" he prompted.

Joseph's head sunk into his hands. When he looked up again, he seemed afraid.

"There's something you need to know." His voice was barely audible.

"Go on," said the detective.

"Michael was with me that evening."

George felt a tingle run up his spine. "Was he with you at 8 o'clock?" he asked. "Did you know he was supposed to be at a meeting with Henry?"

The young man nodded. "What does this mean? I've never put two and two together until now."

"I think it means he knew there wouldn't be a meeting," George said. "I don't suppose you remember what time you met up?"

"He cooked me dinner at his place," Joseph said. "I remember he phoned late afternoon to invite me over. We didn't eat out together in case we were recognised."

"I see," George said. "Was he there the whole time? Could he have slipped out for half an hour?"

Then another thought crossed his mind. How certain were they that Henry had set out in the boat at exactly 7 o'clock? They only had Jasmine's word. A selfish young woman in need of money. Cecilia had often said she couldn't be trusted.

What if Havers had arrived at the house unbeknownst to her? What if he'd forced Henry at gunpoint to row out into the lake? Forensics had simply confirmed the evidence. Had anyone questioned the pathologist about the possible time of death? Or had he simply rubber-stamped the evidence on hand? George knew only too well how hard it was to get forensic work prioritised when there was a major case underway. The police pathologist would've been working all hours on the gangland murder case.

George was getting out of his depth.

A familiar excitement possessed him. The thrill of the hunt. He'd finally found a line of enquiry nobody had thought to explore. Jasmine Paxton had some explaining to do. And so did Michael Havers.

Either could have lied. Or both.

"This certainly changes things," George said. "And it gives you both a motive, doesn't it? Henry might've cut you out of his will if he'd known what was going on."

"Michael said not to worry. That it was probably about Jasmine."

"Yes, your half-sister. Did you know she'd ordered herself a Lamborghini?"

"Of course. She drove it around the estate to show it off to everyone the moment it arrived."

"No, I meant did you know she'd placed the order?" Joseph looked puzzled so he continued. "Or did you find out when the car actually arrived?"

"Don't you just buy them in a showroom?" the young man said. "She simply drove over one day to show it off."

George believed him. He seemed confused by the questioning.

"Think carefully before you answer my next question," he said. "Why did you believe your father was in danger from Jasmine? Why did you warn him?"

He answered almost at once. "It was something I overheard her saying. I don't know who she was talking to. She was on her phone," he said. "Something about coming into a lot of money."

"Why was that a danger to Henry?"

"Jasmine didn't have a job. She was heavily in debt. So where else could the money be coming from?" he said.

"There's another possibility," George said. "Could she have had a sugar daddy?"

"I suppose it's possible," Joseph said after a pause. "She never mentioned anyone. But why would she? She didn't know I was her half-brother. Not then."

It was only afterwards when he was once again lying in bed in the ward that another thought occurred to George. An unwelcome realisation. What if Cecilia had discovered her son was having a relationship with Havers? What if Henry had said something to her about changing his will to disinherit him? That put her well and truly in the frame as well.

He frowned. Surely he'd have instinctively known? And why would she ask him to investigate the death if she herself was responsible? It didn't make sense. But he couldn't rule it out either. He found this deeply disturbing. He'd always been able to keep his personal life and his professional one separate. Had prided himself on being able to do this, after seeing various colleagues have their lives unravel over the years.

Now he understood the dilemmas that'd faced them. How to tread that fine line between revealing his doubts and discovering what he needed to know.

It was a few days later when Sergeant Dawson paid him another visit. "You wanted to know about Jasmine Paxton's finances, Sir," he began.

George smiled. It was nice not to be asked how he was for a change. "What have you found out for me?" he asked.

"You were right," Dawson said. "There's no way she could've afforded a second-hand Fiat let alone a Lamborghini."

"Tell me more."

And Dawson read out the figure by which Jasmine's account was in the red.

George whistled. "What about the bullets? Did the lab find any fingerprints? Was there anything already on file? Was a lab report done when Cecilia fired the gun seven months ago?"

"We're still waiting for the lab to get back to us, Sir," he said. "Here's that file on the drowning."

George opened the manila folder. It contained police reports, the coroner's letter, statements, newspaper clippings and photographs. He examined the photos of Henry lying on the bank of the lake, fully clothed. The police photographer had shot him from various angles.

"Have a look at these, will you?" he said to Dawson after studying them for a few minutes. "Tell me what you see."

Dawson flipped through the photos then looked up, a puzzled expression on his face.

"I thought you said he went out in a boat?" he said.

George nodded. "Go on."

"Why is he wearing those expensive shoes? And for that matter why is he in a white shirt?"

"That's it, Dawson," George said. "He's wearing the wrong clothes. He's dressed for that meeting with Havers, not for going out in a boat."

Dawson looked pleased with himself. "If there's nothing else, Sir, I'd better head back to the office."

George nodded. He was already engrossed in the file. Finally, he felt he was closing in on the culprit.

But first there was another important interview. And Michael Havers couldn't see him until Wednesday of the following week.

His heart lightened. He was due to be discharged from hospital this weekend.

Life was looking up.

The timing proved fortuitous. The day before he was discharged, George's physiotherapist told him he'd be able to use taxis for short journeys, so long as he kept two walking sticks with him for support. Or crutches.

This opened up fresh possibilities.

After feeling cooped up in the hospital for so long, George set himself the delightful task of choosing a nice country pub where he could interview Havers. He settled on The Crooked Door, located a few miles away on the banks of the river.

As his taxi drew up, he admired the old brick building with its four chimneys, nestled against a backdrop of pine trees. Smoke curled from one of the chimneys. Several cars were parked in front. Against the red brick wall a climbing rose rambled irregularly towards the upper windows. How good it felt to be here, with the sun on his face. It was something he swore he'd never take for granted again.

He checked the time. Ten minutes to two. He'd arrived early, from a false sense of pride, not wanting the lawyer to see him hobbling along with his walking sticks.

And it'd give him time to collect his thoughts.

He ordered a pint of ale and found a seat at a wooden table outside overlooking the stream. A couple in a small boat was rowing in circles near the bank. He caught the drift of their laughter and voices but couldn't distinguish what they were saying. He noticed they were wearing waterproof jackets.

The ringing of his phone interrupted his thoughts. It was Sergeant Dawson.

"About those bullets, Sir," he began.

"Yes?" he said.

"You were right. The lab had already checked them," he said. "And they found fingerprints on them."

George put his ale down. "Whose fingerprints are they?" He held his breath waiting for Dawson's reply. But to his surprise it wasn't any of his suspects.

"That's the thing, Sir. We don't know who they belong to," he said. "All the lab can tell us is they don't belong to Jasmine, Joseph or Havers. Their prints were on file. They were taken the day Cecilia went missing."

George forced himself to ask, "Could they be Cecilia's?"

Dawson immediately said, "No, I should've said so straightaway. What do you want me to do now, Sir?"

"Leave it with me, Dawson. I'll have to think about this."

George heard someone call out his name. Turning, he saw a tall man in a striped suit looking in his direction. This must be Michael Havers. He was different to what George had expected. More elegant and also more friendly.

"Thanks for your help, Sergeant," he said, ending the call. And then turned to face the lawyer who was settling himself into the chair opposite.

"You've chosen a lovely pub," his companion said. "I haven't been here before."

"We're spoilt for choice," George said. Something he'd often thought.

As he sipped his ale, he began. "I'm trying to reconstruct the last day of Henry Paxton's life," he said. "I notice you were meant to have a meeting with him at eight o'clock that evening."

"Yes, Henry wanted to make sure his affairs were in order."

George decided to play his cards close to his chest. "Had he mentioned anything about changing his will?" he asked.

"Henry was always talking about changing his will. But he never actually did anything about it." He sipped his beer. "Between you and me, I think he just talked about it to keep his youngsters in check."

"Youngsters. You've used the plural. So you knew about Joseph?" George said.

"Yes. Both he and Cecilia had come to see me about Joseph's inheritance. They didn't want Jasmine to know about it."

"Because- ?"

"You've met Jasmine, I gather? Does she strike you as the kind who'd want to share an inheritance?"

George nodded. "She puzzles me. How did she afford that Lamborghini?"

Havers smiled. "She was seeing my partner, William Smythe. He could afford it," he said. "And he certainly wanted to keep seeing Jasmine."

This was an unexpected development. Would George continue with his original line of questioning?

There was still something he needed to know.

"Do you believe Henry's death was accidental?" he asked. "Did you find it odd that Henry would go fishing at 7 o'clock?"

"I've thought about this long and hard. Joseph's told me you know about our relationship. We had dinner together that evening. Later we decided he wouldn't include that in his statement. He was studying at the time and simply said he was in his room. He lived in a shared house." Havers looked at George with an air of contrition. "I wasn't asked about my whereabouts."

"Do you think any of the family guessed you were involved with Joseph?"

"I've often wondered if Henry had guessed what was going on between us," Havers said. "If that was why he decided to start seeing my partner instead of me."

"So it would've troubled him that you were seeing Joseph?"

"I imagine so," he said. "But I'll never know now."

Then the penny dropped. "Did Henry cancel the meeting with you?" he asked.

"The meeting was supposed to go ahead," Havers said. "But he wanted Smythe to go in my place. He phoned Smythe to let him know late that afternoon. That's why I was free to see Joseph."

"Smythe? That's interesting."

George's mind buzzed. Would this change in the meeting arrangements have influenced Jasmine? He couldn't rule out that it was a factor precipitating her action. If indeed she was the culprit, as Cecilia always believed.

He found it hard to keep Cecilia's perspectives separate from his own, even while knowing this was a mistake.

As they watched, the young couple in the boat finally managed to row in a straight line and headed off downstream.

The two men watched in silence, sipping their beers. And then Havers left.

Once he was out of sight, George phoned Dawson. "I need you to obtain William Smythe's fingerprints," he began. "We need to see if they match the ones on the bullets."

"What if he refuses, Sir?"

"Just tell him we need to eliminate him from our enquiries," George said. "I'll get a warrant if necessary." Then he changed his mind. "No, wait. We'll pay him a visit."

The offices of Smythe and Havers had an imposing air. George couldn't remember the last time he'd seen so much oak panelling.

Havers' partner looked old enough to be Jasmine's father.

"We need to talk about Henry Paxton's death," George began.

The older man's composure didn't change. "I really don't see what that has to do with me," he said.

"I think it has everything to do with you," George said. "Perhaps you'd care to explain why your fingerprints are on the bullets inside Henry's gun? The gun we assume was held to his head to force him to row out onto the lake in a boat that needed repair."

The lawyer's skin turned ashen. "It was that girl," he said. "It was all her fault."

"But it's your fingerprints," George persisted. "You're the one in the frame."

Smythe sighed. "Yes, I admit to putting bullets in the

gun. She said they were blanks. That she wanted to frighten off some poachers they'd had there."

"Just for the record, this is Jasmine Paxton we're talking about?"

"Yes, Jasmine. Henry wanted to disinherit her," he said. "She'd borrowed a fortune from me to buy that car. Nothing was ever enough for her."

"It never is for that kind of woman."

Smythe shook his head. "Once I'd loaded the gun, Jasmine excused herself. This was around 7 o'clock. When she came back, her shoes had mud on them. She told me Henry had decided to go fishing. It seemed odd. I'd driven all that way to help him change his will."

"Did she give you an explanation?" George asked.

"No. She just said he'd changed his mind. And then she asked me to leave. Said she had a headache."

"And afterwards? When you heard that Henry had drowned? Did you wonder what had really happened?"

"I had my doubts, especially because I'd seen mud on her shoes," he said. "But then the coroner said it was an accident and it was a rainy night. My shoes were dirty too."

"But you never came forward to make a statement?"

"Jasmine swore he'd gone fishing. Said she'd lose her inheritance if I muddied the waters." He sighed. "It was wrong of me but I didn't volunteer the information that I'd gone to the house. The only other person there that night was Jasmine's mother and she was in a drug-induced sleep."

George was silent.

"For what it's worth I'd have told the truth if anyone had asked me," Smythe said.

"I'm asking you now," George said. "It's time you made a full statement."

"Did you ever consider the possibility that I killed Henry?" Cecilia was looking straight at him, an expectant look in her eyes. They were sharing a bottle of chardonnay in her garden. Celebrating the arrest of Jasmine Paxton.

Had she guessed?

He could only offer her the truth. She would accept nothing less, he knew that. "You know as well as I do that I have to check every possibility," he said. "I hope my answer doesn't offend you."

"Not at all. I wouldn't have asked you to look into Henry's death if I didn't consider you a good detective." She smiled. "I hope I wasn't on your wanted list very long."

"Not in that sense, you weren't," he said. "Of course, in another sense you're always on it."

"Touché." She raised her glass to his. "So I was right after all? Are you sure?"

"No question in my mind that Henry was murdered," he said. "In the end I had three suspects with strong motives and with opportunity. And amongst them our murderer."

"Do you have a strong enough case to convict her?" she asked.

"I believe so," he said. "There's still work to do but we have enough evidence to stand up in court."

"What about Smythe? He's a dark horse."

"Smythe might be able to save himself. He's been very cooperative since I told him his fingerprints were on the bullets. Mind you, the fact he didn't come forward at the time of the inquest will go against him."

"How did you know the fingerprints were his?" Cecilia asked. "I thought you said there wasn't a match."

George smiled. "Let's just say I put out a line and the fish took the bait."

"You bluffed?"

"That's one way of putting it," he said. "I like to think it was an educated guess."

He raised his glass. "I think we should drink a toast to Henry, don't you?"

But before the glass reached his lips, his phone rang. It was Sergeant Dawson. "We've had a call to Lawnton Canal, Sir. Looks like a murder."

"Right, I'm on my way."

He looked apologetically at Cecilia. "I'm afraid there's never a good time for a body to be found."

Acknowledgements

I'd like to thank the following editors who published these stories and offered encouragement – Tony Lambert, Jude Durrant, Nikki Roberts, Norah McGrath, Alice McIntyre, Clare Cooper, Lotta Gustavsson, Kari Bjornstad, Eva Serner, Veronica Trajkovski-Malheden, Sarah Hemmel, Kristin Sigvaldsen, Liz Smith, Hilary Lyall, Jill Finlay, Mike O'Mary, Belinda Wallis, Cecilia Van Zyl, Lisa Sinclair, Shea Tomkins, Julie Redlich, Emily Skaftun, Tracie Couper, Jodi Cleghorn, Lynn Ely, Liz Ferguson, Debbie Attewell, Gill James, Pat Kelly and Carl Styants.

Thanks to my writing friends for their helpful critiques over the years – especially Lynne Hackles, Kay Gregory, Fran Tracey, Ginny Swart, Kath Kilburn, Rosemary Hayes, Sandie Beswetherick, Su Kopil and everyone else in my online groups. And to Liz, Wendy, and Bruce for their useful advice and ideas.

Special thanks to my family for their encouragement and support - to my daughter Amy for her helpful ideas and for the cover art, to my son Andrew for creating my website, to my daughter Catherine for giving me this title, and to my husband Denzil for proofreading this manuscript.

www.ingramcontent.com/pod-product-compliance
Ingram Content Group UK Ltd.
Pitfield, Milton Keynes, MK11 3LW, UK
UKHW041414180426
11947UKWH00007B/124